— *Indiana Author*

By the same author

JULIE'S SUMMER

JULIE'S SUMMER

Crystal Thrasher

A Margaret K. McElderry Book

ATHENEUM　1981　NEW YORK

Library of Congress Cataloging in Publication Data

Thrasher, Crystal.
Julie's summer.

"A Margaret K. McElderry book."
Summary: Remaining behind to finish high school and
get a job when her family leaves rural Indiana at the
end of the Depression, Julie learns what a destructive
force vicious gossip can be.
[1. Country life—Fiction. 2. Depressions—1929—
Fiction] I. Title.
PZ7.T4Ju   [Fic]   81-3479
ISBN 0-689-50209-5   AACR2

Published simultaneously in Canada by McClelland & Stewart, Ltd.
Composed by American-Stratford Graphic Service, Inc.
Brattleboro, Vermont
Manufactured by Fairfield Graphics
Fairfield, Pennsylvania
Designed by Maria Epes
First Edition

This book is dedicated to my sister,
Jewell Knight Thrasher,
for love given and memories shared

"it's just a tincup full of dewberries . . ."

"There isn't much to be seen in a little town, but what you hear makes up for it."

KIN HUBBARD

JULIE'S SUMMER

Chapter One

It was a warm Sunday in early May of 1935. President Roosevelt had told everyone in the country that prosperity was just around the corner, and Mom and Dad believed him. They had packed up everything and left Greene County this morning for greener pastures and the promised prosperity.

I waved good-bye until the truck that was carrying my family away passed from sight behind the trees. Then I stood in front of the empty house and looked down the road after them. When the grinding sound of the old truck as it labored under its heavy load of household trappings had gone beyond my hearing, a dead silence followed their leaving.

Jase Perry had brought us to these hills during the darkest days of the Depression in an even older, more rattletrap truck than the one Dad was driving this morning. There had been seven of us riding in that old truck with Jase. Four in the front seat, Jase and Floyd Perry, and Mom and the baby, Robert. Jamie, Seely, and me rode on the back with the furniture. Dad had gone on ahead with the wagon and livestock.

Now there were only four leaving the hills. Mom and

Dad in the front seat with Robert between them, and Seely all alone on the back of the truck. Jamie was dead. Drowned in the February flooding of Lick Crick. And Jase was dead too. Taken by his own hand. Four staying in Greene County, I thought, and four leaving. "But they've got a warm, sunny day for going," I said to myself, remembering the cold November wind that had chilled us through and through on that other day.

I should be going. There was nothing here for me. There never had been. But now that the folks had gone, there was even less reason for me to be here. I turned from the road for one last look at the weather-beaten old house that had been our home for the past year or so. The time we had spent here hadn't been so good that I would want to remember it or have it over again, yet I knew it would be a long time before I would ever forget it.

I turned to leave and a moving figure near the edge of the trees caught my eye. A warm feeling of gladness came over me as I recognized Floyd Perry hurrying across the field. He was coming to see the folks before they left, I thought. And he had just missed them.

As Floyd hurried by the barn, he raised his hand and called, "Hey, Julie." My hand answered his, then I stood and waited for him to come to the house.

I had known Floyd Perry all my life. It seemed like no matter where we lived, or where we moved to, the Perrys were always there, neighbors to us. His folks and mine had been friends even before we had been born, and they had brought up both families of kids to feel as close as brothers and sisters, teaching us to call them aunt and uncle. I was in the fourth grade of school when I found out that Floyd was no kin to me at all. It nearly broke my heart.

4

But then after we had grown up a bit, and especially after Floyd had come back from the Civilian Conservation Corps camp in Idaho, I was tickled to death to know that he wasn't kin to me. I could love him any way I wanted to.

"Have the folks gone already?"

He could see that I was the only one left on the place, but I nodded anyway. "I was just leaving."

I don't think Floyd even heard me. He was gazing off down the road as if by staring hard enough he could conjure up the truck and my family the way they were an hour ago. "I thought they would wait to see me before they left," he said.

Floyd seemed suddenly lost, like a displaced person, and spoke as though he was the child my parents had left behind in Greene County. "Since Dad . . . died . . ."— Floyd still couldn't say that Jase had killed himself— ". . . and they put Mother in that asylum over by Richmond, I've come to look on your folks as my own."

I remember the fights I'd had with Dad because he had opened my letters from Floyd, and Mom saying, "Julie, your dad meant no harm. He looks on Floyd Perry as one of his own."

I knew they were hoping that I would marry Floyd as soon as I finished high school and we'd come to live near them. But I had other ideas about that. I'd had my heart set on being a schoolteacher for some time now, and if I married Floyd fresh out of high school I'd never get to college.

Now I took Floyd's hand and turned toward the gravel road. "Let's go," I said. "Dad wanted to get there before dark, otherwise he'd have waited for you. You know he would've. Dad loves you the same as one of his own kids."

I smiled at him and added, "I ought to know. Mom has told me so time and again."

Floyd seemed pleased with my words, but almost immediately his face resumed its troubled expression, and he didn't speak until the house was out of sight. We were nearing the dirt lane that led to Ben Collier's sawmill where Floyd worked and over the hill to the teacher's house where he had room and board. "Would you like me to run home and get Mr. Thompson's car and carry you to Newark?" he said.

I shook my head. "It's not far," I answered. "I can walk it in no time."

"Then I'll walk a piece with you," he said. He turned his back to the dirt lane and without another word, he started on down the road ahead of me

I hurried to catch up and walk with him. Just as I came even with Floyd, a bit of loose gravel rolled under my feet and I stumbled. Floyd grabbed my arm to keep me from falling, then when I was steady on my feet, he slipped his arm around my waist and held me close to him.

Thinking to tease him out of his glum and gloomy mood, I said, "Don't start getting fresh with me, Floyd Perry. Remember, this is Sunday, and we're on a public road in broad daylight."

He took his arm from around my waist and moved a step away.

"I was just trying to stop you from falling."

Floyd spoke so seriously that I had to laugh at him. "Good heavens! Don't you know by now when I'm fooling?"

Floyd smiled then, showing the chipped front tooth that had been broken years ago when he'd tripped and

6

fallen over the chopping block in our woodyard. "You wait till it ain't broad daylight," he said, grabbing me with both arms and hugging me tight to him. "Then I'll close that pretty mouth of yours. And I won't be fooling," he added.

He leaned his face down close to mine. I thought he would kiss me right there and then. But he just grinned like a possum eating pokeberries and commenced to whistle "Foggy, Foggy Dew."

If he had kissed me, it wouldn't have been the first time. Floyd had kissed me every time we met until he was eleven or twelve years old. Then he stopped. He didn't kiss me again until I was past sixteen and he was going on nineteen. Then his kisses had been different. And his chipped tooth didn't cut my lips the way it used to do.

We were almost to where the road forked off toward the Flat Hollow Church when George and Clara Brent stopped their car to speak to us. Clara asked if the folks had got away all right. I said they had. Then she asked if we'd like to ride to church with them. "You can sit on Floyd's lap," she said, with a wide teasing smile.

Floyd nudged me and whispered, "How about it? Do you want to go to church?" I shook my head no.

"Not this morning," I said to Clara. "Mrs. Arthur is expecting me to be at her house when she gets home from church."

Clara smiled and waved as George gunned the motor and took the turnoff on two wheels. A cloud of dust boiled up behind the Brents' little one-seated automobile and hovered over the road, marking their passing, and leaving us fanning the air and choking in its wake.

I was used to eating George's dust, as Mom used to say.

Last summer she had taken Jamie and Seely and me to Flat Hollow Church every Sunday. And somewhere along the road George and Clara Brent would pass us on their way to church. They would always smile and wave, but they never stopped. George couldn't carry all of us in his car, so he wouldn't ask anyone to ride with them. We had buried Jamie in the Flat Hollow Churchyard, and I hadn't been there since. And I wouldn't go back again, except to keep the promise I had made Mom as she was leaving this morning.

"Mom wants me to tend to Jamie's piece of earth and see that he gets flowers on Decoration Day," I said, my eyes following the trail of dust, and my mind leaping ahead to the Flat Hollow Church. "She worries that weeds will overtake his resting place and it will be lost to her."

Floyd took my arm and turned me from the little rock road, and we went on toward Newark. "When the time comes," Floyd said, "we'll go to the graveyard together. Dad lies not far from Jamie and I daresay his grave could bear some looking after too."

We walked slowly, stopping often to rest in the shade of the trees. Now the sun would be on one side, then on the other, and we'd cross the road to keep on the shady side as much as possible. The trees grew right to the edge of the road, and the road twisted up one hill and down the other with a sharp curve at the foot of almost every hill. Deep ravines fell away on one side of the road, and high, tree-covered ridges rose to hide the sun on the other side. The sun was almost directly overhead when we stopped to rest before tackling the last long crooked hill this side of Newark.

"One of these days," Floyd said, gazing at the hill

ahead of us, "I'm going to get me an automobile that will skim over these hills and hollers like they ain't even here."

"If wishing made it so," I said, "you'd have one already."

We smiled at each other, clasped hands, and walked on, each of us dreaming of better days yet to come.

Chapter Two

Church was over and Mrs. Arthur was just entering the side door of her house when we got there. The dress shop, where I worked after school and all day on Saturday, took up the whole front of the house. No one ever used the front door except during business hours. It was a big house. The largest one in Newark. Webb Arthur had built it for his bride over twenty years ago, and when he died in the war two years later, Maud Arthur had turned the two front rooms into a dress shop to support herself and the baby Nancy.

Behind the dress shop there was a huge kitchen where we cooked and ate our meals, and a long wide dining room that passed for a living room. But most of our living was done in the kitchen. Along one wall of the dining-living room, a wide stairway rose to the second story where Mrs. Arthur and Nancy had their bedrooms. A big sewing room took up the rest of the second floor.

Many of the dresses that Maud Arthur bought in Indianapolis to sell in her store had split seams and small rips and tears that had to be repaired before she could put them in her shop to sell. The big sewing room was used to store these things so that the women in the community wouldn't know they were buying damaged merchandise.

I slept, and kept my few things, in a small room built off the kitchen. It had probably been a pantry at one time and didn't have an outside door. But sometime in the past a big window had been cut in the back wall, and I used this window to go in and out of the house to the backyard.

When I'd first mentioned moving in with the Arthurs, Mom had used every argument at hand to persuade me not to go. She said that Maud Arthur was odd-turned, stuck-up, and had a mean streak a yard wide. But I argued that she didn't know Mrs. Arthur, not as well as I did, and she had no reason to belittle her. "If you had to make your living by dealing with people, and working as hard as Mrs. Arthur, you wouldn't feel like socializing either," I said.

When Mom found that she couldn't sway me from going, she had said, "Have it your own way. You're the one who is going to have to live with her. But you mark my words," she added, "that woman is a troublemaker, and there'll be no getting along with her."

It seemed like Mom and me never could see eye to eye about anything.

Now as Floyd and I turned off the road and up the path toward the house, I said, "I'm really lucky that Nancy's mother wanted me to stay with them. If I'd had to go with the folks, I might never have gotten to finish high school."

Mrs. Arthur saw us standing and talking by the gate, and called, "Julie, come on in now. The day's half gone and there's nothing done."

"I'll be right there." I answered, and turned back to hear what Floyd was saying.

"You may find things a mite different here now that

you're alone with no where else to go," Floyd said under his breath. "Could be, you ain't as fortunate as you think." Then, since Maud Arthur was still waiting at the door for me, he said for her ears, "I'll come to see you as often as I can get the teacher's car."

Floyd touched my hand, turned, and started back down the road toward home. I went into the house.

"There'll be no time for lollygagging around with the boys," Mrs. Arthur snapped. "Not if you aim to keep up with your work."

Her words stopped me dead in my tracks. I didn't know any boys. Just Floyd. And he'd never be a hinder to my work. That's what I told Mrs. Arthur. "Floyd won't be any bother."

"Well, see that he ain't," she replied crossly.

Mrs. Arthur had never spoken so sharply to me, and I couldn't understand why she had now. Far as I knew, I hadn't done anything to make her mad. But something had turned her sour all of a sudden. As I went upstairs to tell Nancy that her mother was home from church, I wondered if Mrs. Arthur had some gripe against Floyd Perry that I didn't know about.

Sunday morning was Nancy's time to do as she pleased. Mrs. Arthur said it wasn't necessary for her to help me, so Nancy would wash her long blond hair and put polish on her nails. She offered to polish my nails for me, but I said it wouldn't do any good. Not with the work I had to do.

Nancy didn't have to turn her hand to a lick of work around the house. Mrs. Arthur said that she had other things in mind for her daughter and these things didn't include cooking and scrubbing floors like some common scullery maid.

Nancy Arthur had been my best friend ever since the first day I'd walked into the high school, a year and a half ago, and she was all I could ask for in a friend. But she had a lazy streak, which her mother encouraged, and she lived in a world of make-believe where she seemed to think that, given time, everything she ever wanted would come to her without her having to lift a finger for it.

I knew better. I had been taught that if you want to achieve anything in life, you have to work for it. Dad always said, "Give a day's work for a day's pay." And that's what I tried to do at the Arthurs.

On the Sundays that I didn't go home, I got up and went to the kitchen as soon as I heard Mrs. Arthur come downstairs. Then after she had left for church, I would do the morning chores. These included sweeping the shop and dusting the shelves and dress racks so the store would be ready to open on Monday morning. By the time Mrs. Arthur got home from church, the work would all be done, and I'd have the noon meal ready to put on the table.

I suppose that could be the reason that she was angry today, I thought. I had stayed all night with the folks last night, and when Mrs. Arthur got home from church today, dinner was yet to be made and the work was still waiting to be done.

After a quiet meal, which I had helped her to prepare, Mrs. Arthur mumbled that she had things to tend to upstairs and left the room. I cleared the table, then I went to the front of the house to clean the store and get it ready for business.

13

Nancy came to the shop while I was dusting the shelves and offered to help me. I told her that she could study her lines for the class play while I was working. Her mother wouldn't like it if she came in and caught her doing my work for me.

She smiled and picked up a dust cloth and started wiping the dress racks. "Don't worry," Nancy said. "Mother won't be coming down for a while. She's too busy figuring out ways to rook the townspeople." She grinned impishly, and added. "Don't ever tell her I said that."

Nancy was always telling me things, then making me promise not to tell her mother. As if I ever would. And I in turn confided in Nancy. Things I would never dare to tell another soul. But one day when Nancy said that in spite of all her mother could do, she would someday be a great actress, I kept quiet. I was afraid she would laugh at me if I said that I wanted to go to school and be a teacher. It took brains and money to do that. And I was barely making passing grades in school, and the only money I had to my name was the little bit her mother had paid me for working here.

Feeling sure that we were safe from Mrs. Arthur's prying eyes, Nancy and I wasted all Sunday afternoon rearranging the shop and trying on dresses. "Let's pretend we're having a style show," Nancy said, "and do the whole bit." So we paraded up and down the aisles in the dresses that fitted us, and laughed and giggled as we tried the ones that didn't fit.

I should have been studying for the class exams that were scheduled for the next day, but it was hard to say no to Nancy. Especially when her suggestions offered a bit of diversion from the monotonous sameness of each day.

Nancy didn't seem to notice the never-changing routine of the days. Or if she did, she never spoke of it. She spent most of her waking hours play-acting and pretending that things were different than they were actually. I guess that's why Nancy was given the leading role in the senior class play. She was always playing a part.

I hadn't tried for a part in the school play, even though Nancy had urged me to. I had more than enough to keep me busy just doing my class assignments and keeping ahead of the work that Mrs. Arthur set aside for me to do.

I would hurry from school to spell Mrs. Arthur from the dress shop, or else I'd fix the evening meal and leave her to do the shop books and close up for the day. It all depended on what she'd be doing when I got there. We would eat supper in silence, then Mrs. Arthur would go upstairs to her sewing room, and I'd clean up after the meal. Usually, I wouldn't see her again until the next morning. Nancy would eat a bite later, when she got home from play practice, then we'd push her dishes to one side and study our lessons on the table. Sometimes it would be midnight before we turned the lamp down low and went to bed.

We had just closed the dress shop on Saturday evening when Floyd drove up in Mr. Thompson's car. It had been the hottest day yet, and the shop was like a bake oven. Floyd came in and said, "Wash your face and I'll take you for a ride." I hurried to my room to get ready. I could think of nothing I'd like better than a cool, refreshing ride in the country and wasted no time getting back to the kitchen.

15

Nancy was setting the table for supper, and Mrs. Arthur stood nearby with a deep frown on her face.

"There'll be no joy-riding in an automobile around here after dark," Mrs. Arthur said. "Not as long as you're under my roof."

The sun was just going down and it wouldn't be really dark for another hour yet. I waved my hand to Nancy, who had stopped what she was doing to listen, and went on toward the door. "We'll be back before dark," I said.

"If you want to stay in this house until school's out, you'll heed what I say."

I turned back from the door. I couldn't believe Mrs. Arthur meant that. Even Mom, strict as she was with me, wouldn't object to an hour's ride in a car with Floyd. My eyes found Nancy's and she quickly looked away. She wanted no part of this argument, if it went that far. I looked at Mrs. Arthur's firm set face and unyielding stance and gave in to her.

"All right," I said. "I can live without a ride in the country." I turned to Floyd. "Come on. I'll walk to the gate with you."

Mrs. Arthur raised no objections to that. I opened the door, and Floyd and I left the room together.

"She acts like I'm not to be trusted alone with you," Floyd said.

"It's not that," I replied. "She just wanted to stir up trouble. Seems like she can't stand to have things go smoothly these days, and she thought she'd get an argument out of me."

We talked of other things then until Floyd said that he had to go. He had to get the teacher's car home to him. "Julie, don't fuss with that woman," he said, as he was leaving. "She's got the upper hand now, and there's no way you could win."

I stayed outside long after Floyd had gone, thinking about what he had said. I didn't want to fuss and fight with Mrs. Arthur. I was doing my best to keep the peace and get along with her for the few remaining weeks of school. It wasn't easy for me to do. I was used to speaking my mind and having some say in the things that concerned me.

It was full dark when I finally went into the house. Mrs. Arthur had gone upstairs and Nancy was doing her homework on the kitchen table. I got my books and sat down with her. Nancy smiled and moved the kerosene lamp closer so we could both see to read, but neither one of us said a word. I guess we both knew it would do no good to talk about Floyd Perry or discuss her mother's ultimatum to me.

Things went along at the Arthur house pretty much the same after Floyd's visit as they had before. I did the housework that Mrs. Arthur left for me, worked in the shop, and went to school every day. I worried constantly that my grades at school wouldn't be high enough to allow me to enter normal college later on, and I would have to take the whole year over again.

Nancy and I sat up to all hours of the night studying for tests and doing our homework. Then when that was done, we went over her part in the class play. I'd read the other roles and cue her for her lines. Floyd didn't come to see me again. If he had, I wouldn't have had any time to spare for him.

On the last night before the actual performance of the class play was to take place, both Nancy and I were so tired that we were silly. Neither of us could remember anything. Nancy said she was scared to death that she would get on the stage, then forget her lines.

"I'd be the laughingstock of the county," she moaned. "Mother would be so mortified that she'd close her shop and leave town. She'd never be able to hold up her head and face people again."

I was reading cue lines for her at the time, but I had to stop and laugh.

"Julie, that's not supposed to be funny," Nancy said.

"I know," I said, laughing. "But you remind me of a pregnant old maid. Now that it's too late to get out of it, you worry that your mother will find out and run you off."

Nancy laughed, too. "Mother will throw us both out of the house if she hears you talking that way."

I didn't doubt that for a minute.

The tickets to get in to see the class play cost twenty-five cents, so I didn't go. I would need every penny I had later on when school was out. I knew what the play was about from helping Nancy with her lines. I didn't need to waste my money to hear it again.

Mrs. Arthur went to the play. She said it was her civic duty to go. After all, she reminded me, the money it brought in was to be used to rent caps and gowns for the graduating class. "And that includes you," she said pointedly.

"What will you do here by yourself?" she asked as she was leaving the house. "I suppose Floyd Perry will slip in here the minute that I'm gone," she muttered.

It had been a long time since Floyd had come to the house to see me. He used to walk to town in the evening, after he'd finished work for the day, but I was always busy. And if I wasn't, Mrs. Arthur soon found something for me to do. After the Saturday when Mrs. Arthur had forbidden me to go for a ride with him, Floyd had stopped coming there altogether.

"That's not likely," I told her now. And I thought to myself, "You've seen to that!"

But to my surprise, Mrs. Arthur had no more than cleared the gate and passed from sight toward the school-house when Floyd knocked at the kitchen door.

"I've got the teacher's car," Floyd said, when I asked him to come in. "Why don't you come out for a ride with me?"

I didn't wait to be asked twice. I blew out the light, pulled the door shut behind me, and let Floyd lead the way to the car.

Chapter Three

When the sun goes down in Greene County and the twilight time fades into night, there is a complete blackness everywhere. The dense dark forests and deep pervading hills make a solid wall of pitch black night, broken only here and there by the faint glow of a kerosene lamp shining from some far window. Tonight, the car headlamps made a weak tunnel of light through the darkness ahead and guided us down the rough gravel road.

"I got a letter from Mom yesterday," I said.

I knew Floyd would want to know how the folks were faring.

"She said that the old truck had broken down on them near the village of Jubilee, and they've taken a house there until they can do better."

Floyd's attention was fixed firmly on the steep twisting hill that we were going down, and he didn't answer me. "They are expecting me to come down there when school is out," I went on.

He managed the curve at the foot of the hill, then sat back in the seat. "Are you going to go?"

"I don't know. I can't picture anything for me in Jubilee." I thought for a moment. "When I've got my diploma in my hand," I said, "I've a mind to go to Linton and try to find work down there."

We had reached a Y in the road. The gravel ended at the tail of the Y and paved highway began. One fork led off to the east and the other broke away to the west toward the county seat. Mia Bailey's Diner, where the young people hung out after school and on Saturday night, sat smack in the middle of the Y between the two forks of road. Floyd pulled off to the left and parked near the diner, switched off the lights and motor, then turned in the seat to face me.

"I've been saving my wages to buy in with Ben at the sawmill," he said. "As a full partner, I'd be making twice or three times as much money as I'm getting now. More than enough for us to start on." He moved nearer and put his arms around me. "Marry me, Julie," he said softly. "and forget about getting a job when you graduate."

I'd known he was leading up to this but not how to head him off. I wasn't ready to get married. I had no desire to go straight from being a daughter and a school girl to being a man's wife. There had to be a gap between. An interval for knowing and pleasing myself, before I took on the job of pleasing a husband. I didn't even want to think about it. I'd always known in my heart that one day I would marry Floyd Perry. That was understood. But not yet, I thought now. I've got to be me for just a little while longer.

His lips touched mine lightly, and I moved away from him impatiently. "Don't tempt me, Floyd. I might say yes and marry you tomorrow, just to get away from Mrs. Arthur."

He pulled me close again, and this time I didn't resist

when he kissed me. "It doesn't matter why you marry me," he whispered. "Just that you do."

"I can't now, Floyd," I said gently. "Ask me again later."

"I will," he answered. "You can count on it."

Floyd kissed me, the way you'd kiss a child, then turned to open the car door. "Come on," he said, taking my hand. "I'll buy you a big orange soda."

Other than Mia Bailey, the middle-aged owner, the diner was empty when we walked in. Floyd looked around the room then led the way to a table at the far end near the music box.

"Where is everyone tonight?" Floyd asked, as Mia Bailey set our orange drinks on the table. "I never saw this place so quiet."

"I guess they all went to see that play at the schoolhouse," she answered. "It won't be quiet in here when it's over. Kids'll come swarming in here like flies on a honey pot, everybody hungry and thirsty and in a hurry, and all wanting special attention. . . ."

When it looked as if she would never run out of breath, Floyd broke in to ask for change for the juke box. Nickels, if she had them. Mia Bailey stopped her good-natured complaining and went to get his change. As soon as she was out of hearing range, I whispered to Floyd. "Let's hurry and finish our drink and leave here."

"Not until I dance with you." He smiled at me, then he got up and held out his hand for the fistful of nickels that Mia Bailey handed him.

Floyd dropped several coins into the music box; then as a soft, haunting melody filled the room, he turned to me and lifted his arms. "Just one dance, Julie?"

I couldn't say no to him. Not if my life depended on it. And it just might, I thought, as I stepped into his arms. "Defying her," Mrs. Arthur would call it. Going against her word and joy-riding after dark when I'd been warned not to do it. And now on top of that, I'd added the sin of dancing in a roadhouse.

"We'll have to go home as soon as the music stops," I said. "I don't want Mrs. Arthur to know that I left the house tonight."

Floyd laughed at me for being worried about Mrs. Arthur finding out that I hadn't stayed at home. "You're just a 'fraidy cat, Julie," he said. "She wouldn't dare hurt you."

"Floyd, she can harm me in the worst way and not lay a hand on me. She knows how much a diploma from high school means to me, and she could make me leave her house to punish me and keep me from getting it."

The music ended and we went back to our table. The ice had melted in my glass and I pushed the watery orange drink away.

"I'm ready to go now," I said, and turned toward the door. Floyd dropped some change on the table and followed me out.

"Don't worry, Julie," Floyd said, driving much faster than it was safe to travel on the narrow, winding road. "I'll get you home with time to spare."

I hadn't said a word since we left the diner. The joy of seeing Floyd tonight, going for a ride, and talking to him had been spoiled by my fear of what Mrs. Arthur would do when she heard about it. It did no good to tell myself I shouldn't have left the house. I had. And sooner or later, I'd have to account for it.

The house was still dark when we got there, and I breathed a deep sigh of relief. If Nancy or Mrs. Arthur had been at home the lamp on the kitchen table would have been lit. Even if they had been in bed, there would've been a light. Mrs. Arthur liked to leave the lamp burning with the wick turned low, in case she had to get up during the night.

"So far, so good," Floyd breathed, as he opened the car door for me.

He took my arm and we walked to the door. After a quick peck on the cheek, Floyd said, "When you're ready to go job-hunting in Linton, I'll get the teacher's car and take you."

I guess the relief at not having to face Mrs. Arthur just now had made me bold and a little giddy. I hugged Floyd tight, and said, "Oh, I do love you," before I hurried into the house.

I lit the lamp, turned the wick down low, then I went to my room. I got undressed and ready for bed by the dim light from the kitchen and crawled between the sheets. I left my door open so that when Mrs. Arthur came home, she would find me in bed. Just as though I hadn't left the house all evening.

I heard Mrs. Arthur's heavy steps as she came into the house and closed my eyes, feigning sleep. A moment later, Nancy came in. My door closed with a soft click, then Mrs. Arthur said in a harsh whisper, "Don't ever let me catch you with that kind of trash again!"

My eyes flew open and I sat bolt upright in bed. I thought she was speaking to me. It sounded like she was right there in my room. Then I heard Nancy answering her, and lay back down.

"Liz and Jimmy Hawkins aren't trash," Nancy said. "Their folks have come on hard times and the kids have to wear hand me-downs, but they are just as good as you are."

There was the sound of a slap, then light footsteps running from the kitchen. Mrs. Arthur muttered something to herself, the strip of light under my door was dimmed, and she left the room.

My chest hurt from my held-in breath. I let it out slowly, then lay and stared wide-eyed into the darkness and thought over what I'd just heard. I'd never known Mrs. Arthur to speak harshly to Nancy or hear tell of her striking her. I wondered what had brought it on tonight.

One thing I knew for sure, this was no time for Mrs. Arthur to hear that I had gone for a ride with Floyd. If she'd slap Nancy just for walking home with Jimmy and Liz Hawkins, Lord only knows what she would do to me for disobeying her orders.

I couldn't get to sleep. All sorts of thoughts ran through my mind keeping me awake. Maybe I should just forget about getting a job and going on to college, I thought, and tell Floyd I would marry him whenever he said. Any other girl in her right mind would jump at the chance. He was sober, hard-working, and handsome in an Abe Lincoln kind of way. Yet even as I thought this, I knew that I wouldn't marry Floyd Perry just to be sure I'd have a roof over my head for the rest of my life.

I had leaped at the chance to stay with the Arthurs. I hadn't believed Mrs. Arthur would lay down so many rules and restraints and how uncomfortable they could get to be. And look where that had got me. Boxed in on a sleep-

25

less night with a bad conscience. And if I intended to graduate, I still had a while to put up with the same thing.

I couldn't live here with tonight hanging over my head like Damocles' sword, just waiting for the moment when Mrs. Arthur would confront me with it. I'd have to tell her. I wouldn't wait for her to hear it from someone else. The first thing tomorrow morning, I would tell her myself. With that settled in my mind, I went to sleep.

The next morning I didn't have a chance to tell Mrs. Arthur that Floyd had come to town after she'd left the house last night, and we had gone dancing at Mia Bailey's place at the Y.

Nancy was quiet and didn't mention the school play. But Mrs. Arthur made up for her silences. Someone had told Mrs. Arthur that the Rural Electric Company was bringing electricity to the hills and back country of southern Indiana. Right now, she said, linemen were stringing wires across the hills and hollows into Newark. "Folks figure the lines will be here by midsummer, if not sooner," Mrs. Arthur said. "And they'll be coming right by this house."

She was still talking about the changes she would make when she had electricity when Nancy and I left for school. No one had asked me what I'd done the night before. I wished they had. It would all be out in the open where I could fight it or forget it. Now when she heard it, either from me or someone else, Mrs. Arthur would swear that I had deceived her deliberately.

I started to tell Nancy, but she spoke first. "Did we wake you when we came in last night?" I shook my head no and started to say that I was awake already. Then I realized that would mean I'd heard everything between her and her mother. So I kept quiet.

"Mother's having another of her bad moods," Nancy said. "We'll have to watch what we say and do around her until this passes."

I was glad then that I hadn't had a chance to tell Mrs. Arthur about last night. I knew that she would find it out sooner or later, but I hoped it would be much later when she was feeling better.

I told Nancy that I hoped I wouldn't upset her mother, then changed the subject to the class play, and we talked about that the rest of the way to school.

I knew the minute I stepped into the house that afternoon that Mrs. Arthur had found out I'd been dancing at the Y while I was supposed to be at home. She stood there with her arms crossed on her chest, cocked and primed and loaded with questions. Biding her time till she could fire them at me with both barrels. I knew I was in for it and stopped just inside the door and waited for her to speak and get it all out of her system.

"I knew as soon as your folks were out of the county I'd have trouble with you," she said. "I distinctly told you there'd be no joy-riding in that car with Floyd Perry. Yet the minute my back's turned, you're out riding and dancing, and God only knows what else you've been up to."

She stopped to get her breath, and I waited for her to go on. It would only make it worse for me to talk back to her and deny any of it.

"I won't stand for no sneaking out to roadhouses. Not while you're under my roof. You'll abide by my rules, or you'll get out. And that's all there is to it!"

She glanced toward the front of the house and lowered

her voice. I knew then that Nancy had got home before me and was in the dress shop taking care of business, while her mother was here in the kitchen giving me old Billy hell for disregarding her orders.

"I'm raising my daughter to be a good, decent girl," she said, her voice just above a whisper. "And I won't put up with your whoring around and bringing shame on her name."

The unfairness of this struck me. I wouldn't have taken it from my own mother and I didn't intend to hold still and take such talk from Maud Arthur. Not even if it meant I would be thrown bodily out of her house.

"I didn't sneak out last night," I said hotly. "Why should I? I wasn't doing anything wrong."

A smug, satisfied smile crossed her face. She had what she wanted. She'd drawn blood and got me to argue with her. Mrs. Arthur stepped toward me, blocking my path. and shook her finger in my face.

"If you weren't up to some kind of meanness, why'd you try to hide it? Why didn't you just tell me you went out with the Perry boy last night?"

"You didn't ask me!" I cried. I pushed by her then, and ran to my room, slamming and bolting the door behind me.

After a while I heard Mrs. Arthur call Nancy to supper, and the low murmur of their voices as they ate. But I couldn't catch a word they were saying. Finally, someone rapped lightly on my door, and Nancy asked me to come and eat something. Even when she whispered, "Julie, mother has gone upstairs," I didn't answer her. I turned my face toward the darkness outside the window and wished with all my heart that I had never stepped foot inside the Arthur house.

Chapter Four

Memorial Day came on Sunday following the class play.
Floyd hadn't mentioned it when I'd seen him on Thursday night, but I knew he hadn't forgotten that we were
supposed to go to the Flat Hollow cemetery and decorate
the graves of our dead, just the same as everyone else in
the county would be doing today.

I got up early and I was dressed and ready to leave the
house before Mrs. Arthur ever came downstairs. I figured that I would start walking toward Flat Hollow before she left for church and meet Floyd as he came to
get me. That way, Mrs. Arthur couldn't forbid me to go.
And I felt certain she would, if she knew about it.

I started to leave the house and got as far as the gate,
then I turned around and went back. I didn't dare leave
without telling Mrs. Arthur where I was going. She would
never let me hear the last of it if I slipped away from the
house before she got up. I would just have to take my
chances and hope she'd be in a better humor this morning.

She hadn't spoken to me at all on Saturday. The few
times we'd met face to face, she had looked over my head
and beyond me, as if I wasn't even there. Once when
Nancy had noticed what was happening, she had whis-

pered, "Julie, don't pay any attention to Mother today. She'll get over her spite and anger sooner if you just ignore it." But it had made me mighty uncomfortable to be around her.

For the first Sunday since I'd been at the Arthurs, Nancy followed her mother downstairs for breakfast. I was surprised to see her. But what really amazed me was the way they were both dressed this morning. They weren't going to church, that was for sure. Heavy blue denim cobbler aprons covered their cotton dresses, and they carried wide-brimmed straw hats, the kind we used to wear when we worked in the garden.

"Needless to say. I'm not going to church," Mrs. Arthur said, as she settled herself at the breakfast table. "Denny Sims will be here later this morning to take me to the graveyard. While you girls are gathering flowers to take to Oak Grove," she added, "I'll fix a box dinner and we'll eat with the folks after we get the graves cleared and decorated."

Denny Sims was a second or third cousin to Maud Arthur, and we seldom saw him around Newark. He lived in eastern Greene County and drove the school bus over there. He'd probably have a bus load of relatives that he'd picked up along the way this morning, all going to the Oak Grove cemetery, which was more than an hour's drive north of Newark.

Whether I wanted to or not, I had to tell Mrs. Arthur that I wouldn't be going to Oak Grove with them. There was no way I could avoid it now.

"I'll help Nancy pick the flowers and put them in water," I said. "But I can't go to the graveyard with you. I promised Mom that I would put flowers on Jamie's grave today, and Floyd will be here any time now to take me to the Flat Hollow church." I finished in a rush.

Mrs. Arthur put her fork down. She was looking at me, and seeing me now, and I wished that she wasn't. Her eyes seemed to be boring holes right through me, and I dreaded to hear what she would say.

"Go. By all means," she said, her eyes as hard as rocks. "But you can't take any flowers from here. We need all we've got."

Roses, peonies, and lilacs were in full bloom around the Arthur house, enough to cover half the graves at Flat Hollow, but I wouldn't have taken her flowers even if she'd offered them to me. There were wild flowers and woods fern that we could pick to decorate Jase and Jamie's graves, and Ora Empson and Clara Brent would be happy to give Floyd and me peonies and lilacs to make big bouquets for them. We didn't need Mrs. Arthur's flowers.

"That's all right," I replied. "We've got our own flowers."

Nancy and I put on gloves and cut a tubful of roses; then we filled another tub with long sprigs of lilacs and sweet-smelling peonies. We drew water from the well to pour over the flowers and keep them fresh; then Nancy called her mother and asked if we had enough flowers for the cemetery.

Mrs. Arthur came out to where we had the flowers in the deep shade of the house, then just stood and shook her head when she saw them. "You don't have enough fern," she said. Before Nancy could tell her that we'd picked all there was to find, Mrs. Arthur said, "Run up the road and ask Mrs. Watson if you can have a handful of her asparagus tops. That makes a prettier bouquet than woods fern," she added, "and not so hard to come by, either."

Nancy turned toward the gate, ready to do as she was told, but I held back. It was getting late and Floyd should've been here by now. The Watsons lived away on the other side of their store, out of sight from the Arthur house, and I didn't want to be there when Floyd came here for me.

"Go on!" Mrs. Arthur ordered. "And be quick about it."

I turned my back on her and followed Nancy out of the yard. The sooner I got it done, then the sooner I could get started on my way to Flat Hollow, I thought, as I hurried up the road toward the Watson house.

Mrs. Watson told us they had already picked all the asparagus fern they would need for their bouquets, and there was plenty more left in the garden. We should help ourselves to all we wanted. Which we did. And quickly, too. Breaking the stems off close to the ground and stacking the branches on one arm like we were cording wood.

When we got back home, our arms full of the feathery asparagus tops, Denny Sims was there. The tubs of flowers had already been loaded on the bus, and Mrs. Arthur was pacing up and down beside the bus, waiting for Nancy and me to get there.

"You took your time about it," she said crossly, and reached to take the asparagus tops from Nancy's hands. Then to me, she said, "Don't just stand there! Get on the bus so we can get started."

32

I held the greenery out to her, stepping back from the bus at the same time. "You take this," I said. "I'm not going."

Mrs. Arthur made no move to take the asparagus from my hands. "You are going," she said. "And I don't want to hear another word about it. That fellow Floyd you said would take you to Flat Hollow hasn't shown up. Get in."

"I've got to go to Flat Hollow," I said desperately.

Her eyes flashed with anger as she took a step toward me. I thought she was going to hit me. I guess Nancy thought the same thing. She moved closer to me, and whispered, "Please, Julie, don't argue with her. You'll just make things worse for yourself." She took my arm and I let her pull me toward the bus.

The aisle of the bus was blocked with tubs and buckets of flowers of every color and description. Boxed dinners and baskets of food occupied most of the rear seats. I laid the asparagus tops in with a tubful of wild roses, then stepped over the tub to the first vacant seat. I slid over to sit next to the window, and Nancy sat down beside me. Mrs. Arthur had taken a seat at the front of the bus so she could lean forward and talk to the driver.

After she had settled herself with a loud sigh, I heard her say, "You don't know the trouble I've had with that girl." Then she went on to tell him.

"Don't listen to her," Nancy said, under her breath.

I turned my face toward the window and didn't bother to answer her. I was so mad that my ears were buzzing. I doubt that I could have heard more had I tried. If there is one thing in this world worse than being forced to do something against your will, I don't know what it is, I thought. And I don't want to know, if I have to experience it to find out about it.

At the Oak Grove cemetery, I helped Nancy and the other young people to fill the tin cans, fruit jars, and funeral urns with water. Then we separated the flowers and made individual bouquets to put in the containers. The older members of the families cut weeds, raked the rubbish into piles and dumped it all into the gulley that lay on one side of the cemetery.

When the work was done, and the graves made neat and bright with flowers, the women spread tablecloths beneath the shade trees at the edge of the graveyard and put out the food. Everyone took a plate from one of the baskets and went to help themselves. I told Nancy that I wasn't hungry and went to find a shady spot where I could be by myself.

Oak Grove cemetery was laid out on top of a hill, with no church or dwelling place anywhere near that I could see. And from where I stood, I could see a long way. I wondered why the people had buried their dead so far away from a church or settlement. Maybe there had been one at one time, I thought, but the people had torn it down and moved away.

I sat down, put my back against the trunk of a big tree, and let my eyes wander over the miles and miles of hills and hollows before me. Floyd was out there somewhere. Probably wondering now where I'd gotten to, and why I hadn't waited to go to the Flat Hollow churchyard with him. He would never understand that I'd had no choice but to go with Mrs. Arthur this morning.

He knew she went to church every Sunday morning.

There was no reason for him to doubt that she would do so today. Why hadn't he come for me while she was supposed to be in church? That is what I had expected him to do to avoid facing Mrs. Arthur or having hard words with her about my going to Flat Hollow with him.

A suspicious thought crept into my mind and just hung there, waiting for me to disavow it or to give it credence. Floyd might have come to the Arthur house while Nancy and I were away getting asparagus tops for the bouquets, and Mrs. Arthur had sent him away with some trumped-up story. I wouldn't have put it past her, I thought. She was devious enough to do anything to thwart me and have her own way.

I crossed my arms on my drawn-up knees, then rested my head on my arms. Tears of anger and frustration burned my eyes as I thought of the fix I was in. I wouldn't have felt more helpless if I had been hog-tied and strung from a limb. Mom had asked just one thing of me before she'd left me here. She hadn't said behave yourself, as I'd expected, or told me to write to them. All she had asked was that I take flowers to Jamie on Decoration Day, and I hadn't been allowed to do that for her.

A hand touched my back, then someone sat down beside me. "Julie," Nancy said, "I've brought you a sandwich."

I raised my head and brushed a hand across my eyes to clear my view. "I'm not hungry," I said, and tried to smile. I shouldn't have tried smiling. Not the way I felt right then. My face crumpled, and I buried my head in my arms and began to cry like a baby, senselessly, and for no obvious reason.

Nancy put her arms around me and spoke softly, trying to get me to hush. "Please, don't do that Julie," she said. "Nothing can be that bad."

You don't know anything about it, I thought. You've never been in my shoes, so how could you know how bad they pinch? But the sound of her voice calmed me, and my sobs dwindled gradually to sniffs and snuffles. I sat up, wiped my face on my dress tail, and turned to face Nancy.

"Why does your mother hate me so?" I asked quietly. "I've never done anything to harm her."

"For the same reason she hates me," Nancy replied, her voice so low I could barely hear her. "We're girls, and we're young."

"But that doesn't make sense. There must be something . . ."

"Believe me, Julie. She doesn't need any other reason."

There was nothing I could say to that. Nancy didn't seem inclined to add anything to what she'd said, either. She sat quietly tugging at tufts of grass, then letting the blades drift slowly from her hand, while I digested what I'd learned. It was so unreasonable to be hated just because I was a young girl. I couldn't help being what I was. Only time could change that.

"Wonder what time it is." I broke the silence.

"Oh, my gosh!" Nancy tossed a handful of grass into the air and stood up. "I forgot. I was supposed to find you and tell you they're all ready to go home."

I got to my feet and gave my skirt a quick brush with my hand. "Then we'd better show ourselves," I said. "I wouldn't want to be left here. Dead or alive," I added.

Nancy giggled. "Maybe they'd leave you," she said.

"But Uncle Denny would make her wait for me." Then she got serious and said, "Julie, don't let mother upset you so. It's just a couple of weeks until school's out. Try to bear with her till then."

My eyes met hers, and I nodded. There was no time for anything more. We were at the bus, and everyone was waiting for us.

The sun was going down behind the trees when we got to Newark. It would be dark as pitch in another hour. But late as it was, we were still the first ones back to town. There was not a soul at home in the other houses that we passed. And when we got to the Arthur house, there was no sign of any kind that Floyd Perry had been there and gone while we'd been away.

Chapter Five

This was the Saturday before graduation. Five more days, six counting Sunday, then I could walk out of the Arthur House and need never look back. After we'd got home from the Oak Grove cemetery, Mrs. Arthur had never once mentioned Floyd Perry or brought up the subject of my going to Flat Hollow at any time in the near future.

She had been even more cold and distant toward me. As if I bore no resemblance to the girl she had welcomed so warmly to her home a few months ago. I didn't mind her coolness. In fact, I preferred it that way. I could get along with her, if she left me alone. Which she did.

We worked together and ate at the same table, yet she never spoke directly to me. When it was necessary, like this morning, she would speak through Nancy.

"We'll go to Indianapolis today and pick out your graduation dress," she told Nancy. "I have some buying to do for the store, so we'll get it all done at once." Then with a cold eye for me, she added, "Julie will watch the shop while we're gone and close it at five o'clock sharp. I want supper ready to sit down to when we get home."

They left the house soon afterwards, and I was happy

to see them go. The sawmill where Floyd worked closed at noon on Saturday, and I thought that Floyd might come to Newark to see me this afternoon. I hadn't seen him since the night of the class play when we'd gone to Mia Bailey's place at the Y.

I had expected to be busy today, since it was the last Saturday to shop before graduation day. I knew a lot of the girls hadn't bought a new dress for it yet. But hardly a soul came in. Those who came with the notion to buy left the store as soon as they heard that Mrs. Arthur was in the city buying new stock.

"We'll come back later," they said. "Maybe we can find a good dress at a bargain."

I could have told them that that was a waste of wishful thinking. This shop didn't have any bargains. But I kept my mouth shut, and minded my own business.

On the small wages I got for working here, even if Mrs. Arthur had been willing to sell me a dress, I couldn't have paid the sale price on one. Let alone the price she would've asked for it to begin with. Instead, a while back, I had bought four yards of soft white muslin and a scrap of bright remnant from Bud Watson's general store and made my dress. It wasn't anything fancy. Just a plain, simple dress with a scoop neckline, puffed sleeves, and a fitted waist above a full skirt. The bright belt and piping made it look better than it was.

As I sized dresses and blouses and straightened the sale rack that afternoon, I made plans and daydreamed about the day when I would leave the Arthur house. First thing, I thought, I would need a job. And I knew that wouldn't be easy to come by. Grown men, the ones who could find a job, were working six days a week and ten hours a day for twenty-five dollars. And there were still a lot of people out of work. But I wouldn't dwell on that now. It would just discourage me, and I couldn't afford to lose hope. There would be something I could do to earn a living. I wasn't particular. I'd take any kind of work I could find.

Floyd Perry had said that he would help me find a job when the time came. And even though he hadn't been here to see me for a while, I knew I could depend on him to keep his word to me. Floyd had to work long, hard hours at the sawmill, and he couldn't always get away when he'd like to. Right now they might be supplying light poles for the electric company that was bringing light to the hills. If that were so, I wouldn't see Floyd until the work was done.

But on the other hand, I thought to myself, it could be that he figured the sight of him would set Mrs. Arthur off on a tangent again and make things worse for me than they were already. He'd not show his face here if he thought it would get me in trouble with her, no matter how much he might want to see me.

He knew, and I knew, that Mrs. Arthur was just as anxious to be rid of me as I was to see the last of her. But I couldn't leave Newark before I got my diploma from high school. Without that certificate, I could never hope to enter normal college or ever receive a teaching permit. And that was the one thing I felt I had to have to insure my survival.

I'd thought a lot about survival during these years of the Depression, and teaching school seemed like a sure-fire way to make money and stay alive. While people were starving to death all over the country, and men were killing themselves because they couldn't find work and feed their families, the schools were kept open and the teachers went on working. I didn't know how much money the schoolteachers were paid, but it was a steady income. And they had their self-respect. And that seemed to be the first thing a person lost when they were out of work.

Mom had taught school for four years after Grandmother Curry died and before she married Dad, but she hadn't kept it up, and her license to teach had expired long ago. That had been one of her deepest regrets during the hard times. "If only I'd kept on with my teaching," she'd say, when Dad couldn't find work, "we'd have a little something coming in regularly."

Well, Dad was working regularly now. Their hard times were behind them, and Seely would have an easier time of it when she started high school this fall than I'd had. I didn't begrudge her the better things. I was happy for her.

There hadn't been anyone in the shop for hours now, which meant I'd had a lot of time for thinking. But thinking of Mom and Dad and Seely and Robert was treading on dangerous ground. I was unhappy here and homesick to see them. And there wasn't a thing in the world that I could do about either one but bear it.

I shook myself and thought I might as well lock the door, even if it was early, and go in and start supper. Keep myself busy at something. But before I could put the thought into action, the door opened and a young man entered.

He was a stranger to me. We didn't see many men in the dress shop, and certainly never one like him. Once in a while a family man would come in to pay the balance on something his wife had asked Maud Arthur to lay back for her. But those men were tight-lipped, with a weary, closed-in look about them. They would count out the money slowly and carefully, usually to the penny, then take their purchases and leave the store without one word.

They were as different as daylight and dark from this smiling, open-faced young man in the sweat-stained tan uniform and dusty, mud-caked brown boots. His damp, red-gold hair curled from under an old baseball cap he had stuck on his head, and his short straight nose was sun-burned and peeling. It was plain to see that he had come directly from a job of work to the dress shop, but it was a mystery to me where he could be working here in the hills. There wasn't any work for the people who lived here, let alone a stranger.

"I don't bite pretty girls on Saturday," he said, with a teasing smile. "I save that for the second Tuesday of every week."

I felt the color rise in my face as I realized I had been staring at him. "Oh." I stepped forward. "Could I do something for you?"

"I'm sure you could." He smiled again, showing even white teeth. "But right now, I'd like a gift for my mother. It's her birthday," he added.

As we moved about the store, I could feel his eyes on me, making me self-conscious and awkward. I wished that someone—anyone—would come in so I wouldn't be alone with him. I showed him everything we had in the store, and he shook his head at everything he saw. I was beginning to despair of ever finding something that pleased him.

He didn't seem to mind. He followed me from one thing to another, talking all the while and punctuating his words now and then with a friendly grin. He told me that he was a lineman, working for the electric company, stringing power lines throughout the township. But he only worked until noon on Saturday and went home for the weekend. His folks lived in Bicknell, where his dad worked in the coal mines. He was on his way there, now.

"But I can't go home empty-handed on Mother's birthday," he said. "She would throw her boy Chance right back out the door."

"Chance?" I said, amazed. "Is that your name? I never heard the likes of that."

"Chance Cooper," he said, smiling and moving nearer to me. "My daddy said that he asked my mama to take a chance with him. Then when she did, and I came along afterwards, she called me Chance."

I felt my face grow warm. I was blushing at his words, and I turned quickly to a stack of brightly colored scarfs on a nearby counter. I made no answer to his explanation of how he got his name.

He bought a paisley scarf and a pair of white gloves for his mother finally, and I gift-wrapped them for him. Mrs. Arthur would have charged him a dime for the tissue paper and the piece of ribbon, but I let it go for the price of the purchase.

"Thank you, Miss . . ." Chance stopped. "You know my life history, but I don't even know your name." He gave me another of his teasing grins. "I can't come in here every Saturday afternoon and ask for the girl who blushes," he said.

"It's Julie," I said. "Julie Robinson. But you mustn't . . ."

"I'll be seeing you, Julie Robinson." He touched his fingers to the bill of the baseball cap and left the store.

43

". . . ask for me," I finished, as I watched him stride down the road, get into a dusty old car, and drive away.

This good-looking stranger fascinated me with his smile and light-hearted way of speaking. I'd never met anyone like him. I hugged myself and smiled as I turned from watching him through the window. Already, I was thinking of the next time I would see him. He had said he'd be back, and I held to those words as though he had made me a solemn promise. Even when my common sense told me that it was a line, that he told this to every girl he met, I put the thought out of my mind and assured myself that he meant every word of it.

Floyd Perry, with his dependability, was forgotten for the moment. Chance Cooper had brought a bright rosy glow into my drab, do-nothing life, and I reveled in its light. I didn't even mind the sour look I got from Mrs. Arthur later that night when she could find nothing to complain about the way I'd done things today. I had something else on my mind now besides whether or not I was pleasing her.

A while back, even yesterday, I couldn't have waited to tell Nancy about the dreamy fellow I'd met, but tonight I didn't mention Chance Cooper to her. Even when she whispered, "Julie, what have you been up to? You look like you've just caught the brass ring on the merry-go-round," I didn't tell her. If he never came back, I wanted to be the only one who knew that I'd been looking for him.

After school, on Monday, when I went to the shop to spell Mrs. Arthur from work, Chance Cooper was solemnly eyeing a dress that she was holding in front of him.

My heart leaped with pleasure to see him there, but I was careful to hide it. It would never do for Mrs. Arthur to find out that I knew Chance. And I sure didn't want him to know how glad I was to see him again.

When she saw me, Mrs. Arthur said, "Julie will help you," and handed me the dress she'd been showing him.

I could tell she was out of sorts and quickly losing her patience with him. I took the dress from her hands and smiled at Chance behind her back. When the door closed at the rear of the store, and I knew she couldn't hear me, I said, "Is there anything she hasn't shown you?"

Chance laughed shortly. "Yeah," he said. "Courtesy."

I smiled at his candor and tried to change the subject. "Did your mother like her gift?"

"Very much," he replied. Then he went right back to talking about Mrs. Arthur. "How do you fit in here?" he asked. "Is that woman some kind of kin to you "

I shook my head, then explained that my family had moved away to be nearer my dad's work, and they had left me here to finish out the school year. "Her daughter Nancy is my best friend," I said. "That's why Mrs. Arthur let me stay here." Then I added quickly, "I earn my keep. She pays me a small wage for working here in the shop and helping her with the cooking and housework. But if it wasn't for her, I wouldn't be graduating with the rest of my classmates this Friday."

There was no denying that Mrs. Arthur had been a help to me. Never mind how grudgingly she had given this help. And I wouldn't speak ill of her to a stranger I'd just met, no matter how attractive I thought he was. Dad used to say, "Give the devil his due, but not one iota

45

more." I felt like I had given Mrs. Arthur the credit she deserved. Nothing else.

Chance wore a puzzled expression as he looked at me and shook his head. "She didn't strike me as the kind of woman who ever did anything just from the goodness of her heart," he said. "But you know her better than I do."

"I guess I know Mrs. Arthur as well as anyone ever knows someone else," I said, thinking of the way she had tricked me out of going with Floyd to Flat Hollow on Decoration Day.

"Do you think she would allow you to go out with me some night?"

He didn't wait for my answer, but went on as if it was all settled, and he could come calling at some time.

"My graduation class is having a reunion on Wednesday night at the Ridgeport dance hall," Chance said. "I've been hoping ever since I met you that you'd go with me."

I wasn't expecting anything like this. Not so soon after meeting him. "I . . . I couldn't possibly," I stammered. "I don't know you."

Chance grinned and stepped so close to me that I couldn't move without touching him. "Julie, you know more about me than the kids I used to run around with in school. And that's who we'll be seeing at the dance. Maybe not all of them," he said, correcting himself. "But there'll be a good crowd. Most of the kids I went to school with have married now and moved out of the hills to find work, but the ones who can make it back will be there."

I stood still and silently shook my head no, I couldn't go to the dance with him. It was out of the question for me to even consider it. For more reasons than I cared to mention. "I don't go anywhere on a school night," I said finally, giving him the least of the reasons.

"Why not?" Chance asked. "Are you afraid of what that old witch will do to you afterwards?"

About that time I heard someone moving about on the other side of the closed door to the dining room, not a dozen steps from where we were standing. "Sh . . ." I put my finger to my lips. "She'll hear you."

I didn't think that she could really hear what we were saying, but just the tone of our voice would be enough to bring her into the shop.

"You'll have to go now," I told Chance. "It's time for me to lock up the shop."

He stepped back from me then and turned toward the front door. I followed him. "I'll be here Wednesday night to take you to the dance," he said, reaching for the door-knob. "And don't you forget it."

"You mustn't come here!" Just the thought of what Mrs. Arthur would do then gave me the cold chills. "It would only cause trouble," I said. "And I have to live here until school's out."

"Then I'll wait for you at the schoolyard," he said. I drew back in alarm.

"Think about it. Julie," Chance said softly. "No one ever needs to know but you and me."

He left then, and I locked the door behind him.

I didn't know what I was going to do about Chance Cooper and what he had in mind for Wednesday night. Even if Mrs. Arthur hadn't been so dead-set against whatever I wanted to do, I still couldn't have gone to the dance with him. I didn't have anything fit to wear.

My mind was in a turmoil as I gave the shop a lick and

a promise and closed the dining room door firmly behind me. "Oh, forget it!" I told myself, and went on to the kitchen.

Nancy was setting the table for supper. Mrs. Arthur was nowhere in sight. Nancy looked up when I walked in and said, "Julie, who were you talking to just now? I heard you tell them to forget it."

"I was talking to myself," I replied. Then it all came spilling out like rain from a downspout. I told Nancy how I had met Chance Cooper, about the dance on Wednesday night, and what he proposed to do. Listening to myself, as I related my troubles to Nancy, I couldn't believe the fix I'd gotten myself into while minding the store and my own business.

"What am I going to do? I know he'll come here to the house when I don't meet him at the schoolyard."

She smiled and went on placing silver on the table. "Do you want to go to the dance with him?"

I hesitated for a moment. Did I? "Yes," I said, just above a whisper. "But you know your mother wouldn't ever stand for it."

"Then we won't tell her." Nancy was whispering now. "Wait until she goes upstairs that night, then you leave by the window. She'll never know that you're gone."

"Nancy, I'd never get away with it. She'd know just by looking at me that I was hiding something from her. You know as well as I do," I said, "that your mother has an uncanny knack for ferreting out things that people try to keep from her."

Nancy laughed quietly and glanced toward the stairs. "She can be fooled though, if you put your mind to it," she said. "I know. I've done it. Some of the time when she thought I was practicing the class play, I was out with Jimmy Hawkins. She never knew the difference."

"You fooled me, too," I said. "I thought you liked acting and playing a part so much that you never even looked at boys. I didn't know you liked Jimmy Hawkins," I added.

"I didn't dare to tell you," Nancy said, with another glance at the stairs. "I was afraid Mother would get wind of what I was up to and get the truth out of you somehow."

She stood still and turned to face me, her blue eyes dark and sober. "Julie, I'd do it again, even if I knew she'd find out about it," she whispered. Then, "I'm just as anxious as you are for school to end. Maybe then, I can get away from here too."

I heard the door close at the top of the stairs and moved away from Nancy to start taking up supper from the stove.

Chapter Six

I stayed out of Mrs. Arthur's way as much as I could for the next two days, doing my work quietly and spending my free time in my room. When Nancy winked at me and suggested playing cards on Wednesday evening, I claimed to have a headache and went to my room. Nancy and I had both learned to be sneaky and to keep secrets, I thought to myself.

I slid the bolt, quietly locking the door, then stripped hurriedly to bathe and dress for my date with Chance Cooper. Nancy had loaned me a pair of her sandals to wear tonight, and my white graduation dress was freshly ironed and hanging in the closet, ready to slip into.

I trembled to think of what would happen if I was caught slipping out of the house to meet Chance. Mrs. Arthur would run me off the place and throw my clothes out after me. And there, thought I, would go all my hopes and dreams of ever making something of myself.

I couldn't believe, even while I was getting ready to go, that I was actually willing to risk everything for an evening out with a boy I hardly knew. But I was stubborn. And then I thought, getting caught by Mrs. Arthur was just one of the risks I was taking tonight. Chance Cooper himself was the other.

I might end up walking home from the dance. Or worse. I'd heard the girls at school telling how they'd had to walk home on occasion. One of the girls had said, "One of these times when a fellow says to me, 'Walk . . . or else,' I'm going to say that I'd rather else. Just to see if he knows what he's talking about."

Then someone else said, "Oh, they know! The night when Ashley Hudson, old Tarzan himself, walked me home from the Sweetheart Dance I wrestled him every step of the way. Then just when I was ready to give in to him, he gave up!"

Everyone had laughed, Nancy and I included. Then Nancy had whispered to me that she thought the girls had led the boys on; things like that didn't happen to nice girls. But now I wasn't so sure about that. How did a boy know that you were a nice girl? If Chance couldn't tell what kind of girl I was, I thought, the road would be mighty long and dark walking home tonight.

I blew out the light, and then I noticed that the lamplight that usually showed under my door, had dimmed to a faint line. While I'd been wool-gathering, Nancy and her mother had gone upstairs to bed, leaving the lamp turned low for a night light.

I waited a while longer to make sure they had settled in for the night, then I went to the window. There was a loud screech of wood rubbing together as I raised the window, causing my heart to beat faster and stopping me dead in my tracks. Again I waited, listening for a sound from upstairs. But all was quiet. I lifted my skirt over the low sill and stepped to the ground. When my eyes got used to the darkness, I went quickly around the house and up the road to the schoolhouse.

I felt breathless, excited, and more than a little scared. I'd never gone out with any man except Floyd Perry and, near as I could tell, Chance Cooper wasn't a thing in the world like Floyd. The closer I got to the schoolyard, the slower I walked. I hoped he wouldn't be there, crossed my fingers and prayed that I would be stood up. Then I saw his car lights blink on and off, and I knew I was committed to see this night through; come what may. I stopped, hesitating and unsure of myself, then I took a deep breath and went forward to meet him.

"I'm glad you decided to go," Chance said quietly. "It wouldn't have been any fun without you."

I stepped into the light, then crossed it quickly to the dark on the other side. "If I get away with this," I said, as I got in the car, "I'll never lie and be sneaky again as long as I live. So help me," I breathed.

Chance laughed. "Stolen apples are always the sweetest."

I didn't believe that, but I couldn't argue the point. Maybe he knew better than I about such things. This was my first experience at stealing anything. And even though it was only a small chunk of time, getting hold of it hadn't been sweet. Right now, as I sat next to Chance, moving swiftly down the road toward Ridgeport, it was making a bitter taste in my mouth like a bite of a green persimmon.

Chance talked about the old friends and classmates that he was expecting to see at the dance, but I hardly heard a word he said. I was too worried about the outcome of this evening, and wishing it was already over.

The class reunion square dance was in full swing when we got to the Ridgeport dance hall. Five sets of dancers, made up of four couples each, were do-si-doeing around the floor, while a tall, slim man in a black outfit called the steps. The calls were strange to my ears.

"A bird flies out, and the crow hops in," the caller chanted in a singsong voice, while a woman skipped out of the circle and a heavy-footed man stamped in. The other dancers promenaded around the ring, then took the bird and the crow into the circle, and two others dropped back to start the whole rigmarole over again. I was fascinated by the dance, but it looked too complicated for me to ever learn it.

Chance assured me that it was simple to catch on to. He'd teach me, he said. When the next dance started, Chance pulled me onto the floor where we were joined by three other couples. The caller shouted, "All join hands," and after that, he lost me. I turned left when I should've gone right, I went around the cage instead of through it, and when he called, "Grab your partner, promenade home," I ended up with a man I'd never seen before.

Chance rescued me, and I held on to him until my head stopped spinning. "Aren't you glad you came?" he asked, with a big grin.

I just nodded my head. I was too out of breath to speak.

Chance introduced me to his friends as Cinderella, and I let it pass. I thought it was just as well that no one knew my name. It would take a little longer for word to reach Mrs. Arthur that I'd been here. All I needed was two days of grace, then it wouldn't matter what she heard about me. I would be gone from her sight.

The men took turns calling the dance steps that night so no one would miss dancing. When it came Chance's turn to be the caller, I sat on a bench along one wall and watched as the dancers went through the complicated dance steps as smoothly as clockwork. If they had been frozen in motion, I thought, the picture of their colorful movements would have made a lovely piecework quilt.

The dance ended at midnight with a slow waltz. Chance said, "The last dance belongs to the one what brung you," and put his arms around me. I followed his lead as if we had been waltzing together all our lives. I leaned into his arms and forgot everything during that last dance but the music and the pleasure of the moment.

His lips close to my ear, Chance whispered, "You just fit in my arms . . . for dancing," and pulled me up tight to him. I went stiff all over and missed a step. He laughed softly, and held me even closer. "What's the matter, Cinderella? Did you lose your glass slipper?"

I stepped back, breaking his hold on me, and walked off the floor. I didn't care how it looked to the others at the time. I was thinking of myself. With the long dark road to Newark ahead of me, it wouldn't do for him to think I approved of his hugging and squeezing. He would get the idea that I was leading him on. I'd rather have him mad at me now for walking off the dance floor than have him angry later when he found out that I didn't play night-games. And maybe even accuse me of asking for it.

I didn't have much faith in Nancy's belief that a man wouldn't use force on a nice girl. I thought it depended more on the kind of man he was than the sort of girl he was with. It didn't prove a thing to me that Jimmy Hawkins hadn't tried to get fresh with Nancy when she slipped out to meet him. He had to face her in school the next day. And worse than that, her mother, if Nancy complained about him.

If Chance Cooper had it in mind to try something on the way home, neither of these thing would stop him. I had no one to complain to, and he would have no reason ever to face me again.

Chance followed me to the car and slid in under the steering wheel. I got into the car on the other side and snuggled as close as I could get to the car door. Neither one of us said a word. He started the motor, and the rear wheels of the car threw loose gravel as we roared away from the dance hall.

The nights in Greene County must be blacker and darker than anywhere else in the world. And this night seemed to be the darkest ever. The weak light from the car headlamps showed us the way, but it didn't light up the inside of the car. Chance's voice came out of the darkness, low and earnest. "You don't need to be scared of me, Julie. I wouldn't hurt you."

My throat was tight and I had to try twice before I could speak. "I'm not scared," I lied. And kept my hold on the door handle. If the car stopped, I was going to be out that door and running before he could reach me.

Going to that dance with Chance Cooper had been a stupid, stupid thing to do, I thought. I could be at home, safe in my own bed right now, with nothing more terrible to look forward to or contend with than Mrs. Arthur's sharp tongue. Yet I was here in a car, on a dark road where anything was apt to happen, and probably would.

But nothing did happen. Chance switched off the lights and motor when we got to Newark and let the car coast as near as he dared to the Arthur house. He reached across to open the car door for me and found my hand still gripping the door handle.

"Julie," he said quietly. "I asked you to go with me tonight so I'd have a girl for the dance. If I'd had anything else in mind, I wouldn't have picked you for it."

I scooted out of the car and ran toward the house, my face hot and burning with shame. I'd made a fool of myself for no reason. He hadn't even thought of me as a girl. He just wanted a dance partner.

I hoisted myself over the window sill and into my room, silently praying all the while that Mrs. Arthur wouldn't be waiting there to catch me and throw me back out the window. Even after I was safely in the room, and there was no sign of anyone else ever being there, I couldn't believe that I'd gotten away with it. I still half expected to hear Mrs. Arthur call my name and demand an explanation for coming in through the window at this hour.

Late as it was when I got to bed, I was still the first one up the next morning. I had the coffee on and breakfast nearly ready when Mrs. Arthur and Nancy came downstairs. Nancy asked me how my headache was this morning, and it took me a moment to remember that I had supposedly gone to bed with a sick headache the night before. "It's fine now," I answered.

Mrs. Arthur said, "If you paid attention in class, you wouldn't have headaches from reading and studying half the night by a kerosene lamp." Then she went on to say she couldn't wait for the power lines to reach Newark so she could have electric lights like other civilized human beings. "Not that I have to depend on it to live well," she muttered.

Nancy rolled her eyes, making a face behind her mother's back, and answered sweetly, "Yes, mother, we know."

We finished breakfast and got out of the house and on our way to school as quickly as possible. I didn't want Mrs. Arthur to have the time to study my face and start asking questions. I just knew that she'd be able to tell that I was hiding something, if she got a good look at me.

Nancy knew that I had something to hide, and she started asking questions as soon as we were out of the house. She couldn't believe that Chance Cooper hadn't kissed me, that he hadn't even tried to. "You don't mean it," she said. "Didn't he even try to put his hand inside your blouse or under your skirt?"

I shook my head. "Really, Nancy, as for any of that kind of thing, you would've thought I was his sister. Or even his brother."

I didn't let on to her how glad I'd been at the time to be treated like his sister. "He said he only wanted someone to dance with," I said. "And that's all we did."

"Are you going to see him again?"

"I doubt it," I said. "He didn't mention it. Besides, I won't be here after Saturday," I added.

We were quiet the rest of the way to school. Then as we were going into the schoolhouse, Nancy giggled and said, "Isn't it a stinking shame that we can't tell those girls, who think they know it all, about last night? Wouldn't their mouths drop?"

"Oh, Nancy, you mustn't," I said. "No one else must ever hear of it."

"I wouldn't tell on you, Julie. You know that." Then as if she was thinking out loud, Nancy said, "I guess that's our punishment for sneaking out to do something. No matter how much we'd like to, we can't ever tell anyone about it later."

For the next two days I held my breath every time Mrs. Arthur looked at me or opened her mouth. Then it was Friday evening, and I felt like I had it made. I would get my diploma tonight. And after that, I wouldn't have to worry about her again.

Chapter Seven

When she was ready to leave for the commencement that evening, Nancy looked beautiful. It was a good thing that I hadn't known beforehand how gorgeous her dress was. I might have been ashamed to wear my homemade cotton one. Now it was too late to worry.

We stood together before the full-length mirror on the shop's dressing room door and hugged each other as we hadn't done in a long time. Nancy said that we made quite a picture. I agreed with her. She, with her blond hair smooth and shining above the saffron-colored silk, and I sat beside her, my dark auburn hair hanging in loose waves to my shoulders and wearing a homemade white cotton dress, made a clear picture of contrast.

"Best friends, forever," Nancy said to our reflection in the looking-glass.

My reflection smiled and nodded, then I turned away from the mirror. I knew this would be our last night as close friends. Her mother would see to that. But I couldn't let Nancy know how I felt. It would spoil the evening for her. We had waited too long for graduation day to let anything put a damper on it now.

It was full dark when we left to walk to the schoolhouse.

Mrs. Arthur carried a flashlight, but she kept switching the light from one side of the road to the other, and we still couldn't see where we were walking.

As we turned into the schoolyard, the beam of light struck Floyd Perry full in the face, and Mrs. Arthur drew in her breath, startled.

"You nearly scared me to death," she said, and kept the light aimed at his face.

Floyd looked handsome. Almost like a picture in a magazine. He had on a new dark suit, white shirt, and necktie, and he had had his hair trimmed since I'd seen him last. But the best part was his smile, chipped tooth and all, aimed straight at me. I don't know who reached out first, but all of a sudden we had our arms around each other and we were both laughing and talking at the same time.

"I rode to town with the teacher," Floyd said. "But I couldn't sit still and wait any longer."

At the door to the auditorium Floyd left us to return to his seat next to Mr. Thompson. Mrs. Arthur took a chair that was reserved for the parents in the front row. As Nancy and I went to put on our caps and gowns, I found myself wishing with all my heart that Mom and Dad were seated on that front row tonight. They would be so proud to be there.

For the candlelight procession that preceded the handing out of the diplomas, we were lined up alphabetically according to our last names. Nancy was one of the first two leading the procession. I was near the end of it. It was a wonder that we didn't set fire to the building with the lighted candles, or at the very least, the person next in line to us. But it went off without a hitch.

When Mr. Andes, the principal, called my name, I didn't think my legs would carry me to the stage. But I managed to get there, shake his hand, and accept my diploma. I didn't stop at my seat as the others had done. I walked straight by it to the door and out into the cool, dark night.

I thought I was going to throw up. And if I did, I wanted to be alone when it happened. The door behind me opened, letting out a band of light as someone else came out, then closed again, leaving the schoolyard in darkness.

"Julie, are you all right" Chance Cooper was standing beside me. "You were so pale when you left the room, that I followed you out here."

I was surprised to see him. I never expected ever to hear from him again. Not after the way I had behaved toward him.

"What are you doing here?" I asked rudely.

"You went to my reunion, so I came to your graduation. It's as simple as that."

I turned to walk away from him, but I was still lightheaded and I stumbled. Chance quickly took my arm and held me until I was steady on my feet. "Are you all right?" he asked again.

"Stand away from her!"

Suddenly, Floyd was there in front of us. His hands were clenched fists at his side, and his face showed up as white as his shirt front. "Mister, I told you to move," he said, the words dropping slowly from between his teeth.

Chance put his arm around me protectively. "Julie?" he said, questioning Floyd's right to be there.

"I'll take care of Julie!" Floyd grabbed my arm, pulling me toward him, and shoved Chance aside as he did so. "She don't need any help from you," he added.

Commencement exercises were over and people came streaming out the door, staring at us as they passed by. Some of them stopping to watch and listen. Chance made a lunge at Floyd, and I threw myself between them. "Stop it!" I cried. "Stop it this minute!"

I might as well have been screaming to the wind for all the attention they paid to my words. When they had wrestled each other to the ground, I pushed my way through the crowd that had gathered around them and ran to lose myself in the darkness.

Tears of hurt and anger blinded me as I stumbled headlong down the rough road, hurrying to find a place where no one would find me. I left the road at the first dirt lane I came to, and a few steps farther on I came upon a tree that had fallen along the wayside. I slumped down on the tree trunk and bawled until I thought I'd drained every drop of water out of my body. When I couldn't cry anymore, I got to my feet and started walking slowly back to town.

The lamp on the kitchen table was lit, sending streamers of light from the Arthur house, when I got there I knew that Mrs. Arthur would be waiting for me in the kitchen, but it never once entered my mind to go around to the back and climb in through the window to avoid meeting her. I opened the door walked in and met Mrs. Arthur's fury face-to-face. I knew that I must look a sight and I could tell from the way she was looking at me that she new exactly why I was in such a state.

Nancy hadn't come home yet. Not that I could expect

her to help me. She couldn't afford to speak out against her mother in my behalf. She still had to live with her. But when Nancy was around, Mrs. Arthur was more apt to hold her tongue and soft-pedal her words.

"Look at you! You're a disgrace," she said, as soon as the door closed behind me. "Acting like a slut and making a spectacle of yourself with those two men." Then she added piously, "It's a blessing your folks weren't here to see you."

I didn't try to stop the boiling anger that I felt toward the woman in front of me. It had been building up for weeks now, and until this moment I'd had to keep it all inside and not let it show.

"Leave my parents out of this," I said. "There was nothing for anyone to see but a disagreement between two boys." My words came spilling out loud and hot. I didn't care if the whole town heard me talking back to her.

Mrs. Arthur's face seemed to swell and turned a livid red, like she was about to burst a blood vessel. "Just a little disagreement, huh!" she screamed. "It looked to me more like two dogs fighting over a bitch in heat!"

I forgot that she was my best friend's mother, that she had given me a place to sleep and eat until I finished school. I'd had all I could stand from her. I wanted to strike out with my hands, to hit her, but instead I screamed right back at her, aiming to hurt her with words.

"You're a disgusting, evil-minded, vicious old woman," I cried. "And I hope your tongue falls out for the hateful things you've said to me!"

I ran to my room, slammed the door, and shoved home the bolt so she would know I had locked her out. She tried

63

the doorknob and pounded on the door, demanding that I open it. When I wouldn't answer her, she shouted, "You be ready to leave my house by morning!"

I opened the door and stood in the opening. "I'll not step one foot from here until I get my pay for these past two weeks," I said.

Maud Arthur had had her back to me when I started speaking, but then she whirled around to face me, her face red and hard with anger. "You'll not get one red cent from me," she said. "Your room and board have cost me more than any wages you might have coming." She turned and left the room. A moment later I heard the sound of her heavy steps going up the stairs to her bedroom.

I closed the door with a bang, then threw myself across the bed. I had been counting on those two weeks' wages to help tide me over until I found a job. Now I didn't know what to do.

After a while, I knew there was only one thing I could do under the circumstances. Go home to Mom and Dad. Even though I didn't want to go, it would give me a place to live until I found work and got a place of my own. And they would be happy to have me there. I didn't know where they lived, but it wouldn't be hard to find them in a town as small as Jubilee.

I packed everything I owned into an old suitcase that Clara Brent had given me when I moved away from home, raised the window, and slipped through to the backyard. I had made up my mind to walk to the Y in the road tonight, then catch the first bus from there in the morning. Tonight, the long walk on the dark road to the Y didn't frighten me. Anger and determination had driven all fear from my mind. All I could think of was getting away from this house.

I hadn't gone ten steps from the window when Floyd said, "Julie, I was just coming to talk to you."

"Go away. Haven't you caused me enough trouble for one night?"

"That's what I wanted to talk to you about," he said. "I'm sorry I raised a ruckus at the school, but I didn't know that fellow was a friend of yours."

"And you couldn't wait to find out, could you?"

"Aw, Julie, don't be mad. Chance Cooper and me have had a long talk and we've got our differences squared away. He ain't mad no longer."

"I don't care to hear about it." I started on by him toward the road.

Floyd seemed to notice my suitcase for the first time. "What's this?" he asked, and took the heavy bag from my hand.

I stood still to tell him that Mrs. Arthur had ordered me out of her house because of the fight at the school. "And I'm leaving right now," I said.

I felt my voice start to break. I knew if I spoke one more word I would start crying. It seemed like any time that I was filled to the brim with anger, tears rode on the crest of the waves, and the least little thing would cause them to spill over.

Floyd didn't say anything until he had carried my suitcase back to the house and heaved it into my room. Then he took my arm and guided my steps toward the road. "We'll walk awhile, Julie, and decide about what you're going to do."

"Mr. Thompson has gone on home," Floyd said, as we walked aimlessly along the road. "If he'd waited awhile, I could've got his car and taken you wherever you wanted to go. But I can't let you start walking away at this time of night."

There were two graveled roads that crossed in Newark, and twice that many well-worn paths and wagon tracks coming out of the hills and running into town from other directions. Floyd chose to follow a dark path that led up the hollow and away from the main road. Since he was still holding my hand, I went with him.

It was easy to talk to Floyd in the darkness. Not that we ever had any problem communicating. We could look at each other sometimes and know what the other was thinking. Just like now. I could almost feel Floyd wanting to know what had really caused the trouble with Maud Arthur. And I wanted to tell him. But I wanted to explain it in my own way so he would understand my side of it.

"I suppose you could say that this all started the night I went for a ride with you, while Mrs. Arthur was at the class play," I began. "She nearly had a fit when she found out that I had left the house, and since then she has watched me like a hawk, just waiting to catch me at something shady."

"Where does Chance Cooper fit into the picture."

"She doesn't know about Chance," I said. Then I added quickly, "Or at least she didn't until tonight."

"Neither did I," Floyd mumbled under his breath.

After a few steps, he stopped and turned me to face him. "Tell me about this Chance fellow, Julie. Where did you meet him, and why would he feel he had a right to fight for you?"

"When you talked to him, what did he say?"

"That you were friends," Floyd replied. "Nothing more."

"I don't know why he thought he had to defend me," I said. "We barely know each other. He came into the shop one day to get a gift for his mother, then he stayed to talk for an hour. I guess he was lonely," I added.

When Floyd didn't say anything, I went on talking. He seemed to expect it. "I was feeling lonesome that day for you and the folks when he came in, and his friendly chatter cheered me. You hadn't been to see me for weeks," I said defensively. "You didn't even show up on Decoration Day, like you'd promised to do, to take me to the Flat Hollow cemetery."

"Hold on there, Julie!" Now Floyd was on the defensive. "I came to get you that morning, but Mrs. Arthur told me that you and Nancy had already gone to the graveyard."

"She lied to you," I said flatly.

"I know that now," he replied. "But at the time, I saw no reason to doubt her word. The house was shut up, and she was waiting beside the bus for Denny Sims to finish loading the flowers so they could leave. I looked around awhile," Floyd added, "but I saw no sign of you and Nancy anywhere."

Hearing Floyd's account of what happened that Sunday morning, made me mad at Mrs. Arthur all over again. "That horrid woman," I said. "She didn't tell me you'd been there looking for me. I thought you'd forgotten." I didn't add that later I'd figured she'd sent him away.

Floyd was quiet for a moment, then he asked, "Is that why you went to the square dance with Chance Cooper?

67

You thought I'd forgotten you?"

So he knew already that I'd gone to the class reunion with Chance, I thought. I wouldn't have to tell him about it.

"Maybe that was partly the reason," I answered slowly. "But mostly, Floyd, I wanted to go with him. He seemed like a decent sort, and I hadn't had any fun for such a long time."

And did you have fun?"

"I enjoyed the music, and I liked the people I met there," I replied. "You'd have liked them too, Floyd. They all seemed so carefree and happy. And you know we haven't seen many people like that lately."

Floyd found my hand again in the darkness, and we walked on in companionable silence. Finally, Floyd broke the silence. "I can't take you dancing," he said. "Not with the hours I'm working at the sawmill. And I don't have the right to forbid you to go with someone else. But you're my girl, and you know it," he added with a little laugh. "I guess I'll have to be content with knowing that for the time being."

"I like Chance Cooper," I said quietly. "But that doesn't mean that I love you any less. He was just someone to pass the time of day with until I could see you."

We walked without saying one more word until we came to the wagon tracks that led up Widow Hollow, then we turned back toward town. "Where were you headed tonight when I met you?" Floyd asked. "Were you going to find Chance Cooper?"

"I never thought of it," I answered honestly. "I was going home to Mom and Dad."

"Do you want to go home, Julie?"

I shook my head, then I realized that he couldn't see my answer in the darkness. "Dad's got enough mouths to feed," I said, "without having me pile in on them. But I didn't know where else to go."

Floyd put his arm around me and pulled me close to him. "You don't need to go home, honey. I'll take care of you. Tomorrow," he assured me, "I'll take you to Linton and find you a place to live."

Floyd saw me safely back to the Arthur house, and after promising to see me early the next morning, he left to walk the four miles home to Mr. Thompson's house.

I went to bed almost at once, but not to sleep. I curled myself around the extra pillow on my bed and thought over the evening just passed. Nothing had gone the way I'd expected it to. That is, nothing except Floyd's reassurance that he would take me away from here tomorrow. That still held true. But all the other hopes and dreams that I'd held for this day, and the joy I had thought to feel at graduation, just weren't there. They had evaporated and faded away like gray wood smoke in a heavy fog, leaving me feeling as lost and unwanted as a poor relation at a family reunion.

My only consolation was that on the morrow I would be leaving this place behind me. I'd get a good job, have a nice place to live, and I'd be happy. I could hardly wait for morning.

Chapter Eight

I was up and dressed before dawn the next day, and waiting impatiently for Floyd to get there. I was eager to start for Linton. I heard the car stop at the gate and picked up my suitcase. I wanted to get away before Mrs. Arthur came downstairs and caused more trouble. It wouldn't be in her nature to let me leave quietly.

I had reached the kitchen door when Nancy came racing down the stairs, barefoot, and wearing a thin nightgown. She threw her arms around me, hugging me tight. "Oh, Julie, I wish I was going with you."

I returned her hug, then stepped away. "Your time will come soon," I said, and went on out the door, closing it softly behind me.

I knew that jobs were scarce, but I didn't expect them to be nonexistent. Floyd and I walked up one street in Linton and down the other looking for help-wanted signs. But there were none to be seen. Floyd told me that the merchants placed a notice in their shop windows whenever they needed help. It cost too much to run an ad in the newspaper. Not to mention the horde of people who would have to be turned away.

The little cafe where we stopped for lunch had a wait-ress-wanted sign propped on the counter near the cash register, but Floyd said that I shouldn't ask for the job. "You wouldn't like it," he said. "It's one big hassle, with very little pay. We can do better than that for you."

After lunch, we walked the streets again. I was ready to give up and go back and ask for the waitress job, when Floyd stopped at the hardware store. "Let's go in here," he said. "I've got a speaking acquaintance with Wendell Hazel who owns this place." He grinned and opened the door for me. "Maybe Wen knows of someone who needs some good inexperienced help."

Wen Hazel smiled when he saw Floyd and came to meet us with his hand outstretched. He moved lightly and easily on his feet for a heavy-set man. I figured him to be in his early forties. There was quite a bit of gray showing around the edges of his close clipped dark hair, but his blue eyes were keen and bright in his smooth, youthful-looking face. He and Floyd talked about the weather—how hot it was—and discussed business. It was poor.

When the amenities were over, Wen Hazel was ready to sell hardware. "What can I do for you today, Floyd?"

"Seems like Ben and I nearly cleaned out the store the last time I was here," Floyd replied. "I don't need a thing in that line today." He kind of laughed, ill at ease to be asking a favor, and motioned to me. "But I'd take it as a real kindness if you could tell me of anyone who needs help here in town."

Floyd took my hand, as if I might run away if he didn't hold on to me, and told Wen Hazel, "Julie graduated from high school yesterday and she's eager to go to work and make her mark in the world."

71

Wen Hazel smiled and shook his head. "I could've used you last week," he said. "But I just hired Verna Clayton for the job." He paused and thought for a moment. "There's not much hiring going on right now, but I did hear that Halcie Hissem would need someone at the dime store before long. Other than that," he said, "I can't think of a thing."

We thanked him for his time and turned to leave the store. Before we reached the door, Wen called Floyd's name and stopped us. "I don't know if you'd be interested," he said to me, "but Foster Allen and his wife are looking for a girl to live in and help Esta for a while."

I hesitated. This sounded too much like what I had just left at the Arthurs, and I wasn't looking for another situation like that. I started to shake my head to say I wasn't interested, but Wen Hazel spoke up before I could refuse it.

"Think about it for a minute," he said. "You'd have room and board at the Allens', and you'd be right here in town if another job came up for you." He smiled and added, "That's the main thing when you're job hunting. To get hired, you've got to be there when they need someone."

I thought of how little money I had to last me until I found work, and I knew that I couldn't afford to be choosey. I said that I would go and talk to the Allens. But first I'd like to apply for the job at the dime store. "When Halcie Hissem needs help," I told them, "I want her to know that I'm available."

Wen Hazel gave us directions for finding the Allen place, wished me luck, and we left the hardware store. Floyd said he knew the woman at the dime store to speak to, and he would go along with me. I would have preferred going in alone. I thought it would make me look more dependable if I walked in alone and asked for work.

When I first saw Halcie Hissem, I wasn't so sure that I wanted to work for her, even if she'd have me. She was a tall bony woman who looked to be close to fifty years old, with high cheek bones and a long thin Roman nose that looked fit for taking the stitches out of a patchwork quilt. I thought that she would probably be a sour, demanding woman to work for, with not one grain of humor to leaven or sweeten her disposition. Then she smiled at Floyd, and I noticed that her brown eyes were soft and warm with pleasure at seeing him.

Halcie Hissem's smile of welcome changed to a wary look of doubt when Floyd told her where I come from, and why we were there. "I don't care about hiring someone I don't know," she said. "Especially a scrap of a girl from the hills around Newark."

She looked me over from head to toe, as if she expected to find straw in my hair and mud still clinging to my shoes, and allowed that she could take my name, just in case. "But I've always had an older woman to help in the store," she murmured. She went to the rear of the store and got an application form and gave it to me.

While I was filling out the work questionnaire, Halcie Hissem fired a steady barrage of questions at me. Where were my parents? Why was I here, and not there with them? Couldn't I get along at home? I told Floyd when we left the dime store that now she knew more about me and my family history than I did. "I never saw such a nosy woman," I said.

"She's particular about who she works with," Floyd

said. Then he laughed and added, "Halcie is especially careful about who she leaves in charge of her cash register."

I could see her point. These days, when cash money was so scarce and hard to come by, a day's take-in at the dime store would look mighty promising to a desperate person. I could understand why she would be leery of hiring a stranger off the street or, in my case, out of the hills to clerk in her store. Halcie Hissem was of Mom and Dad's generation, and they weren't given to trusting strangers.

"In a way," I said, following my line of thought, "she reminds me of Mom. And even though Mom and me can't get along worth a hoot most of the time, I think I could get on with Halcie."

Later when we were on our way to the Allen house, I told Floyd, "I sure hope I can get the job with her. Clerking in a dime store would beat doing housework and tending kids, nine ways from Sunday."

"You'd do well to forget about that dime store for the time being," Floyd said, "and concentrate on getting this job with the Allens." Then, as if it had been on his mind a while, he said, "We've still got to find a place for you to stay tonight."

"If the Allens hire me, I won't have to worry about a room for tonight," I said. "Room and board come with the job." Then I noticed the house just ahead of us. "Floyd, there's the Allen place now!"

Floyd put on the brakes and stopped suddenly in front of a small one-story white house. I smoothed my hair, brushed at the wrinkles in my skirt, and took a deep breath.

"Wish me luck." I turned and went quickly up the walk toward the front door.

There was no one at home. The house was too still and quiet for anyone to be there. But I knocked at the door anyway and waited to see if someone would answer. "There's no one here," I called to Floyd. Then I stood on the porch and waited like a dummy for him to tell me with a wave of his arm to come back to the car.

"They've probably gone to do their trading," Floyd said. "And they're not apt to be home until after the stores are closed. We'll get you a room just for tonight, and you can talk to them tomorrow," he added.

Finding a room for one night was easy to talk about, but not so easy to do. Floyd said that a disreputable crowd hung around the only hotel in town, and it was no fit place for a girl alone. "Our best bet," he said, "is to try and find a private home that takes in overnight travelers."

We drove all around town hunting for a tourist home. I was beginning to think that I'd have to go home with Floyd when we finally saw the sign ROOMS TO LET tucked in the corner of a window. Feeling like we were at last making headway, we got out of the car and went up to the front door.

The woman who answered our knock said that she didn't have an empty room in the house. But had we tried the Everett place over on First Street? They let out rooms by the night.

Floyd replied that we hadn't but we would. He thanked her, and we went.

At the Everett house, the man looked Floyd and me

up and down, and said, "Try the cabins out at the junction!" And slammed the door in our face.

"I hadn't thought of the cabins," Floyd said, when we were back in the car. "But that would be real handy for us. There's a big truck-stop restaurant at the junction. We could eat supper there tonight, and you could get breakfast in the morning."

The Junction Restaurant and Truck-Stop was about five miles north of Linton, where state road 59 crossed highway 54. Six rough log cabins sat close together in a semicircle, and partly hidden behind the restaurant. I didn't like the looks of the cabins, but I knew Floyd wouldn't leave me there if there was the slightest question in his mind about the place.

I waited in the car while Floyd went inside to inquire about a room for me. Even though this was our last hope. I almost wished there wouldn't be a vacancy. This would be an awful spot to get stranded, I thought.

There wasn't a house, barn, or any other kind of buildings within sight of the junction. The truck-stop had been built in the middle of a cornfield, and the cornfield stretched all the way to the wooded hills around it. "They should've called this place the Oasis," I told Floyd, when he came back to the car. "It seems to be the only watering hole for miles."

He grinned and handed me a skeleton key on a dirty string. "Here's your pass to a tent for the night," he said. Then he got serious. "You'll be all right. I've seen the cabin, and it's snug and clean."

We ate supper at the restaurant, then Floyd carried my suitcase to the cabin and set it inside the door. "I've got to get Mr. Thompson's car home to him," he said. "He don't mind that I use it, but he always wants it on Saturday night."

"You should get a car of your own," I said. "Then you wouldn't have to depend on the teacher's car for everything."

"I aim to do that," he said, "one of these days."

But I knew he wouldn't. Not as long as Mr. Thompson made it so handy for Floyd to drive his car. After promising to be back the first thing tomorrow morning, Floyd left for home.

I watched Floyd out of the parking lot, then I went inside and locked the door. The cabin was stuffy and smelled of stale, unused air. I crossed the bare concrete floor to the one small window and swung it open, then I turned to take stock of the room. There was a sway-backed bed, cane-bottomed chair, and a time-scarred dresser in the way of furnishings. In the corner, behind a faded curtain, I found a rust-stained toilet and wash basin. I turned the spigot and a dribble of water, as red as the clay banks and gullies, ran into the sink.

I left the water running, hoping it would clear, and sat down on the bed. I had gotten out of the Arthur house and away from Newark, but what had I landed in? I was no better off now than I had been this morning or yesterday, I thought. Worse, if anything. I still had to find a job and some place to live. And after tomorrow, I'd be on my own. Floyd Perry couldn't afford to neglect his work to look after me.

I washed my face and hands in the dingy water and got ready for bed. The job as a mother's helper at the

Foster Allens' house was looking better all the time. I prayed that I wouldn't get there too late for the job, that someone else hadn't already taken it.

The sound of rain on the roof of the cabin woke me the next morning. I had no idea of what time it was and, for a moment, I couldn't think where I was or what I was doing there. Then I remembered, and all the frustrations of yesterday filled my mind and brought back the hopelessness that I had taken to bed with me. Well, today would be different, I told myself, and leaped out of bed. If I wanted a job, I would have to go out and find it. Work wouldn't come here looking for me.

I had finished dressing, and I was checking the room to see if I was leaving anything behind, when I heard footsteps on the gravel path in front of the cabin. A moment later, there was a rap on the door and Floyd called my name. I grabbed my suitcase and hurried to open the door.

Chapter Nine

We were sitting at a table near the window of the Junction Restaurant, waiting for our breakfast to be served. My suitcase was sitting in a third chair. Floyd ran a hand over his wet hair, brushing it back from his forehead. "The teacher didn't come home last night," he said. "I had to walk through the rain to the Colliers' this morning to get the key to Ben's flat-bed truck to drive."

The rain seemed to be slackening off now. The bit of sky that I could see from the window appeared to be cloudless and clearing.

"Floyd, there was no big hurry for you to get here," I said. "Had you waited awhile, you wouldn't have got wet." I motioned toward the patch of blue sky. "The rain's about over."

"I figured you'd want to get right over and talk to Foster Allen and his wife and get your bid in for that job," Floyd said. "The way it is, they might've already hired someone."

"Oh, Floyd, don't say that. I've got to get that job."

The waitress brought our food, and we ate quickly. We were both anxious to be on our way to the Allen house. If they had already hired someone else, then the search would start again for a place where I could stay while I looked for work. Only this time we'd be hunting for a boarding house, where meals came with the room.

"It may be next to impossible to find a suitable boarding house," Floyd said, as if our minds were running on the same track.

I agreed with him. "But I'll take whatever I can get," I said. "And make it do."

We got up to leave. Floyd took my arm with one hand and my suitcase in the other. Just as we got to the door, the door opened and a group of men came in. We stepped back to let them by, and I noticed Chance Cooper was with them. He saw us at about the same time.

Chance looked at the suitcase in Floyd's hand, then at my face, with a doubtful, unbelieving expression. He motioned for the other men to go on without him and stepped over close to Floyd and me.

"Julie," he said. "I went to the dress shop to see you, but the Arthur woman told me you'd gone away. She didn't say that you'd left with Floyd."

His voice carried to the nearby tables, and the people stopped their eating to stare at us and listen.

"I'm just driving Julie to her new job," Floyd said, speaking for me, but loud enough for all to hear. "I didn't see you there when Julie was ready to leave."

He threw the key to the cabin onto the counter, shouldered his way by Chance, and opened the door for me. "Let them make what they will of that!" Floyd mumbled, as we hurried across the parking lot to the truck.

"I've got no use for that Cooper fellow," Floyd said, helping me into the truck. He went around and got in on the other side, settling himself under the wheel. "There's something about him that sticks in my craw and puts my teeth on edge."

"I like him," I said. "I think he's nice."

"Julie, you don't know a thing about men," Floyd retorted. "And I'm telling you right now, I don't want you to have a thing to do with him."

I didn't answer him. Likely as not, I'd never see Chance Cooper again. But if I did, I thought, I'll be the one who decides whether or not to be friends with him.

We didn't speak another word all the way to town. I doubt that we could've made ourselves heard over the rattle and roar of the truck, even if we'd had anything to say to each other.

When the Allen house came in sight, Floyd stopped the truck, got out, and came around to help me to the ground. He held me for just a breath of time and whispered, "Good luck, Julie."

I ducked my head in answer, turned from him, and ran up the street to the house.

The rain was barely a sprinkle by now. I'd have had to stand stock-still in it to get wet. Yet in spite of that, I felt damp and bedraggled as I waited on the Allens' front porch for someone to answer my knock.

The door was opened by a young man wearing bib overalls, white shirt, and a beard. For a moment, I just stared at him. Beards weren't common on men of his age, only the very old men let their facial hair grow. I caught myself and quickly stated my business. He stepped back from the door and motioned for me to come inside.

"My wife will talk to you," he said. "She knows more about that than I do." He stooped to pick up the two little boys who had appeared suddenly beside him, one on each arm, and turned away. "Wait here," he said over his shoulder. "I'll send Esta in to you."

While I waited, I looked around me. I was surprised to see the room in such a mess. Everyone I knew might have a cluttered house during the week, but they always had it cleaned up by Sunday, just in case company dropped in unexpectedly. From the looks of things, dirt and disorder didn't bother Esta Allen one whit, be it Sunday or weekday.

I thought that only some poor fool, or one desperately hard-up for work, would even consider taking on the job of bringing order to this cluttered-up place. Then I reminded myself that I could fit into either of those categories and prayed silently that the Allens would see fit to hire me. I folded my hands in front of me and waited quietly for one of them to come and tell me whether I stayed or went.

"I can keep the house clean, or I can take care of the young'uns," Esta Allen said, as she came across the room to meet me. "But I'll be switched if I can do both at the same time." The words came out in spurts, like she was putting her foot down harder on one word than she did on the other.

She swept a stack of clothes to one end of the couch and told me to sit down, then she sat beside me. "Mending that I'll never get done," she said, pushing the clothes farther away from her.

Early as it was in the day, Esta Allen already looked tired and harassed, like she had put in a full day's work and couldn't see where she had accomplished a thing. I smiled at her. "I could do that for you," I said quietly, pointing to the mending. "I could clean your house and cook, too, and be glad for the job," I added quickly. "But I want you to know at the start, it would be just until I can find other work."

"That's good," she said. "Because this job won't last long. We can't afford to keep full-time help. But Foster thought that a hired girl could help me for a few days and bring some kind of order around here." She smiled, as if she didn't put much stock in Foster's idea, then went on to explain. "He thinks once I get the house cleaned from one end to the other, then I can keep it neat and handle the young'uns without any further help."

Esta Allen had been picking at her skirt, making pleats with her fingers, then smoothing them out while she talked. She raised her head and looked closely at me for the first time. "You don't look strong enough to do hard work," she said.

"Oh, but I am," I answered quickly. Then to add weight to my words, I said, "I've worked in Mrs. Arthur's dress shop at Newark and done most of her housecleaning for nearly a year now."

Esta nodded her head. "That Maud Arthur," she said, knowingly. "If a body can please that woman, they can do anything. When did you leave her place?"

I felt my face grow flushed and warm. "Yesterday morning," I replied. "I didn't please her all the time."

My words seemed to please Esta Allen. She smiled and asked, "Could you start work for me today?"

I got to my feet, my thanks rolling off my tongue like syrup off hot pancakes. "I'll get my suitcase and be right back," I told her.

The rain had stopped. The sun was shining. And suddenly, it was a beautiful day. I ran all the way to the truck. Floyd was sitting on the running board, head down, and his hands clasped around his knees. The very picture of despair.

"Cheer up, Floyd! I got the job. She wants me to start work right now."

He got up without a word and took my suitcase out of the truck and set it on the sidewalk. He had that lost look about him, like he'd had the day my family moved away and left us, and I hated to just pick up my bag and walk away from him.

"You'll come to see me, won't you, Floyd? I'll be looking to see you."

He put his hands in his pockets, as if he didn't know what else to do with them, and gave me a long look like he thought he'd never see me again. Finally he said, "Darn it, Julie! I don't want to leave you. What if things don't work out here for you? What then? Where would you go?"

I put my arm through his, just to touch him. "I'll be fine, Floyd. There's no need to worry. You've brought me to good people."

He held me close to him for a moment, then I pulled away and went up the walk to the house. Long after I was inside, I heard the old logging truck roar past the house on its way back to Newark.

That night, I wrote a letter to Mom saying that I had a good job, and I wouldn't be coming home this summer. As I sealed the envelope, I thought of how my life had changed practically overnight. Had Floyd Perry not met me as I was leaving the Arthur house on Friday night, I would have been on my way home. More than likely, I'd have been there by now.

Chapter Ten

The time at the Allen house passed swiftly and smoothly. I was there nearly three weeks before Halcie Hissem called me to come to work for her at the dime store, and it seemed like no time at all. I hadn't seen Chance Cooper since our brief encounter at the junction, nor had I heard from Floyd Perry. I hadn't expected to see Chance, but I did think it strange that Floyd hadn't come back to find out how I was getting along with the Allens.

That first Monday morning I was there, Esta showed me where she kept the cleaning paraphernalia and gave me free rein to do the work at my own pace. "There's your department," she said, with a wave of her hand. "Do it to suit yourself."

And I did. There was never any pushing or hurrying me from Esta. I cleaned her house from one end to the other, one room at a time, and when I fell into bed at night, I was too tired to care about anything but my rest. Water for washing and scrubbing floors had to be carried from a pump in the back yard and heated on a kerosene stove on the back porch. Then, when I had finished with it, I lugged the dirty water to the far end of the yard and dumped it into a drainage ditch that bordered their ground.

Esta Allen had a wood-burning range in her kitchen, but she said she never used it in the summertime. It made the house so hot they couldn't bear it. All the food was cooked on the porch stove, then carried into the kitchen and placed on a long porcelain table where we ate our meals.

I looked after the Allen children while Foster and Esta went to town on Saturday to do their trading. But other than that time, Esta took care of the children and saw to their needs. I thought it was just as well that she did. I was more adept at handling a broom and dust pan than I was with the diapers.

Foster Allen paid me eight dollars and room and board for every week I worked for them. That was good wages. A lot of men worked all day for only a dollar. Mostly, Mr. Allen treated me like company, yet he teased me like one of the family. When I saw him in the morning, before he left for work, he'd say, "Julie, when are you going to get yourself a beau and get married?" Then when he came home in the evening, he would put a surprised look on his face, and ask, "What! Are you still here?"

He'd laugh, I'd blush, then he would turn away. He never seemed to notice me the rest of the time. That was the only contact I had with Foster Allen, but I liked him.

Esta gave me two free half-days, and Sunday afternoon was mine to do as I wished. She left it up to me to pick which half-days I wanted during the week. I choose the first Tuesday morning after payday. I wanted to go downtown. It was a long walk so I started early, hoping to get back before the day got too hot.

The house was clean, the windows washed, and the piled-up mending was all done. Esta and I had stitched and patched and darned socks every night after supper, while we listened to the radio. Now I needed something for my hands to do while I sat idle in the evening.

The storekeepers were just opening their doors when I got downtown. A young woman with short-cropped hair, and wearing men's overalls and a work shirt had set up a fruit and vegetable stand in the shade of Burns' grocery store awning. She spoke as I went by and turned her head so her eyes could follow where I went. I didn't wonder about her. I had my mind on the yard goods counter at Wickes Department Store two blocks away.

I wished my way through the ready-made dresses and fine silk underthings at Wickes, then spent nearly an hour picking and choosing three different patterned length of cotton material in the dry goods section of the store. I felt like four dollars was too much to pay for the yard goods, but I was getting enough material for three dresses. And I would need better clothes than I had now if I aimed to work out in public. My other two dresses that I had worn to school had had most of the life and color washed out of them.

I went to the dime store to get thread and needles and bias tape that I'd need to make the dresses. It was the same as Wickes sold, only cheaper. And I had to go where my money had the most buying power.

Halcie seemed pleased to see me. I told her where I was working and added quickly that it was just a temporary job.

"You come and see me on your day off," Halcie said. "I'll show you all you'll ever need to know about clerking here. By the time Rosie leaves, you'll be able to step in and do her job without a hitch."

I promised Halcie that I'd do that and left the store walking on air. Though my feet barely touched the ground, there was a purpose and directness to my steps. I wasn't just killing time now, waiting for something to happen. It had happened. I had a job.

I didn't consider what I was doing at the Allens a real job. Anyone could do housework. I'd been doing it all my life. The dime store was public employment, a job to be proud of.

I could hardly wait to get back to the Allen house to tell Esta about it and show her the soft cotton material I had bought at Wickes. I would start laying the pattern and cutting the cloth this afternoon, I thought, as I hurried toward home. Then tonight after supper, I'd baste the pieces together and have a dress all ready to sew and finish on my next free day. If Rosie could just hold out at the store for one more week or ten days, I could have the dresses made and be ready to start work at the dime store, with nothing else on my mind but pleasing Halcie Hissem.

Esta looked at the three lengths of dress goods and felt the texture between her thumb and first finger. She asked what I had in mind to do with it. Where are your patterns? she asked. When I told her I had planned to use the dress I had on for a pattern—I couldn't afford to buy one—Esta went and got a pattern she had for a tailored shirtwaist dress and brought it to me.

"This would make up into a pretty thing," she said, laying the shirtwaist pattern against the pale green striped material. "We can take it in at the waist, shorten the hem, and it will do just fine. There's not that much difference in our sizes," she added.

She was right about that. Esta was a little taller than I was, and a bit thicker through the middle, but to a careless observer we would seem to be the same size. Watching her now, while she was expressing her enthusiasm for sewing and offering her help, I thought Esta didn't look much older than I was either. She seemed to have grown younger and more alive, more aware, in just the few days that I'd been here.

The first dress we made was the pale green striped shirtwaist one. After lunch, I set up the ironing board and began to iron the clothes I had washed on Monday. Esta cleared the table and spread the dress goods across it, smoothing the material with her hands. Then she took the ragged tissue-paper pattern from its tattered envelope and began to lay it in place. I had forgotten to buy straight pins from Halcie, but Esta said not to fret. She had a world of them tucked away and went to get them.

For the rest of the afternoon, she pinned and tucked and cut out dresses, putting every scrap of material to some good use. When all three dresses were cut out, ready to be basted together, Esta rolled the pieces, each in a wrapping of its own color, and laid it aside.

"We'll do a little basting on your dresses after supper," Esta said, getting out the potatoes and meat for the evening meal. "Then tomorrow morning, I'll set up the sewing machine for you to use."

I had finished the ironing and I was starting to put the ironing board away. "Just leave it up and set it back out of the way," Esta said. "We'll need it again in the morning to press the seams."

And so it went for the rest of the week. We didn't fall behind on the housework or slack it in any way, but it didn't take us nearly as long to get it done. The kids were kept clean, well fed, and happily entertained with empty thread spools, which we strung on colorful scraps of material that we had tied together. Mr. Allen found no reason to complain, either. His supper was always ready on time, with a fresh-baked pie or cake cooling on the sideboard.

That Sunday afternoon, Foster and Esta Allen took the boys and went to the country to see her folks. I went to the matinee at the Tivoli theater and stopped at Peggy's Cafe after the movie for a hamburger and a Coke. I was home before dark with a long, empty evening ahead of me.

My dresses were all done except for the hemming. And Esta Allen believed like Mom when it came to sewing on Sunday. She said, "Every stitch you sew on a Sunday, you'll take out with your nose later on." I respected her beliefs and left my thread and needle alone.

As long as I could keep busy, I was all right. But sometimes just before I went to sleep at night, I would get so lonesome for my family, especially my little brother Robert and my sister, Seely, that I thought I couldn't bear it another day. This was one such night. I got out a pencil and paper and I wrote a letter to Mom. I told her that I hadn't realized how much I loved them all—not until I was so far away from home and couldn't see them or hear their voices. And I wanted to see them in the worst way. But I didn't mail the letter. The next morning I tore it up and threw it away. It would've made Mom feel bad to know I was unhappy. Even for a little while.

My eighteenth birthday came and went while I was with the Allens. I didn't mention it to anyone. We had never made a fuss about birthdays at our house, and it was unheard of to give gifts to each other the way Chance Cooper did for his mother. In my whole life, I could remember only one time when I had ever gotten something for my birthday.

That had been my twelfth birthday. We had lived on the big farm then. Threshers were helping Dad to harvest the wheat, and I was helping Mom in the kitchen, preparing a big noon meal to feed the men. A few minutes before time for the men to come in from the fields to eat, my sister Seely came to the kitchen.

Seely is five years younger than I with skin so fair we can see through it. But that morning, her face was burned red from the sun, and her bare arms and legs showed deep scratches from the briar patch. She carried a tin cup in one hand, and the other hand covered the top of the cup.

"Happy birthday, Julie," she whispered, and offered the covered cup to me.

She had taken me by surprise, and I hesitated.

"It's just a tin cup full of dewberries," Seely had said softly. "But it's all I've got to give you."

Now, on my eighteenth birthday, I rubbed my eyes with the back of my hand and it came away wet.

This was no time to be thinking of Seely and home. Halcie Hissem had called me to say that this was Rosie's last week. I was to start to work for her on Monday. And today, I was going to look for a place to live. Esta Allen said that she had stayed at Mrs. Brown's boarding house until she married Foster. Maybe I could get a room there. I promised her that would be the first place I'd go to look for a room.

"You should wear a hat to keep off the sun," Esta said, as I was leaving. "A day like this, you're apt to have a heat stroke."

I laughed and replied that I didn't own a hat. But I would walk on the shady side of the street until I got downtown.

It was hot, no doubt about that. At least ninety degrees even on the shady side of the street. It would be a little cooler when I got downtown where tan canvas awnings shaded the store fronts, and the sun didn't strike me directly.

I stopped to talk to the woman at the fruit stand. I hoped to buy some dewberries from her, but she told me they were all gone. "Dewberries came on early this year," she said, "and they didn't last long. I guess it was the hot weather," she added.

There was a cool breeze on the corner, and I lingered awhile. The woman had the voice of a young girl. I thought at first that she was about my own age, but after I looked at her more closely, I could tell she was nearer to thirty than twenty. The short red hair that curled naturally around her heart-shaped face had faded to the dull, rusty shade of a robin's breast, and there were fine lines around her green eyes and wide, smiling mouth. She had on the overalls and blue workshirt again today, but there was no way that anyone could have mistaken her for a man.

She offered me fresh raspberries, but I smiled, shook my head, and moved on down the street. I could feel her eyes on me until I turned the corner on Maple Street.

I followed Esta's directions down rough brick sidewalks and across streets that had no sidewalks of any kind, and finally found Mrs. Brown's house at the far edge of the business district. Here the brick sidewalk was ruptured and swollen by the roots of the old trees that had come to the surface in places.

The house was one of the fine old homes that had survived the progress of the town, but to be self-sustaining now, its rooms were rented out and strangers lived under its roof. A small radio repair shop had sprung up on one side of the house, and a neighborhood grocery store was doing business on the other side.

Mrs. Brown eyed me suspiciously when I walked in and asked her if she had a room to let. I had no luggage, not even a purse. I carried my money tied in a handkerchief in the pocket of my new green dress. She was sitting behind a huge old desk in the front hall, and she made no move to get up or show me a room. "How long do you figure on staying?" she asked.

"I expect I'd be here as long as the job lasts at the dime store," I replied. "Esta Allen told me that she lived here until she got married, but I don't aim to get married," I added.

At the mention of Esta's name, she sat up straight in the chair, then leaned toward me, her voice dropping confidentially. "How is Esta? Is she still living with that man?"

I nodded my head. "She and Foster Allen have two kids now," I said. "I've been working for them this summer."

Mrs. Brown smiled then for the first time and heaved her heavy body out of the chair. "Then if Esta's not coming back," she said, "I guess I could let you have her old room at the head of the stairs."

With one hand on the banister, she pulled herself up the steps and unlocked the first door on the landing.

"You have the use of the kitchen and the front parlor," she said, still puffing to get her breath after the climb. "And I expect everyone to clean up after themselves," she added.

I smiled, nodded again, and followed her into the room. I couldn't believe the size of it. There was a big double bed with a high wooden headboard, a matching dresser, mirror, and an easy chair. A small stand-table sat close to the chair and held an electric lamp for reading. A wide double window, framed in white net tie-back curtains, looked out over the side yard and the radio repair shop.

"You'll have to share the bathroom with Verna Clayton who has the room next to yours," Mrs. Brown said. "But that shouldn't be a problem. She's neat as a pin."

I turned from the window and glanced in the direction of the bathroom. "It's lovely," I said. "I'll take it."

"The rent is three dollars and a half a week, or twelve dollars a month," she said. Then added, "Most of my people pay by the month."

I untied the knot in my handkerchief and paid her a month's rent. Then I told her my name so that she could make out the rent receipt and said that I would be moving in on Saturday. That would be my last day at the Allens.

"If you don't figure on getting married," Mrs. Brown said, looking up from the receipt she was writing, "what do you aim to do with yourself? You can't work for Halcie Hissem all your life long."

"I'm going to be a schoolteacher someday," I replied promptly.

I'd never told that to another living being, but it came just as naturally as breathing to tell this woman that I was only marking time at the dime store until I could save enough money to go to college.

"You'll want to talk to Millie Edwards," Mrs. Brown said. "She lives here with her aunt. They have the room across the hall from you, next to Martha Griffin." She handed me the rent receipt. "Millie teaches at the one-room school in Ellis, then helps out in the office at the canning factory during the summer. She has to, to make ends meet," Mrs. Brown added. "Old Miss Edwards is not able to help, and that little school just pays her pauper wages."

I said I'd be happy to make her acquaintance. Then I thanked Mrs. Brown and went quickly on my way. I couldn't wait to get home to tell Esta Allen that I had found a room at Mrs. Brown's boarding house—her old room, if I could believe what Mrs. Brown had told me.

Chapter Eleven

When I got back to the Allen house, Chance Cooper was sitting on the porch talking to Esta and playing with the two little boys. I hadn't spoken to Chance since the night he and Floyd had fought in the schoolyard. Floyd had done my talking for me that morning at the Junction Restaurant when we saw Chance there.

He smiled all over, like a kid on the last day of school, and said, "Hi, Cinderella," just as though we had been seeing each other every day.

Esta got up to take the children inside for their naps. I waited until the door closed behind them. "How did you know I was here?" I asked, sitting down on the porch steps. "I never thought to see you again."

"I just found out where you'd disappeared to," Chance replied. "The power company bought poles from Ben Collier's sawmill for the stretch of line into Newark, and I just happened to see Floyd at the mill. He told me that you were working here for Foster Allen."

"So you and Floyd are talking now, instead of fighting," I said, with a bite of sarcasm.

Chance grinned and slid closer to me. "I don't carry a

grudge," he said. "Nor hold any hard feelings toward
Floyd."

"Ha! That's big of you, I'm sure!" I moved to the
end of the step out of his reach.

Esta came back to the porch then with a big pitcher of
cold lemonade and stopped any reply that Chance might
have made.

"Did you see Mrs. Brown about a place to live?" Esta
asked, as we sat sipping the cool drink.

I felt again the excitement of having my own key to a
room in town. But I quickly smothered it and answered
Esta as if I was used to living alone in strange towns, and
this was nothing new.

"Mrs. Brown asked about you," I said calmly. "She
wanted to know if you were still married to that man.
When I told her that you were, and you had two children,
she said, 'Then I guess I can let you have her old room'."

"At the top of the stairs!" Esta laughed.

"That's the one." I laughed with her.

"Are you moving again? I've just now found you,"
Chance said.

"Julie starts work at the dime store on Monday," Esta
said. "Didn't she tell you? That's all we've heard around
here." She smiled at me, then added, "We'd like to keep
her, but it's time she was on her own."

I'd never considered myself backward nor slow to
speak up. Yet lately, it seemed to me, there was always
someone who spoke up in my place. Esta was right. It was
time I stepped out on my own and started speaking for
myself. Beginning right now.

Esta was telling Chance how to find Mrs. Brown's

97

boarding house, the street and house number.

"If you can find the place," I said, as if I had my doubts that he could, "come by sometime and I'll cook supper for you."

He grinned wickedly and addressed his remark to Esta. "Do you think I'd be safe to eat her cooking?"

"I wouldn't try it any time soon." Esta laughed. Then, "Speaking of supper," she said, "I'd better get ours started. Foster will be home soon and there'll not be a bite ready for him."

Esta went into the house. Chance got to his feet and said he had to go too. "We had to wait for the pole-setters this afternoon," he said. "So I just left work and drove into town to see you."

"Do you have the electricity as far as Newark yet?"

"That town is lit up like a Christmas tree," Chance answered. "We've come quite a ways on this side of Newark already." He grinned and added, "I'm getting closer to you every day."

As he was getting into the car to leave, Chance asked, "Does Floyd Perry know that you're moving into a place of your own?"

I shook my head. "I haven't seen Floyd," I said. "Not since he brought me here."

"Then I'm one step ahead of him." He smiled, waved, and drove away.

I was busy for the next two days washing and ironing my things and cleaning Esta's house for the last time. I had expected Esta to tease me about Chance Cooper and ask me why I hadn't told her that I had a beau. But we worked together and got along just the same as we always had. She didn't bring up his name, and I didn't refer to him in any way. Once in a while I would catch her eyes on me, and she'd have a puzzled look on her face, but if she wondered about Chance and me, she never said so.

I was all packed and ready to leave the Allen house by noon on Saturday. Esta insisted that I wait until Foster got home from work so they could drive me to the boardinghouse. While we were waiting for Foster, I remembered a scarf that I had left on the porch and went to get it.

I opened the screen door just as Mr. Thompson's car stopped in front of the house. "It's Floyd!" I cried. "Oh, Floyd!" I ran down the walk to meet him. He met me halfway and held me close in his arms, like he'd never let me go.

"Oh, I've missed you so."

"I've missed you, too," Floyd said. "But I thought it best not to come here where you work."

"My work here is finished," I said. I took his hand and we started up the walk to the house. "I found a room in town and I start working at the dime store the first of the week."

Floyd smiled. "I know," he said. "That's why I'm here. Wen Hazel told me that Halcie had called you to work for her, and I came to move you to town."

I just shook my head. "And I was afraid you wouldn't know where to find me," I said.

Esta Allen was surprised when I walked in with Floyd. Her eyes went from my face to Floyd's then back to mine. I was still holding Floyd's hand, and after that one quick look at Esta, I hadn't taken my eyes off him.

99

"I take it that you know this young man," Esta said, with a smile.

"This is Floyd Perry, Esta. We've known each other all our lives."

Floyd smiled and nodded to Esta, then he turned to me. "If you're ready, I'll take you to your boarding house."

I left the room to get my suitcase, but I heard Floyd telling Esta, "I room with the schoolteacher over beyond Newark a-ways, and I'm using his car. I promised him I'd have it back there early this evening."

"I didn't hear Esta's response. And I didn't hear her follow me to my room. But when I turned to leave, she was standing right behind me.

"You sure had me and Foster fooled," she said, just above a whisper. "Going out with two men at the same time and not one word to us about it."

She paused, and I wondered what was coming next. I didn't want to leave here with Esta's disapproval. But I didn't feel like I was obliged to tell her everything that went on in my life, either. I kept still and waited for her to go on.

"You know what they call a girl that goes out with more than one man at a time, don't you?"

"Yeah," I said. "Very lucky."

"Julie, it's not like you to be flippant," Esta said, reprovingly. "I only meant to be helpful."

"I wasn't being sassy to you, Esta," I replied, keeping my voice low so Floyd wouldn't hear me. "But how would you feel? In the past eight weeks, I've gone for one ride with Floyd and to one dance with Chance Cooper. You can hardly call that going steady with either one of them."

I stepped around her to leave the room, and Esta put her hand on my arm and stopped me. "That Chance just wants to play with you," she said, her tone serious. "But Floyd is in love with you."

"Floyd loves all us kids," I replied just as seriously. "And we love him."

She started to say more, but I moved away from her to the door and went to join Floyd in the front room.

As we were leaving, Esta called after us, "Don't you two be strangers here. You come and see us. Hear?" We waved and promised we would and forgot the promise the next minute.

Floyd sat in the easy chair and talked to me, while I unpacked my suitcase and put things away. Mrs. Brown wasn't there when we arrived, so I couldn't introduce Floyd. I knew it was against the rules to have company upstairs at the boarding house, but Floyd had come to my room anyway. We had left the door wide open so that when Mrs. Brown came in, she could see there was no hanky-panky going on between us.

"As soon as I'm finished here," I said, "we'll go to the grocery store and lay in supplies. That kitchen won't do me a bit of good if I don't have something in the house to cook."

Floyd jumped up suddenly. "Darn!" he said, and sat back down. "Wen Hazel wants us to have supper with him and Angie Abram tonight at Peggy's Cafe. I said I would ask you and let him know."

That would take care of supper tonight, but what would I do tomorrow? The grocery stores would be closed on Sunday. I had thought that I would cook supper here tonight and have Floyd stay and eat with me. I wasn't ready to meet new people yet. Even if they were Floyd's friends and he would be there with me.

"Well," Floyd said. "What do I tell Wen? Yes or no?"

I was still hesitating. "Floyd, I don't know Angie Abram."

"Sure you do." He laughed. "Angie works the fruit stand there in front of Burns' grocery store."

My mouth dropped open. "The woman in the overalls?" I asked with amazement. "Is she Wen Hazel's woman?"

"It's not generally known," Floyd said. "But Wen's been courting Angie Abram on the quiet for more than a year now, trying to talk her into marrying him. But she won't hear of it. I'd say that Wen hopes to persuade Angie to change her mind by taking her out in public where everyone can see what his intentions are toward her," Floyd added.

"She must think a great deal of him," I said, "to see him secretly for so long a time. I wonder why she doesn't want to marry him."

Floyd spread his hands as if to say it was beyond him why Angie didn't want to marry Wen. "How could I know Julie?" he asked softly. "I don't even know why you won't marry me."

I didn't want to talk about that. I'd told Floyd of my hopes and dreams of becoming a schoolteacher, but he had just laughed and said that I was aiming too high. That a girl without a penny to her name was better off married and raising a family than wasting her time dreaming about being a schoolteacher one day. I walked over and stood by the window, looking out over the radio shack but not seeing it. A moment later, Floyd came and stood near me. We were near enough to touch, but I knew we were miles apart in our thoughts.

Finally, Floyd said, "Listen!"

I listened, but there wasn't a sound to be heard anywhere.

"I don't hear a thing."

"That's what I mean. We must be the only ones in the house."

"I guess we are," I answered.

"Then why are we whispering?"

We looked at each other and burst out laughing. We laughed until we were both weak in the knees and fell across the bed gasping for air. When he could get his breath, Floyd said, "I feel better now."

I raised myself on my elbow and leaned over him. "Me too," I said. "I haven't laughed like that since . . ." and stopped. I couldn't remember the last time.

"Not since the night your folks moved into the hills to be near us," Floyd said quietly. "And we stuffed strawticks in the barn loft for you kids to sleep on that night."

"I'd forgotten about that time."

"I haven't," he said. "I mark that night as the end of our good times and the beginning of the bad. The way things were that winter, and for a long time afterwards, I couldn't even tell you that I loved you."

Floyd's words had brought it all back to mind, and I was seeing again the tall gawky boy who had tried to put straw down the front of my blouse. I bent closer and kissed the boy. But the man he was now, pulled me down against him and started kissing me over and over again.

"Julie, are you up there?" Mrs. Brown called from the foot of the stairs.

We were on our feet in an instant, and the next moment I answered her from the open door.

"I'm here," I said, and hurried to the landing so she could see me.

"I didn't hear you come in, but I thought I heard voices from your room."

"You did," I replied. Then added, "We were just leaving to go to the grocery store."

"Then I won't keep you." She turned and disappeared into the inner part of the house.

"You'll have to do your trading later," Floyd said, when I got back to my room. "Wen wanted to eat at five, and it's ten after, right now." He held out the watch to show me the time, then put it back in his pocket.

"Just as long as I don't come home without groceries, it won't matter," I said. "But Mrs. Brown will be watching to see if I get them."

Mrs. Brown was nowhere in sight as we went down the stairs, but I had the feeling that she was watching from somewhere nearby as we walked out the front door and closed it behind me.

Wen and Angie were waiting for us at a table set for four, near the back door at Peggy's Cafe. "We didn't know if you were coming or not," Wen said, when we were seated. "But we waited and hoped, and here you are."

Floyd said, "I should've let you know, but I went to see Julie's room at the boarding house, and we kind of lost track of the time."

He touched my hand and I raised my eyes to his face. His eyes were soft and warm with love as they met mine. For a short breath of time I forgot we weren't alone, and I returned his look of love with interest. Then I thought, if

104

I can see his love in his face, the others can see it in mine. I lowered my eyes and turned my face away.

Angie Abram laughed softly. "Julie, I'm glad you're here," she said. Then, "Did you get all settled in your new home?"

She had on dark slacks this evening, with a soft, short-sleeved white blouse opened at the throat. The women around here didn't wear trousers and frowned on those who did, but slacks seemed to suit Angie. Somehow, I couldn't picture her in a dress.

I answered Angie, grateful to her for trying to put me at ease. "Isn't it funny," I said. "We've spoken at the fruit stand, but we never knew who each other was until tonight."

Her smile spread to her green eyes, making them sparkle like dew on early spring grass. "Oh, I knew who you were," Angie said. "Wen told me a while back that Floyd's friend Julie was helping Esta Allen for a while. When you came walking to town from that direction, I knew that you had to be Julie. From my stand on the corner," she added, "I get to know just about everyone who goes by there."

"That would be interesting," I said. "I like watching people. There's so many different sorts and shapes to wonder about. But there is something else that I wondered about too. Where do you get all those vegetables and stuff that you sell at your stand? Do the farmers bring them to you?"

Angie laughed, pleased and not a bit put off by my questions. "I raise my own vegetables. Have for years," she answered. "And pick most of the berries, with the help of my brothers. There's only two of the boys left at home

105

now." Angie added. "The others joined the three C's as soon as they were old enough, and like our dad before them, they forgot all about the rest of us as soon as they were out of sight."

There was nothing I could say to that, so I kept quiet. After a moment, Angie asked, "What about you, Julie? What are you doing here alone?"

I turned to Floyd, half expecting him to make some reply to Angie, but he and Wen were talking about automobiles and they weren't paying any attention to what Angie and I were saying.

"I'm not alone," I said. "Floyd's here with me. And I have friends." I smiled at her. "Four, now, counting you and Wen Hazel."

I thought that my answer would amuse her, but instead, a look akin to pity crossed Angie's face and concern for me filled her voice. "Julie, aren't your folks living?" she asked gently.

"Oh, yes." I hadn't meant to imply that they weren't. Somehow, I had just assumed that Wen Hazel had told her my circumstances earlier, when he'd told her who I was and what I was doing here.

The waitress came to take our order. I waited until she had finished and left the table, then I went on to tell Angie about my family. I felt that it was only fair that she should know about mine, since she had volunteered the information about her own family.

"Dad and Jase Perry, Floyd's dad, brought us to Greene County nearly two years ago," I said. "Mom never liked it here, and I can't say that I blame her. Not long after we got down here, Floyd's dad died and they took his mother away. Then my brother drowned in the spring flood water and, after that, wild horses couldn't have held Mom here. They moved away this spring as soon as Seely was out of grade school, but I stayed behind to finish high school," I added.

"I don't understand how your mother could've left a girl your age to fend for herself," Angie said. "I'd think she would be worried to death about you."

I had to smile at the notion of Mom ever worrying that I couldn't take care of myself. She had been the one who always said, "Have it your own way, Julie. And may heaven help anyone who dares to go against you." But I didn't tell Angie that.

"Floyd's family and mine were closer than kin," I told her. "Mom won't worry as long as Floyd and I are together. She knows he will see that no harm ever comes to me."

"Then Floyd Perry is more than a friend to you," Angie said, her soft low tone making it sound like a question.

"How can anyone be more than a friend?" I answered her question with one of my own. "That's the dearest thing one person can ever be to another," I said.

Angie just looked at me and shook her head, her face the very picture of puzzled disbelief. I could almost hear the wheels of her mind turning, as she thought, "No one can be that dense." And I wanted to smile.

I knew what she had meant by her soft-spoken question. I wasn't entirely ignorant of what went on between men and women. But sometimes I pretended ignorance to avoid talking about it. I didn't consider the supper table the place to discuss such things, especially when it pertained to my relationship with Floyd. That was between the two of us, and I didn't think it concerned anyone else. Not in the least.

Chapter Twelve

The neighborhood grocery store was still open, so Floyd stopped the car to let me out there. He wouldn't go in with me. He said that the teacher would be waiting for his automobile, and he still had more than an hour's drive to get home.

"I've not been able to get the teacher's car the way I used to," Floyd said. "He's keeping company with a widow-woman who works at the Junction, and he's usually gone to see her by the time I get home from work at the sawmill."

I was surprised to hear that Mr. Thompson had a woman friend. "He always struck me as a confirmed bachelor," I said. "Too set in his ways and notions to ever look at a woman."

Floyd smiled and moved his head slowly from side to side. "Belle Bundy is a fine figure of a woman, even at her age," he said. "She's enough to turn any man's head. Especially one like Mr. Thompson.

"But I did ask him about using the car some Sunday to take you to Flat Hollow," Floyd went on. "He said to let him know when you wanted to go, and I could drop him off at Belle's on the way in and pick him up there later, on the way home. You're to say when," he added.

"I'll let you know," I said.

We talked for a moment, then he kissed me good-bye and drove away. I went into the grocery store to do my trading. The clock on the kitchen wall at the boarding-house showed just a little after eight when I got there, yet I didn't see another soul anywhere.

I put the things that I'd bought into the big, nearly empty, refrigerator, flipped off the kitchen light, and went upstairs to my room. As I unlocked the door, I could hear low, soft music coming from the radio in the room next to mine. The one where Verna Clayton lived.

Later that night, after I had turned off the light and gone to bed, I could still hear the radio going next door. I wondered what else Verna Clayton did, besides listen to the radio, from the time she left work at the hardware store in the evening until it was time to go back in the morning. I was going to have those same hours to fill somehow, I thought.

I used to read a lot when I was at home. But after I started working for Maud Arthur there was never any time for it. She and Nancy didn't read. There wasn't a book in her house, and she had no patience with anyone who wanted to spend their time with one. That was something I could do now. First thing tomorrow, I'd go to the public library and get myself some books to read.

Verna Clayton came to the kitchen the next morning while I was eating my breakfast. We exchanged a few words, then I asked her how to get to the library from here.

"I'm not much of a hand myself for reading," Verna said. "But I guess with you going to be a schoolteacher, you'd have to do a lot of reading."

News sure travels fast is this house, I thought. Then I smiled at her, and said, "I suppose I would, if I was studying, but this is just to pass the time after I get off work at the dime store."

"I know the woman who works at the library," Verna said, breaking an egg into the hot grease from her bacon. "But it's not open today. Martha Griffin just works from ten to two in the afternoon, and that's during the week," she added.

I finished washing the dishes I'd used and put them away. "I'll have to arrange to get there on my lunch hour from work one day," I told Verna, and left her to her breakfast. I hadn't found out where the library was, but in a town of this size, it wouldn't be hard to find.

I made my bed, dusted, and ran the carpet sweeper across the worn, faded rug. I couldn't tell any difference in my room, but now I felt like it was clean. I had my bath while Verna was downstairs and cleaned the bathroom. Then I got dressed to go out to the movies. I met Verna Clayton on the stairs as I was leaving and started to smile at her. But she didn't look up as she went by me.

Mrs. Brown was sitting at her desk at the foot of the stairs. I knew the minute she called my name that she had been waiting for me, and she had grown impatient with the wait. There was not a flicker of friendliness about her today, and her eyes were dark and sober.

"I thought you understood that men aren't allowed past this spot," she said, tapping the desk with her finger. "You can see your friends in the parlor until ten o'clock at night. Any night of the week. But you can't take a man to your room!"

Her fingers tapped in time to very word, then came down hard on the last few, like driving home a nail in solid oak. I felt my eyes get wide, the way my little brother Robert's eyes used to do when he wanted us to believe his innocence, and I knew that I must look the picture of guilt.

While I stood there, flushed and tongue-tied, trying to find an excuse for breaking the rules the first night in her house, Mrs. Brown said, "I won't warn you again."

I swallowed, and spoke, my voice coming out low and squeaky like an eight-year-old child's. "I didn't think you'd mind if Floyd went upstairs to see my room," I said. "Floyd is like one of my family, and I wanted him to know that I had a nice place to live. I've never been on my own before," I added.

Once I got started, I couldn't seem to find a spot where I could stop talking. Finally, Mrs. Brown interrupted me to say that it was all right. No harm done this time. "But I've got five girls living here," she said, "and I can't allow one to break the rules, then expect the other four to abide by them."

I said that I understood. It wouldn't happen again.

"I know it won't," she said simply. She got to her feet and moved to the front of the desk. "From now on, Julie, have him wait in the parlor and we won't have any trouble." She smiled at me and went toward the back of the house. I turned and hurried out the door.

Trouble was the last thing I ever wanted from Mrs. Brown. I felt like I could consider myself lucky this time

112

that she hadn't asked me to give up my room, right there and then. The notion never crossed my mind that Mrs. Brown might need the rent money, that in times like these she was just as anxious to keep that room rented as I was to live there.

The brightness of the sun and the noonday heat nearly drove me back inside to my room. I stopped and squinted my eyes against the sudden brightness and looked around me. Huge old trees grew along both sides of the street and their thick leaves dappled the street and sidewalk with shade and held the glare of the sun at bay. I put up my hand to screen my eyes from the light and hurried toward the first patch of shade.

I thought this would be a good time to acquaint myself with the neighborhood that I had moved into and determine which route would be the shortest way to work from here. I had plenty of time. The movie wouldn't start for an hour yet. I turned the corner at the first cross street and walked slowly toward town.

I counted seven blocks from the boardinghouse to the dime store. Not more than fifteen minutes, even poking along the way I'd been doing. I walked ahead to the end of the block, then turned and started back through town to the theater. The doors would be open and they'd be selling tickets by the time I got there.

As soon as I turned the corner, I saw Chance Cooper pacing back and forth in front of the movie house. Waiting for its doors to open, I supposed. About the same time that I saw him, he turned and saw me. He waved a hand, then hurried to meet me.

"I was looking for you," he said, when he stopped beside me.

113

"How did you know I'd be here?"

"Esta Allen told me that you liked to go to the movies on Sunday, so I bought two tickets and just waited for you to show up."

As I went into the darkened theater with Chance, I wondered what else Esta Allen had told him while I wasn't there to hear it.

It seemed cool to me when we first went inside, but by the time the cartoon had ended and the main feature began, it seemed hotter in there than it was outside. Others had come prepared for the heat. All around us, paper fans swished quietly as they moved the stale air back and forth in front of their faces.

It was a Nelson Eddy and Jeanette MacDonald movie, and we sat through it twice. I noticed that many others did the same and remarked on it to Chance. He said that some of the people didn't have anywhere else to go. That they would sleep here until the last show was over, then the ushers would throw them out. "Twenty cents is a cheap price to pay for ten hours sleep," he said.

Heads turned and shushed us for talking. We got up and moved to the very last row of seats. The people back there weren't watching the movie. They had their arms wrapped around one another and were cuddling and kissing. We could talk all we wanted to back here, and they wouldn't even notice.

"These back rows are busier than lovers' lane on Saturday night," Chance whispered.

"I wouldn't know . . ." I started, then suddenly the lights came up bright and the movie was over. Hands went up to shade their eyes against the light. Girls straightened in their seats and hurriedly smoothed their hair. Chance grinned at me, and we got up and left the theater.

"I have to pick up my car at Andy's garage," Chance said. "But we could walk to Hinkle's and get a hamburger before I take you home."

Hinkle's was a little hole-in-the-wall place, Chance said, with just a counter and stools to sit on. "But they serve the best hamburgers in the country," he added.

Wen Hazel was just leaving Hinkle's when we walked in. He smiled and said, "Hey, Julie." Then he looked past me, expecting to see Floyd, I suppose, and I caught the surprised look that crossed his face before he grinned, and said, "Haven't seen you for a while, Chance. Where have you been keeping yourself?"

Chance told him that he'd been stringing power lines out in the boondocks, and he didn't get to town very often. "But now that Julie's moved here, I expect you'll see quite a bit of me this summer," he added.

After a few words, Wen Hazel left the diner, and we took the two stools that had just been vacated at the end of the counter.

"Did you see the look on old Wen's face when he saw me?" Chance asked.

"He's a friend of Floyd's," I replied. "I think he was expecting to see him with me."

Chance laughed. "It's a cinch he wasn't expecting to see me."

Later, when we were on our way home, Chance brought up Wen Hazel's name again. "Wen doesn't care much for me," he said. "He used to be married to my mother's sister, and they'd be at our house for dinner every Sunday. But after Gayle died the way she did, Mother couldn't stand the sight of Wen. She still can't. It wasn't his fault," Chance added quickly, "but Mother blames him anyway."

"Why blame Wen?" I asked. "He couldn't help it if his wife died, could he?"

Chance thought a while before he answered. I could tell that he had batted this question around in his mind himself. "Wen was away on a two-day buying trip for the store when Gayle put arsenic in her tea and drank it," Chance said. "He wasn't even there." Then, "Mother says that if Wen had been at home with Aunt Gayle, where he belonged, it never would've happened. Gayle would be alive today."

"That's unfair to Wen," I said. "You can't condemn a man for something like that."

"I don't," Chance replied. "But he thinks that I go along with the way Mother feels about it, and he doesn't want to have anything to do with me."

"Maybe he will change his mind when he sees that you don't hold any hard feelings toward him," I said. "He's going steady with Angie Abram now, so he must be over the worst of his hurt and ready to start a new life for himself."

Chance gave me a quick glance, then looked away. "So old Wen's got himself a girl," he said softly.

I nodded my head. "They had Floyd and me to supper with them last night," I said. "Floyd says they've been going together for a year, but they've just now decided to let everyone know about it."

My words had taken him by surprise, but he rallied at once. "Maybe things will start looking up for Wen, now that he's stepping out with Angie Abram," Chance said. "It's about time they did."

I said that I hoped so. I liked both Wen and Angie. Then I changed the subject, and we talked of other things until we got to the boardinghouse.

I didn't ask Chance to come in with me. I stopped at the door and thanked him for the movie, and the hamburger afterwards. "Now, I won't have to fix any supper," I said.

"How about Tuesday night?" he asked. "What are you having for supper?"

"The same thing I'd intended to have tonight," I answered. "Cheese sandwiches."

"Good. I'll see you Tuesday night," Chance said. "I like leftovers."

He waved a hand to me, took the porch steps two at a time, and went whistling down the street, headed for Andy's garage, far on the other side of town, where he had left his car.

Mrs. Brown was sitting at her desk talking to Verna Clayton and another woman when I went in. She raised her hand in a beckoning manner and called me over.

She introduced me to Martha Griffin, who worked at the library. Then she said, "Julie, you should've brought Floyd on inside with you. I like to meet the friends of the girls who live here."

"That wasn't Floyd," I said. "He couldn't get to town today. I met Chance Cooper at the movies and he walked home with me."

I went on upstairs, but I saw the raised eyebrow look that passed between the three women. I thought nothing of it until later. Then I realized how they had taken my words, and I blushed with shame. They thought I had picked up a strange man at the theater and let him bring me home.

Chapter Thirteen

Monday morning I awoke early and couldn't get back to sleep. As a precaution, in case I overslept, I had taken my bath the night before. Now all I had to do this morning was to wash the sleep from my eyes, which I did, and get dressed for work.

I took special care getting ready for my first day of work at the dime store. I tried on all three of the new cotton dresses I had made at the Allens and finally settled for the pink floral-patterned one. I didn't wear makeup, just a dusting of face powder, and the pink dress seemed to add color to my cheeks. There was nothing I could do about my worn and scuffed oxfords. I'd put polish on them, but they still looked bad. They would just have to do, I thought. I wasn't going to fuss about something that I couldn't help. Besides, no one worked in new shoes.

As I was going downstairs to fix my breakfast, I heard an alarm clock clanging in Verna Clayton's room. That was something else I would need. From now on, I would be living by the clock. Be at work at nine o'clock, lunch hour at one, back at two, and off work at six o'clock. Except on Saturdays. The store was open until nine that

119

night. I would buy a clock from Halcie today, I thought. I couldn't count on waking early every morning.

It was half past seven by the kitchen wall clock, and I had the room to myself. I dropped two slices of bread into an electric toaster, took the butter from the refrigerator, and poured myself a glass of milk. Half an hour later, my breakfast dishes were washed and put away, and the kitchen was ready for the next roomer to use.

It was a nice morning for walking to work. The sun hadn't burned away the night's coolness yet, and there was just enough breeze to make the leaves tremble on the huge old trees that grew close to the sidewalk. But I had to watch my step. The tree roots had grown under the sidewalk and buckled the bricks. In many places, I had to walk in the grass to avoid the jagged raised pieces of broken brick.

When I turned the corner at Burns' grocery store, I expected to see Angie Abram at her fruit stand. I thought I could talk to her for a while and pass some time. But the stand was still covered with the old tan tarp, and Angie was nowhere is sight.

Wen Hazel was sweeping the sidewalk in front of the hardware store when I got there. He stopped sweeping, crossed his hands on top of the broomstick, and rested his weight on the broomhandle.

"Good morning," I said.

"It is at that," he replied, and cast a glance at the cloudless sky. "But it will be another scorcher later on today."

"No doubt it will be," I said, and started to walk on.

Wen called my name, and I stopped and looked back.

He motioned for me to wait and started walking toward me.

"I didn't know that you were acquainted with my nephew."

"Well, yes." I hesitated. "I met Chance when we were both working in Newark this spring."

Wen slipped his arm around my shoulder and bent his head close to mine. "What does Floyd Perry think about sharing you with Chance? Or doesn't he know it?" Wen squeezed my shoulder, as if to say my secret was safe with him.

I moved away from Wen Hazel. I didn't like the way he touched me or the things he had to say. "Floyd knows that I've been seeing Chance Cooper," I said. "But if you want to know how he feels about it, you'll have to ask him yourself. I don't speak for Floyd Perry."

I could have added that Floyd didn't speak for me either, but I was in a hurry to get to work. I left Wen Hazel standing in the middle of the sidewalk and went on to the dime store.

It was a quarter to nine by the bank clock across the street when Halcie Hissem unlocked the door to the dime store and let me in.

"You can start by straightening the shelves and counters," she said, not once pausing on her way to the rear of the store. "Turn on the front lights and open the door at nine. When that's done, come back here and help me check this shipment," she added as she disappeared behind a stack of boxes.

From that time, until after one in the afternoon, I didn't stop moving. We changed the shelves and rear-

121

ranged the stockroom. We unpacked the truck load of merchandise and put price tags on each piece. I waited on customers, rang up a few sales on the cash register, and went across the street to the bank for change. I was too busy to even think about Floyd or Chance Cooper, let alone worry about Wen Hazel's opinion of me.

When Halcie finally told me to go to lunch, I was too tired to walk the five blocks to Peggy's Cafe to get something to eat. Instead, I stopped at Burns' grocery, bought a bologna sandwich and a bottle of Nehi orange, and took it back to the store. I ate my lunch in the back room, my feet propped up on Halcie Hissem's desk.

At six o'clock I couldn't have said which part of my body had the most aches and pains. I think my feet and my back were tied for first place. But when Halcie said, "Now that you've been here awhile, how do you like it?" I managed to smile and answer, "Fine. Just Fine."

"Then run on home," she said, "and I'll see you tomorrow."

Run? I thought. She had to be kidding! I could barely walk.

As soon as the door to my room closed behind me, I started shedding my clothes. The first thing that came off were my shoes, and the rest came off fast so I could take a bath. I filled the tub to the rim, then I sat and soaked the aches and pains until I remembered that I shared the bathroom with Verna Clayton. She would be home soon. And no doubt, she would be just as eager as I had been to get in here.

I got out of the tub, cleaned it, and wrapped my old pink chenille robe around me. Then I lay down on the bed and propped both pillows behind my head. I thought

I'd just rest a minute, then I would go downstairs and fix some supper. I closed my eyes, and I could feel my body go slack from the tip of my toes to the top of my head.

I awoke in the middle of the night, hungry enough to eat a bear. I was afraid to go to the kitchen for something to eat. I wasn't sure what Mrs. Brown would have to say about it. She might have a rule against using the kitchen at this time of the night, and I sure didn't want to break another of her rules and get called for it. Tomorrow, I promised myself, I would get some fruit and candy to keep in my room for times like this. Then I remembered that I hadn't gotten an alarm clock today to get me up in the morning.

The next morning, I awoke to the roar of running water, and the feeling that I had overslept and missed something. Then I recognized the sound as Verna Clayton filling the bathtub, getting ready to go to work. I started to leap out of bed, then I discovered I was tangled up in the bedspread. The corners were lapped over me like a note in an envelope.

I threw back the bedspread and got out of bed. Then I put the pillows in place and smoothed the sleep wrinkles out of the cover the best I could. It still looked slept on, but that couldn't be helped. I waited to get dressed, hoping that Verna would get done in the bathroom so I could go in there. But I finally gave up that hope, and went ahead and put on my clothes.

It was seven-thirty by the kitchen clock when I went to fix my breakfast. I had plenty of time before I had to leave for work, but I couldn't shake the feeling of a pressing urgency. I sat at the workbench—a shelf, really, that was built onto the wall—to eat my toast and drink a glass of milk. I wasn't as hungry this morning as I'd thought I would be after going to bed without supper. I ate slowly, then as soon as I was finished and I was on my feet again, I felt a terrible need to hurry back to my room.

There wasn't a sound from the bathroom. I tried the door and thought, Thank God! when it opened under my hand. I couldn't have waited much longer.

A few minutes later, I straightened the seams in my stockings, picked up my purse, and felt as ready as I'd ever be for another day at the dime store.

I followed the same route I had taken the day before, and the nearer I got to the store, the slower I walked. I wondered why I had ever thought that working for Halcie Hissem would be so great. I hadn't asked how much money I would make working at the dime store, or even found out when I would get paid. But considering the hours I worked, it should be a great deal more than I had ever made doing housework.

Halcie and I got to the store at the same time. She turned on the front lights this morning as soon as we went through the door, then she went directly to the cash box and began to count the money. I went to the back room, put my purse on the shelf, then returned to the front of the store to find out what my job would be today.

Halcie finished counting the change into the cash drawer, and closed it. "Julie, you wait on the customers as they come in, and stay close to the door." She looked pointedly at the cash register. "I've got some business to take care of in the office," she added.

She went to the little back room, but before she closed the door between us, she called over her shoulder to me. "Just yell, if you need me. I'll hear you."

124

I didn't need Halcie, so I didn't see her again until she came to tell me it was lunchtime. I could leave whenever I wanted. I got my purse and went out at once.

Angie Abram was sitting on the high bench behind her fruit stand at Burns' grocery. I waved and gave her a hey as I went into the store to get a sandwich, and she returned my greeting. When I came out a few minutes later, she motioned me over to the stand.

"How's the new job?"

I sat down on the end of the bench and took out a sandwich before I answered her. "I thought that job would be the death of me yesterday," I said. "But today, I can't find enough work to keep me busy. "So," I added with a laugh, "I guess I'll live till Saturday."

"Have you met any of your neighbors at the rooming house yet?"

"I've talked a little with Verna Clayton, and I've spoken to Martha Griffin. But I haven't met the Edwards ladies that live down the hall from me."

"You'll like Millie Edwards and her aunt," Angie said. "They mind their own business and they don't mix too much with the others."

"I like Mrs. Brown and Verna and Martha," I said. "But I haven't seen much of them since I moved in there. We each have a certain time to use the kitchen, so we won't be in anyone's way, and everybody's busy with their work or something the rest of the time. It's so quiet around that house that sometimes I feel like I'm the only one who lives there," I added.

"The day may come when you'll wish you were," Angie said. "Verna and Martha are just like this." She crossed her first two fingers. "Or closer. And between the two of them, they can make things pretty lively for anyone who crosses them."

I didn't aim to rub anyone the wrong way. Especially not the people I had to live in the same house with. I figured if I kept my mouth shut, followed Mrs. Brown's house rules, and did my part, I wouldn't have a thing to worry about. But now Angie talked like that wouldn't amount to a sieve full of sea water as far as Verna and Martha were concerned.

"I don't understand about Verna and Martha," I said. "They seemed all right to me."

"It's the things they say that you have to watch out for," Angie said. "Why, before I could get my stand set up this morning, I heard that you were making eyes at Wen Hazel and cosying up to him behind my back."

She had spoken so casually and offhand that I thought she was teasing me. Wen had told her about speaking to me yesterday morning, I thought, and now she's kidding me about it. I started to make light of her words, but then I saw her face and hushed. Angie was deadly serious. There wasn't a trace of warmth or friendliness on her face, and her eyes were like green glass.

I slid off the bench and stood up. "I don't know what you are talking about," I said.

"Oh, you know very well what I'm talking about," Angie said. "You just didn't expect me to find it out."

She was in no mood to listen to any explanation I had to give, and I wasn't going to argue with her. Besides, I wasn't sure that I wanted to explain anything to her. Anyone who could be friendly one minute, then cold and accusing the next breath, didn't deserve any answer. I turned without a glance in her direction and stormed back to the store.

I had more than thirty minutes left of my lunch hour, and I couldn't just fume away my anger sitting in the back room of the dime store. I asked Halcie how to find the library, and when she said it was just two blocks away on Morton street, I went there.

I needed something to read to pass the time in the evening, but that wasn't the only reason I went to the library. I wanted to see Martha Griffin. If she was the one who had been talking to Angie Abram and getting her all stirred up, I wanted to know why.

Martha Griffin greeted me pleasantly and went out of her way to be helpful to me. She gave me the library card that I asked for and showed me around the big room as if I was a guest in her home, pointing with pride to the reference books and the new set of encyclopedias. When I told her that I was on my lunchtime, that I'd just stopped in for a mystery book to read after work, Martha brought the latest mystery novels to the desk for me to choose one.

As I was leaving the library, she said, "Julie, whenever you want a book, just let me know. I'll bring it to the house for you."

I hadn't mentioned Angie Abram to Martha. After two minutes in her presence, I simply couldn't see that pleasant, dumpy little gray-haired woman as a trouble-maker or a threat to anyone's peace of mind. I took my book and hurried back to the dime store in a far better frame of mind than when I had left there.

I remembered to buy an alarm clock from Halcie. Fifty-nine cents. And I took it to the back room and put it on the shelf with my purse and book, so I wouldn't go home without it. Then I went back to work, but my mind wasn't on it. I couldn't seem to shake the thought of Angie Abram. Her strange behavior didn't fit what I knew about her. Though I didn't know her well, Angie hadn't struck me as a jealous, spiteful person.

I couldn't understand why she had changed so much since we'd had supper together on Saturday night. We had gotten along so well then, and I'd thought that she liked me. I tried to tell myself that I couldn't care less how an old maid in men's overalls felt about me. But I did care—I liked Angie Abram. And besides that, I was real short on friends right now.

We hadn't had a customer in the store all afternoon, and Halcie and I were taking advantage of the time to clean and polish the counters. I was washing the candy case in the big front window, when I saw Angie headed for the door. I looked around for Halcie Hissem. She could wait on her, I thought. But Halcie was nowhere in sight. I bent my head over my work and pretended that I hadn't seen Angie come in.

"Julie, I want to talk to you."

I looked at her then, and through her, as if I had never seen her before in my life. It's your nickel, I thought. Start talking.

Angie seemed uncertain about how to begin, and I didn't say anything. If she had it in mind to apologize, I wasn't going to make it easy for her. Finally, she said, "Julie, I feel like a fool. Lord knows, I've acted like one."

I could agree with her there, but I thought it best not

to say so. She hesitated a moment, then she took a deep breath and plunged on with what she had come here to say. "I never should've listened to that woman in the first place," Angie said. "But when she mentioned Wen and the new girl at the five and ten, I had to find out what story she was peddling now.

"She said that Wen had his arm around you, brazen as could be, and the two of you had your heads together, laughing and talking as if you were the only ones on the street.

"I told her that she was mistaken," Angie whispered. "There was a good reason for anything she had seen. But after she'd gone, I began to have my doubts. It could be true. After all, what did I really know about you?"

'I never heard anything so ridiculous," I said. I was mad clear through. "You ought to have more sense than to believe something like that!"

"I know better now," Angie said. "And I'm so ashamed of myself. . . ."

"What changed your mind about it?" I broke in on her words of apology.

Angie smiled cautiously, ready to take it back if I didn't reciprocate. "I talked to Wen after you left me," she said. "He told me that he had stopped you yesterday morning to ask about his nephew, and you had stalked off, mad at him too, for butting into your business. Julie, I didn't even know that you knew his nephew, Chance," she added.

"Seems to me, there's a lot you don't know," I retorted.

A customer came into the store and I went to wait on her. The woman looked at several things and finally selected a greeting card and gave me five pennies to pay for it. I rang up the sale, then turned back to where Angie was still waiting. The break in our talk had relieved the tension in me. I didn't feel quite as hostile toward her now.

"Can't we just forget that Wen Hazel ever spoke to me?" I said, picking up the conversation where we had left off earlier. "It didn't concern anyone else, and it wasn't important in any way."

"We can forget it," Angie replied. "But there's others who won't. In this town, whenever a pretty young woman smiles at a man and stops to talk to him, it's important to those who are watching."

Halcie Hissem called from the rear of the store and asked if I needed any help. I answered that I wasn't busy. I was just talking to a friend. She looked at Angie and dismissed her with a glance.

Angie had started to smile, her green eyes coming alive again. But then she looked at her faded blue overalls and shirt, and said with a touch of bitterness, "It's nobody. Just Angie Abram."

I knew she was referring to Halcie's look of small regard, and I didn't know how to answer her remark or Halcie Hissem's unspoken one. I held my tongue and waited. I didn't have long to wait.

"I used to come right out of the fields to bring the vegetables and stuff into town," Angie said. "Then I'd sell it from the back of the pickup truck. When I set up my stand there on the corner, the women were used to seeing me in my shapeless overalls, so I didn't change. They saw that I didn't pose any threat to them," she went on, "so they left me alone. After a while, the women just seemed to forget I was there."

"One of them remembered this morning," I said dryly.

Angie smiled. "Once it got out that Wen Hazel and me were going steady, I was accepted on approval as one of them. And as such, they think that I'm entitled to know whenever some girl is getting too close to my man."

They weren't doing Angie any favor, and I told her so. "With the older women keeping tabs like that on the girls," I said, "what do they do to pass the time in this town?"

"Not much," Angie replied. "If a girl is seen with a different man every time, or stays out later than the women can stay up to watch, they'll tell it around that she's a whore. So to be on the safe side . . ." She shrugged her shoulders, and didn't finish.

"Why couldn't the girls do something together? I was going to ask you to go to the movies with me some night."

Angie was shaking her head no. "They'll give you a bad name for that, too," she said. "Just let two girls start buddying around, going to the show or sharing a room together, and right away the word gets around that they're queer. The same thing goes for the men," she added. "And if there's a hint of homosexuality about a man, he's scorned like the plague."

"I never heard the like," I said. "I don't even know what you're talking about."

Angie shook the short red curls back from her face, and gave me a look of astonished disbelief. "Julie, I thought I grew up green, but you've got me beat a country mile. Honestly, don't you know anything?"

I mumbled, "Not about anything like that." And Angie went on to explain what she meant. I listened open-mouthed with amazement.

131

"They say that there are people who are born hermaphrodites," she said. "They can be either men or women. But I don't believe any such thing. I've never seen anyone around here who looks or acts any different than I do. I think it's just something the old folks tell the kids to keep them in line." Then she added, "Didn't your ma ever warn you about them?"

I shook my head. "No, she never did," I said. "But if Mom had heard about this kind of person she'd have said that if the good Lord made a body that way, it wasn't up to us to judge them." I smiled at Angie and added, "More than once I've heard her threaten to take the hide off us kids if we dared to poke fun at someone just because they were different."

Halcie came out of the office and the look on her face told me that I had been idle long enough. "I've got work to do," I said. "But I'm glad you came to see me."

"It was my pleasure," Angie said simply. And left the store.

"I didn't know that you were acquainted with Angie Abram," Halcie said just a step away.

"She was the first person I met in town," I replied. Then remembering the way she had looked at Angie earlier, I said, "What have you got against her?"

Halcie seemed honestly surprised at my question. "Bless you, Julie. I've no hard feelings toward Angie. She tends her own business and minds her tongue. Same as I do," she added.

"From what I've heard of this town," I said, "she's the only one. Except you," I added hurriedly, sorry now that I had misread her look at Angie and accused her unjustly. "I've been here three days, and already someone has tried to cause trouble between Angie and me," I told her why Angie had come to the dime store, and what she had said.

"Pay no attention," Halcie said. "They can only hurt you and cause trouble if you let them. I always let talk like that go in one ear and out the other, and I'd advise you to do the same," she added.

I said, "Yes, ma'am," and got busy turning off the overhead fan and the lights. Then Halcie and I got our things from the back room and left the store together.

I was surprised to see Chance Cooper waiting for me. I hadn't even thought of him for two days. Then as he got out of the car and came walking toward me, I remembered that I was supposed to make supper for us tonight.

"I'll have to take a raincheck on that meal," Chance said. "Mother's not feeling well, and I have to go home to Bicknell to see her." He grinned and opened the car door for me. "But I can give you a lift home on the way."

I hoped that the relief I'd felt at his words didn't show on my face. I hadn't realized on Sunday when I'd blithely invited him to supper tonight that I would be too tired after working all day to cook for myself, let alone a hungry man.

But I was grateful for the ride home, and I told him so. "Those few blocks to work in the morning are not so bad," I said. "But after being on my feet all day, they seem endless going home."

"How do you like working for Halcie?" Chance said. "I've heard that the five and ten does more business in one day than the other stores do in a week."

"I don't know about that," I said. "But I like working for Halcie Hissem. I think she's nice."

"How about me?" Chance grinned. "Do you think I'm a nice guy?"

He pulled the car to the curb in front of the boarding-house and switched off the motor. "You didn't answer me," he said.

"I'm thinking about it," I said.

"Think of me while I'm gone," he said, reaching for the starter switch. "I haven't time to wait for your decision now."

I got out of the car and waved him on his way with a smile.

Chapter Fourteen

Millie Edwards was just turning up the walk to the house as I got out of Chance's car. She was getting home from the canning factory early today, I thought. It was usually dark when she got home.

"I hear you're going to be a schoolteacher," she said, when we met at the door.

"I hope to someday," I replied. "If I ever get the money laid by to go to college."

Millie Edwards gave me a tired smile. "Teaching school is a good profession," she said. "But not in Greene County. We get paid the lowest wages of anywhere in the state." She shook her head as if puzzled why this should be and reached to open the door. "I guess though I ought to be thankful that I'm working. A lot of the schools closed down hereabouts, and the teachers couldn't find a place to teach afterwards."

She started on inside, but I stopped her. "I didn't know that schools ever closed their doors," I said. "I thought a schoolteacher could always get a job and make a living."

"That used to be true, I suppose," Millie said. "But the Depression changed everything."

She smiled at me, then turned and went in the house. I closed the door after her, then quietly followed her up the stairs.

This was something I hadn't thought about. It didn't make sense to me that a school would shut down just like a factory. Children were not parts and pieces of machinery or a product to be set aside and finished later, when times got better and money was more plentiful. But Millie Edwards had been a schoolteacher for a long time. She should know what she was talking about. For the first time, I began to have doubts about the soundness of studying for a teacher's permit.

I waved at Angie as I hurried by the fruit stand and gave her a hey. I didn't have time to stop and talk this morning. I had neglected to pull the alarm tab on the new clock when I wound it, so it had let me oversleep. When I finally woke up, I had barely enough time to get dressed and make it to work before nine.

I seemed to be running behind the whole morning. I would start to do something, then get called away, and I never would get back to finish the work. It was frustrating. I thought of Esta Allen, the way she always seemed to be an hour late and a day behind in everything, and I no longer wondered at her feverish rushing from one thing to another. She was just trying to catch up with yesterday.

On my way to lunch I met Wen Hazel halfway between the fruit stand and the hardware store. He grinned sheepishly when he saw me and raised his right hand, palm outward, in the Indian peace sign. "Julie, could I speak to you for a minute?"

I nodded, then waited quietly to hear what he had to say.

Wen Hazel shifted his weight from one foot to the other and rubbed a hand over his smooth-shaven chin. "I think I know my nephew a little better than you do," he said. "And I feel like it's my place to tell you about him."

"I'd rather find out about Chance for myself," I said.

"Julie, I'm trying to warn you," Wen said. "Chance doesn't care a hoot about anyone but himself. And he never will. I don't know what kind of game he's playing with you," he added, "but I wouldn't like to see you get hurt."

"No one's going to get hurt," I told Wen. "I may be green, but I'm not an idiot. I can take care of myself."

I moved away from him, anxious to be rid of his company. Chance had told me that Wen Hazel didn't like him. Now, I believed him. And I didn't intend to listen to another word against him. I murmured that I had to get my lunch and walked on.

When I got to the fruit stand Angie Abram called me over. "I was watching for you," Angie said. "I saw Wen stop you. What did he want this time?"

She threw in the question as if it was of no importance to her. But I noticed that her face was stiff and still as she waited for my answer.

"Wen wanted to give me some fatherly advice," I replied. "It seems that he's afraid I'm getting in over my head with his nephew."

"It took him long enough," Angie said. "He knows how some people will see that and what they'll say. I'll have to talk to him about it."

"Angie, when you do, I wish you'd tell him to leave me alone," I said, letting all the indignation I felt toward Wen Hazel come out in my voice. "I don't need him to tell me how to run my life or who to spend my time with," I added.

Angie smiled at my fuming and nodded her head. "I'll tell him," she promised. Then on a more pleasant note, Angie asked me to have supper with her on Friday night. "At Peggy's Cafe," she said, smiling impishly. "And bring Chance Cooper with you if you want to."

I said that I might do that very thing and went ahead to the grocery store for my usual bologna sandwich.

After I got to work on Friday morning I found out that Friday was to be my day off, and pay day was usually on Monday.

"But since you've just started with me," Halcie said, "and you may be running short of money, I'm going to give you a week's pay today. But from now on, it will be every Monday. So spend your pay wisely," she added.

I waited until I was outside the store to open my pay envelope. Then I couldn't believe what I found in it. I looked at the five dollar bill and the two ones, and rubbed them with my fingers to see if a bill or two had stuck together. They hadn't. There was just seven dollars.

I had expected twice this amount. I couldn't see how I could possibly live on seven dollars a week. Three and a half for rent. Three fifty for meals. My mind went blank. I couldn't do it. And at this rate, I would never get to college. There would be nothing left over to save for it.

I walked toward the boardinghouse in a daze. There was no thought in my mind of spending my pay. I was too intent on how to save some of it. Maybe I could find a cheaper room. I had three weeks until my rent came due. That would give me time to look for something else. In the meantime, I would put back four dollars out of every pay envelope to cover the rent, in case I couldn't find anything cheaper, and to save a little each month as well.

When I got to my room I sat down with a pencil and paper and tried to work on a budget. I even made a menu for each day of the week and wrote a grocery list to cover the menus. I figured that I could eat breakfast all week on a nine-cent box of rolled oats, and with a small piece of cheese, or hamburger and tomato, a twelve-cent package of macaroni would cover several meals.

I had spent nearly a dollar for lunches this week. From now on, I would come home for lunch or carry something to work with me in a brown bag. By cutting out bought lunches and cooking all my meals, I could make do on what I had. But it wouldn't allow for anything extra.

Worry over the slim margin I had left myself to get by on drove me to my feet. And the probability that I couldn't do it kept me going with stubborn determination. I changed the bedsheets and cleaned the room. Then I took the sheets to the basement, along with the dresses and underthings I had worn this week, and washed them. While these things were drying on a line in the backyard, I went to the library for more books. I hadn't made allowance for movies in my budget, so that meant I would be reading quite a bit.

Later that afternoon I went next door to the little grocery store for the items I had listed for the week. I got everything on the list, and I had change coming back out of the three dollars. I took the stuff home and stored it on the shelf that Mrs. Brown had allotted me in the kitchen.

The worry was still with me, but it didn't seem so weighty now that I had food in the house to last the week, money put back toward next month's rent, and a little bit of change in my pocket.

My time for using the kitchen in the evening was from six-thirty to seven-thirty. The same as Verna Clayton's. But tonight Martha Griffin, who had the four-thirty to five-thirty hour, was fixing supper for herself and Verna. They would eat as soon as Verna Clayton got home from work, Martha said. And I could have the kitchen all to myself. I took a book that I'd brought home from the library and went to the parlor to read until they were finished.

I had just started the book when Chance Cooper came to the door, asking for me.

"Mark your place," he said, when I met him with the book in my hand, "and I'll buy you dinner at Peggy's."

I'd forgotten that I was supposed to meet Angie for supper. Even if I'd thought of it, I couldn't have gone. I could get half my groceries for the price of a meal at Peggy's Cafe. But this was different. This wouldn't cost me a thing.

I accepted at once. "Just give me a minute to get ready," I said. And ran up the stairs to change my dress.

When I was figuring out how I was going to live on what I made at the dime store I hadn't taken into consideration the possibility that Chance or Floyd might be buying my meals some of the time. I couldn't count on it, but if one or the other of them took me to supper just two nights out of very week, I'd be able to get by on what Halcie paid me and I wouldn't have to look for another place to live.

At the restaurant, the first person I saw was Angie Abram. Wen Hazel was at the table with her. "I should've known he'd be here," I thought, as I waved at Angie, then turned and followed Chance to our table.

"Did you know they were going to be here?" Chance whispered.

"Angie asked me to have supper with her," I answered. "But she didn't say that he'd be with her."

Chance laughed shortly. "Why wouldn't he be?" he said under his breath. "I heard this week that he's been sleeping with her since way last winter. After that," he added, "the least he can do is to feed her."

I caught my breath, then let it out with an angry whisper. "I don't believe that!"

Chance's face turned red under his suntan. "Here they come," he said. "Why don't you ask them?"

"All right! I will!"

But I didn't. They both looked so happy that I couldn't bear to spoil their evening by repeating the dirty gossip that Chance had heard.

Wen and Angie stopped at our table to talk for a moment, then they went on their way. As soon as the door closed behind them, Chance started in on them again. I said he had a dirty mind. And I didn't want to hear another word about Wen Hazel and Angie Abram for the rest of the evening.

He hushed, but I still couldn't get them out of my mind. I wondered how anyone could start a story like that about a nice girl like Angie Abram. And how could

141

I possibly let it go in one ear and out the other, the way Halcie Hissem had advised me to do. It seemed to me that someone ought to do something about stopping such stories. But I had no idea what that would be, or how to go about it.

Chapter Fifteen

Halcie Hissem and I barely had time to say good morning to each other the next day before the store filled with shoppers. I had it in mind to ask Halcie if she had heard any talk about Angie and Wen Hazel, but I couldn't do it with all these people in the store.

Most of them were strangers to us. There were just a few of the regular customers in the bunch. Once as Halcie and I met in a crowded aisle, she smiled and whispered, "Looks like the bus just got in," and laughed as she went on by me.

I knew that Halcie was referring to one of the customs around here during the school year. A schoolbus driver would take his bus back into the hill country, pick up the men and women who had no way to get to town, and bring them to Linton to do their trading. Invariably, the whole bus load of people would descend on one store at a time, causing mass confusion and much disorder before going on in force to the next store. We couldn't expect the bus until after school started in the fall, but meanwhile, the crowd we had this morning would be more than enough for us to handle.

Halcie had warned me earlier in the week that Saturday would be a busy day. We'd have no time to get away for lunch. I should bring something from home, and we would take turns going back to the office for a bite to eat, she said. So I had expected to be busy, but never in my wildest imagination had I envisioned a day like this.

We were busy right up to nine o'clock closing time. When the last shopper reluctantly left the store, Halcie quickly closed the door and locked it behind him. Her shoulders sagged, and she gave a weary sigh as she looked at the disheveled shelves and counters, and the gum and candy wrappers that littered the aisles.

"Just leave it be," Halcie said, when I brought the broom and started to sweep the floor. "I'll do that tomorrow. I have to come in to do the books and make up the bank deposit. I might as well sweep and straighten the counters while I'm here."

I took the broom back to where I got it.

"Get your pocketbook," Halcie called to me, "and bring mine as you come. You can ride with me tonight," she said. "I can't have you walking these streets after dark. No telling what you'd run into," she added.

I appreciated the ride home. And I told her so. "Not that I'm afraid to be out after dark," I said. "But I'm about ready to drop in my tracks."

Halcie laughed softly. "You'll get used to it," she said. "There'll be days when things are so slow at the store that you will wish for a day like today."

"I doubt that," I said.

She stopped the car in front of the boardinghouse and after saying, "I'll see you Monday," she drove away. I went slowly up the walk and into the house. I had never been so tired in my life.

I thought when I went to bed that night that I could sleep right through Sunday without moving a muscle, but my body's built-in alarm clock woke me at seven, as usual, and habit made me get out of bed. I had never been allowed to stay in bed at home unless I was ailing. If I was well and awake, I got up. Tired didn't buy any bedtime.

I had my breakfast, came back upstairs and tidied my room, and then I wondered what to do with the rest of the day. It wasn't noon yet. Too early to expect to see Floyd. He wouldn't be here until later in the afternoon. If he came at all.

I washed my hair and towel-dried it, then I went to the front porch where the sun and wind could finish drying it. I was brushing the tangles out of my hair when Chance Cooper drove up to the house and stopped. He grinned and waved, then he got out of the car and came to the porch.

Chance pulled a chair over next to me and sat down. "How about driving down to the river with me?" He asked. "I'll take you for a boat ride to the river bridge and back." As if that was an added attraction to get me there.

"I can't leave the house," I said. "I'm expecting Floyd any time now."

"He won't be here," Chance replied, rather smugly. "I saw the fellow he rooms with and Belle Bundy leave the Junction more than an hour ago. Headed for Terre Haute, her brother said. So you can stop looking for Floyd Perry today. Belle and the teacher won't be back till midnight," he added.

"How do you know so much about it? I wasn't aware that you even knew Mr. Thompson."

"I never saw him until today," Chance replied. "But I know Belle Bundy. I string wire with her brother Bill every day and share his cabin at the Junction. Besides that," he added, "I know that old car that Floyd drives."

"Mr. Thompson doesn't own the only automobile around Newark," I mumbled. "Ben Collier's got a truck Floyd can drive. I'll just wait and see if he's coming or not."

Chance got up and put the chair back where he had found it. I thought he was leaving. But he went only as far as the top step to the porch and sat down again. "I can be just as stubborn and hardheaded as you," he said, his jaw tight as a steel trap. "I'll sit right here until Floyd Perry shows up."

We sat there not saying a word. Neither one of us willing to be the first to speak and break the silence. After five long minutes of this, I thought how childish we were acting. Here we sat, hot and uncomfortable and mad at each other, when the river was cool and waiting for us just a few miles away.

"I'm not doing anything this afternoon," I said quietly. "Why don't we go for a boat ride down the river?"

Chance shifted quickly on the step to face me. He was as surprised as I was at my words. "You mean that?" I smiled and nodded my head. "Then let's not tarry," he said.

Chance said his folks owned a fishing shack on White River. But when we got there, I found that the shack was a solid, weather-tight cabin, fit to live in the year round. His dad had left an old canoe at the cabin to use whenever he went fishing. Chance put the canoe in the water, then he showed me how to paddle it, and keep it on an even keel.

We drifted down White River beneath the huge branches of the old trees. Sometimes the leaves were so thick overhead that we couldn't see the sun. When we reached the big iron bridge across the river, we turned back and paddled slowly upriver to the cabin.

The canoe rocked and tipped to one side when Chance jumped to the river bank. I cried out, and he turned back to give me a hand out of the canoe. We both took hold to pull the canoe out of the water, then we fell to the ground laughing and out of breath when it was done.

I hadn't noticed the time on the river. Drifting or paddling on the water, it had seemed timeless. But now, lying here and looking at the sky, I saw that the sun was low over the hills and it would soon be dusk on the river.

"Aren't you glad now that you came canoeing with me?" Chance asked softly.

I turned my head to look at him. Chance had his hands folded under his head and his eyes were closed. He looked for all the world like a man with nothing on his mind but a short nap.

"Yes," I said. "But we can't stay here much longer. It will be dark soon."

He opened his eyes and sat up. "There's a bed and a lamp in the cabin," he said, his eyes holding steadily on my face. "We could stay here tonight."

I didn't ask what he meant by that. When he said bed, I knew what he had in mind. I got to my feet and moved a few steps away.

"No, we couldn't," I said. "That would ruin every-

147

thing. Tomorrow we wouldn't even be friends any more."

I turned and walked away from him. It had been a perfectly wonderful afternoon and now I felt like he had spoiled it.

"Oh, hey, Julie!"

I heard him calling me, but I didn't stop or look back.

"Wait a minute, Julie." Chance caught my arm and turned me around to face him. "You don't want to play favorites among your friends," he said. "You were at the Junction with Floyd Perry, why not stay here with me?"

It took me a minute to realize what he was saying. Then the implication struck me. "Is that what you think of me?" I asked angrily. "That I spent the night in a cabin with Floyd? He didn't even see the inside of that cabin. Or ask to," I added.

I jerked my arm free of his hand and ran up the road to the car. A moment later Chance opened the door on the driver's side and slid behind the steering wheel.

Without a word, he started the car and eased it over the deep ruts and bumps of the dirt lane and onto the highway. We didn't speak again until we were almost home.

"I don't know why you're so mad," Chance said. "Everybody knows Floyd rented that cabin and you stayed there. I saw you myself, leaving there together the next morning."

"I don't have to explain anything to you," I said, "but I will. Floyd is too good and honorable to have anyone think a mean thought about him. He got that cabin at the Junction just to provide a place for me to sleep. He wasn't thinking of what people would say about it. He was taking care of me until I could make it on my own."

Chance didn't say anything. It was getting dark, and he switched on the headlights and fidgeted with the dimmer switch. After a while, he said, "Julie, feeling as you do about Floyd Perry, why did you go out with me that first time?"

"I don't know," I mumbled. Then a picture of Chance flashed through my mind, the way I had seen him the first day he had come into the dress shop, and I knew why I'd gone to the dance with him.

"I'd never met anyone so light-hearted and so alive," I said quietly. "You acted like every day was a holiday and you were going to make the most of every minute. Everyone I knew took life so seriously," I added. "I wanted to see what it was like in the carefree world you lived in."

Chance looked at me, then quickly back at the road. It was too dark to see the expression on his face, but when he spoke, his voice was soft and low.

"Julie, opposites truly do attract each other," he said. "The first time I saw you, you were such a solemn, serious girl that I couldn't get you out of my mind. I wanted to see you smile, to make you laugh, and watch your eyes lose that sad, lonely look. I filled my days thinking of things to do to make you happy. But I seem to have said and done all the wrong things," he finished quietly. "None of it worked the way I thought it would."

"It's not your fault that it didn't work," I said. "You've tried to include me in your fun and games. I guess I've just never learned how to play."

Chance left me at the boardinghouse with a short goodnight and went on his way. He hadn't said anything about seeing me again, and I couldn't think of a single reason why he'd want to. I was out of my depth with Chance, and it was time I got back to shallow water where my feet could touch bottom.

From now on, I thought, I'll stick to my own kind. Floyd might not be as exciting as Chance Cooper, but we came from the same background and had the same memories behind us. And best of all, we understood each other.

Chapter Sixteen

Mrs. Brown caught me as I was crossing the hall to the stairs and gave me a note that had been left for me while I was away.

"I was looking for you earlier," Mrs. Brown said. "But then someone told me they'd seen you leaving in an automobile with some boy."

She went on talking, but I wasn't listening. The note was from Floyd. He had written to say that he would see me for supper at Peggy's Cafe on Friday night, unless something came up and the teacher had to use the car.

I folded the note back into its original creases and stuck it in my pocket. I planned to read it again when I got upstairs and away from Mrs. Brown's chatter.

"Did you enjoy the movie?"

Her words caught me halfway up the steps to my room. I answered over my shoulder and kept on going. "I didn't go to the movies, Mrs. Brown. Chance Cooper and I went canoeing down on White River."

Something about the look on her face told me that she had known all along that I hadn't been to the movies. That was just her way to find out where I had been all afternoon.

It was about noon on Monday that Nancy Arthur came to the store to tell me good-bye. Already, the day showed signs of being hotter than usual. Everyone was wilting in sleeveless cotton dresses, but Nancy looked as fresh and cool as a long drink of spring water in a two-piece linen traveling suit.

She smiled as if she was uncertain of her welcome after two months apart, but at my glad cry, she rushed to meet me with open arms.

"I'm leaving Mother's house," she said. "I can't stand her raving and ranting and her constant spying on me any longer. I thought if you weren't happy here, you could go with me," she added hesitantly. "We could leave Greene County together."

I shook my head no. I couldn't quit a good job. Not even for my best friend. "Why don't you stay here?" I asked. "You could sleep with me until you found a room of your own."

"This will be the first place she comes looking for me," Nancy said. "I have to put more than twenty miles between me and that store before she finds out that I've gone."

Halcie Hissem came out of the office then and motioned at her watch. It was time for me to go to lunch. I waved at her and said, "I won't be long," and took Nancy's arm. "Come on," I said. "I'll walk you to the bus station."

"I'm not going to the bus station," Nancy said, when we were outside the store. "She'll be checking the trains and buses, and I can't afford to leave a trace behind me."

"Then how are you going to get out of town? You can't just walk away."

Nancy gave a little laugh and put out her fist with the thumb extended. "I hitched a ride out of Newark on the Holsum Bread truck," she said. "And I've made a deal with him. As soon as he finishes his deliveries here, he is going to take me on to St. Louis. I don't know where I'll go from there."

"Do you have any money, Nancy?" I had twenty-eight dollars saved in a baking powder can under my mattress. If she needed it, it was hers. And she knew it.

"Bless you, Julie." Nancy hugged me, then stepped back and smiled at me, though her eyes were misty. "You keep your money," she said. "That's one thing I don't need. Mother doesn't know it yet, but I collected for every hour I ever worked for her, and added a little bonus for myself while I was at it, before I ever left there this morning."

Nancy stopped at the corner and put out her hand. "This is where I leave you," she said. "That's my ride waiting for me across the street."

I pretended I didn't see her hand and hugged her close. "Take care," I said. "And keep in touch."

Nancy turned quickly and started across the street, her head held high and her shoulders squared away as if she was prepared to meet anything that came her way head on.

As I walked back to the store, I hoped that Nancy had as much grit and backbone as she pretended to have. She would need it and more to fight her mother's attempts to drag her back to Newark. It wouldn't be just Nancy that Mrs. Arthur was after. She'd want every penny of her money back also. And knowing Maud Arthur the way I did, I knew she wouldn't give up on either one very easily.

One way or another, she would find Nancy and bring her to account for her actions.

I was wringing wet with sweat when I walked into the dime store. I brushed my damp hair away from my face and said to no one in particular, "God, it's hot!"

Halcie eyed me sternly for a moment, then she said, "Julie, don't you think He knows it?"

Friday was my day off work, but this Friday Halcie had called me to come and help her at the store. She was swamped with customers. She said this wouldn't happen often, but if I didn't mind . . . I said I didn't mind. I could always return my books to the library and do my shopping on my lunch hour during the next week.

But I did mind. I was to meet Floyd Perry at Peggy's Cafe for supper around six. And I had to work until six. I hadn't seen Floyd for more than two weeks, and I'd wanted to look my best for him tonight. But now that I'd had to work, it would rush me just to get to Peggy's in time to eat supper with him.

I didn't go home before I went to meet Floyd at Peggy's Cafe. I went straight from work to the restaurant. And when I stepped through the door at Peggy's, I nearly turned around and walked back out.

Floyd Perry was there waiting for me. But so were Chance Cooper, Wen Hazel, and Angie Abram, all sitting at a table together, and watching the door for me. I hesitated a moment, then I went on toward the table as if I had expected to see them all there and I was looking forward to their company. Angie seemed apprehensive about the gathering, but Wen Hazel was leaning back in

154

his chair with a sly, amused grin as if he was enjoying every minute of it.

Floyd and Chance got to their feet as I came to the table. I motioned for them to take their seats. "Sit down," I said. And apologized for being late. They both remained standing. I stood between them, waiting to see if Floyd wanted to sit at this table with Wen and Angie or take another table where we could be alone.

"I'm not staying to eat," Chance said. "I only came by to tell you that I'm sorry about last Sunday evening. I never should have said such a thing to you."

"Forget it," I said quickly. "I have already."

I turned away, hoping Chance wouldn't say another word about last Sunday. He had kept his voice low while he was talking to me, but from the smug, satisfied look on Wen Hazel's face, I knew he had heard every word and he would try to make something out of it.

I glanced at Floyd, then looked away. He had heard Chance, and his blue eyes bore down on Chance as cold and hard as blue steel. Chance Cooper was the only one there who seemed to be at ease.

"Julie, I have to go home this weekend," he said. "But could I talk to you Tuesday evening?"

Floyd didn't wait for me to answer Chance. He doubled his fists and took a step toward him. "It sounds to me like you've already said too much to Julie," Floyd said. "Anything you have to say to her now, you'll have to say right here. Then you'll leave her alone."

"You keep out of it," Chance said. "This is between Julie and me. And she can speak for herself."

Suddenly a giant of a man, with arms like stove pipes,

appeared in our midst. He put one huge hand on Floyd's shoulder and the other on Chance and spoke so softly to them that afterwards, I wasn't sure he had spoken at all.

"You got a quarrel," he said, moving them toward the back door. "Then you take it to the alley. Start any rough stuff in Peggy's, and I knock your heads together and break your necks."

He slapped them lightly on the back, opened the door, and pushed them gently outside. Without a glance at the rest of us, he closed the door and went back to the kitchen.

Wen Hazel shoved himself away from the table and got to his feet. "I was afraid this would happen," he said, with a reproachful look at me. "But you wouldn't listen to me." He turned his back and went outside after the boys.

"Wen's right," Angie said. "You should've paid heed to his word. Since you didn't, what are you going to do about those two boys now?"

"Not a thing," I replied shortly. "I'm going home and leave them to each other." I turned and hurried from the room.

Angie caught up with me just outside the door. "You can't leave now," she said. "You're the cause of the fight, and you've got to see it through to the finish."

My face was wet with angry tears and more coming on all the time. "No I don't," I flared out at her. "They fought the first time they saw each other and they've wanted another fight ever since. Now they've got it." I sniffed and wiped my face with my bare hands. "I hate them both," I muttered between swipes and sniffles. "They can beat each other's brains out for all I care."

156

Angie reached for my hand and held it. "You don't mean that," she said.

I took back my hand. I wasn't feeling too friendly with Angie right then, or any of the rest of them. "Go back to Wen Hazel," I said, "and leave me alone!"

She just stood there, so I walked off toward home. When I turned the corner on Ash Street, she was still there, looking down the street after me.

"Now, you've done it," I thought, and the tears started all over again.

With Nancy Arthur gone out of the county, Angie Abram was the nearest thing I had to a girl friend. But after tonight I probably couldn't count on that any longer. I would have to learn to control my temper and my tongue or I wouldn't be able to keep a friend long enough to name them friend.

It was coming on to twilight now, and under the big trees that lined the street it was full dusk. No one could see that I was crying, but I tried to stop it anyway. I wished just once I could lose my temper without bawling about it. Especially, when I was mad at myself— like right now.

I must have walked the back streets of town for hours thinking about Floyd and Chance Cooper and wondering what I was going to do about them. I wasn't ready to give up Chance. I wanted to go on seeing him whenever I could. But I didn't want to make Floyd mad at me, either.

I knew that Floyd would be aggravated and out of sorts when he found that I hadn't waited for him, as he would put it, "to settle with Chance Cooper." But I couldn't bear to be there and see Chance get hurt. As big and strong as Floyd was, Chance wouldn't have a prayer of coming out of the fight unharmed. Floyd would be mad for a while, but he'd soon get in good humor again. It wasn't his nature to stay angry for long.

Floyd was more than likely looking for me right now. He would want to see me before he went back to Newark. But I didn't want to see him. Not yet. When I felt sure that he had given up on finding me tonight and left town, I went home. The house was dark, except for the dim hall light, and I got to my room without seeing a soul.

Work was real slow at the store the next day—more like the middle of the week than a Saturday. Halcie said that people must have got their days mixed up. "Busy as we were yesterday, I should've known we wouldn't do much business today, even if it is Saturday and their usual day to do their trading." When things hadn't picked up by late afternoon, Halcie sent me home. She said it would make up in part for working on my day off.

As I left the store, Chance Cooper called my name and hurried across the street to meet me. I noticed that he had a walnut-sized bruise high on his cheekbone but other than that, he looked fine. I was glad to see he wasn't hurt any worse.

"I thought you were going home to Bicknell when you got off work today," I said, as he fell into step beside me.

"I couldn't leave town without seeing you first," he replied with a lopsided grin. "You might get the impression that Floyd Perry had scared me away."

I made no reply to that but walked quietly along beside him while he went on to apologize for the night before. "I hope you'll forget about last night," he said. "And go to the show with me Monday evening. I promise I won't embarrass you again," he added.

When I still didn't say anything, Chance gave a short laugh and touched the bruise on his face. "I don't know why you're so mad about it," he said. "You can see it hurt me worse than it did you." Then he laughed again.

I stopped dead still in my tracks and faced him. I hadn't blamed him before. The fight had been forced onto him. But now, because he was making light of it, I did.

"Everything is a joke to you," I said. "A big laugh for Chance Cooper! Well, Mister, I don't think you're a bit funny."

I started on down the street but he caught my hand and held it. "You haven't been listening to me," he said soberly. "I'm trying to tell you that nobody can keep me from seeing you. That I really like you a lot, Julie."

"You've got a strange way of showing it!"

I jerked my hand free and hurried away from him. He stayed where he was and made no move to follow me. My steps faltered. I wanted to go back and tell him that I knew how he felt. I liked him a lot too. I started to go to him, but just then he turned back the way we had come and I let him go.

Later that evening while I was fixing my supper, Mrs. Brown came to the kitchen and said there was a young man asking for me at the door. "He looks like he got the worst of a bad argument," she said, and followed me out of the room.

I expected to see Chance waiting at the door, but instead Floyd stood there. He was still in his work clothes and, to my surprise, he looked worse than Chance Cooper. Floyd's nose was naturally big, but tonight it was red and swollen to twice its normal size. Suddenly, I hated Chance for hurting Floyd this way.

It slipped my mind completely that Floyd had started the fight to begin with and that he deserved every bump and bruise that Chance had given him. All I could think of now was that Floyd was hurt, and Chance Cooper was responsible for it.

"I was fixing something to eat," I said gently, and swung the screen door wide open. "Come on back to the kitchen and have supper with me."

Floyd sat at the table and smiled sheepishly when he saw me watching him. "I didn't know if you'd be speaking to me," he said. "I sure made an ass of myself last night."

"You did that, all right," I replied, smiling and forgiving him for it.

"Darn it, Julie," Floyd said with feeling, "Why do you persist on seeing that fellow when you know how I feel about it? I get so mad I can't see straight just thinking of him here with you." He leaned across the table toward me and lowered his voice. "Don't go out with him again, Julie," he begged. "Let's get back to just you and me. The way it used to be."

I was all mixed up in my feelings. I wanted to please Floyd, to make him happy and say I wouldn't see Chance Cooper again. Yet I liked Chance. Just the thought of not seeing him again gave me a sinking feeling all the way to my toes.

160

"After the way I spoke to him earlier this evening," I said quietly, "Chance probably won't ever come back."

"That would be better still," Floyd said, satisfied with my answer. "With him out of the picture, things will be right between us again."

It was full dark when Floyd left the boardinghouse to go home. But streaks of red left over from the sunset, stretched wide swaths of color across the sky and lent a rosy glow to the horizon. I walked to the car with Floyd and leaned close for his kiss before he drove away.

Kissing Floyd came as naturally to me as breathing, I thought, as I went back to the house. And they both seemed equally important to my existence.

Chapter Seventeen

About an hour before closing time on Monday, Halcie Hissem handed me the familiar brown pay envelope and said, "Julie, you will find a little extra in there today. It's not much, but I like to show my appreciation whenever I can."

I exclaimed over the extra three dollars I found in the envelope and thanked Halcie for it. "This will really come in handy," I said. But I didn't tell Halcie how handy it would be. With this raise in pay, I wouldn't have to dig into my savings. I could live on what I made at the store and even add a little to my savings each week toward my college expenses.

Halcie leaned on the counter near the cash box and gazed around the store at the neat shelves and counters and the clean floor. There wasn't a customer in sight, and there hadn't been since noon. We probably hadn't waited on six people all day long.

"Julie, why don't you go ahead home? There's no sense in both of us standing around here for an hour doing nothing."

She didn't have to coax me to go. I got my purse from

the back room, waved at Halcie, and happily left the store.

Angie Abram saw me when I was still a half block from the vegetable stand and waved. Angie hadn't taken offense at the way I had left her at Peggy's on Friday night. She had told me the next morning that she'd found the evening more entertaining than the Sunday funnies in the *Indianapolis Star*.

"What are you looking so happy about?" Angie asked now, as I stopped at her fruit stand. "Did a rich uncle just die and leave you a million dollars?"

"It's not quite a million," I said, and laughed. "But I feel rich just the same. Halcie Hissem gave me a three dollar raise in pay this week."

"That's reason enough to smile," Angie said. She seemed as pleased as I was about the extra money that I'd be getting from now on. "I'd say that's a call for a celebration," she went on, her smile lighting her whole face. "You should get dressed up and do something special tonight to mark the occasion."

I laughed at the notion of me getting dressed up for any reason. "Angie, I couldn't do that if the Prince of Wales was coming to town just to see me," I said. "The best I have to my name are the three cotton dresses that Esta Allen and I made while I was at her house this spring. And I wear them to work every day," I added.

Angie gave me a strange look. "You ought to do something about that," she said seriously. "Every girl should have one good Sunday dress, whether she wears it or not." She added under her breath, "I do."

Then, she said, "Julie, Wickes is having a sale today.

163

Why don't you slip over there and spend some of your new-found riches on a good dress for yourself?"

For a moment, I was tempted to do as Angie had suggested. Then I reminded myself of all the other uses I could put the three dollars to and shook my head no.

"I don't have any need for a new dress," I said. "I wouldn't have any place to wear one, if I had it. Chance asked me to go to the show with him tonight, but I was mad at him at the time and I didn't even answer him."

Angie smiled and brushed the short red curls back from her face. "That's a shame," she said, looking not a bit sorry. "Now, you will have to celebrate your raise all by yourself."

"I may do just that," I said. And went on toward home.

I'd had no intention of doing anything when I left Angie except going home, fixing my supper, and finishing the book I'd been reading. But by the time I had gotten to the boardinghouse, I had talked myself into going out for supper and a movie. I deserved that much, I told myself.

As soon as I got home, I set about getting dressed in the best I had to wear. Yet, after I was ready to go, I put off the moment of leaving my room. I felt self-conscious about going out by myself. And not only that, but Mrs. Brown might think it strange, and heaven only knew what Verna Clayton would have to say about it. I wished again for the hundredth time that Chance would come by. Even if I hadn't said he could.

Now that the time was at hand, I couldn't do it. I would feel foolish walking into Peggy's Cafe alone and eating all by myself. I wouldn't enjoy my supper, nor the movie afterwards, just wondering what the people around me were saying about it. I turned away from the door and went to change my dress.

The sound of Mrs. Brown's voice calling my name stopped me. I opened the door and stepped to the landing. "Julie, there's a young man to see you," she said, from the foot of the stairs.

For a moment, I thought I had hypnotized myself into hearing what I wanted so much to hear. But when I looked toward the door, I could see that I wasn't dreaming. Chance Cooper was there waiting for me. I quickly closed my door and went to meet him.

Chance was always clean and neat, but tonight he looked as though he had just stepped out of a band box in sharply creased tan slacks and a short-sleeved shirt to match. The bruise had faded from his face, or else the new sunburn covered it from sight. He grinned sheepishly as I opened the front door, and said, "Am I too late to take you to supper?"

I gave him the best smile I could come up with, and answered, "Chance, you're right on time."

He took my arm going down the porch steps and held it as we walked up the street.

"First, we're going to Peggy's Cafe," Chance said, almost defiantly. "Then we're going to the show."

I just nodded my head and agreed with whatever he had in mind to do for the evening. I was too happy to have him here with me to disagree with anything he had to say.

I figured that Chance had chosen to eat at Peggy's Cafe to show anyone who was interested that if he hadn't won the fight in the alley on Friday night, he hadn't exactly lost it either, since I was there with him tonight.

"My car conked out on me coming in from the Junction," he said, "and I had to get Andy to pull me into town."

"How will you get back to your cabin?"

"Andy said he'd have it fixed and running again in a couple of hours. But it's unhandy being without it and making you walk to the show and back."

"I don't mind walking," I said. "We never had an automobile at home and I'm used to walking."

I told Chance a little of what it had been like living over by Newark, and he told me how he had grown up. The way he spoke of catching snakes when he was a boy and how he handled the hot electric wires now, it occurred to me that he still hadn't grown up. He was still playing with fire and showing off for the attention it would get him.

The Depression hadn't effected Chance's life as it had mine and Floyd Perry's. His dad had continued to manage the coal mines just as though nothing had happened. And when Chance graduated from high school, he had bought him the car he was driving now.

"That's when I found out there was a Depression," Chance said. "I couldn't find a job to support myself and my automobile. The boys I graduated with left the county to look for work, but I stayed at home with Mother and Dad and waited for better days.

"I'd work for Dad at the mine once in a while just to get gas money," Chance went on. "But I didn't like it. When I saw in the *Indianapolis Star* that the Power Company wanted men to string electric lines through the back country, I drove up there and got a job. A lot of men are afraid of the hot wires," he added. "But I don't mind them. They keep me on my toes and my mind on my work."

While he was talking, I thought how different his growing up had been from Floyd's. Floyd hardly had time to be a boy before he'd had to act like a man. And his dad hadn't made it any easier on him, either. Harder, if anything. Again it struck me that a wide, wide gulf lay between Chance and Floyd. And it was brought home to me more than ever that I belonged on Floyd's side of the crevasse. I knew nothing of the world Chance spoke of, and I was content to leave it that way.

Later back at the boardinghouse, Chance said, "Borrow a pair of overalls from Angie's brother. You're going fishing with me Friday night."

Before I could answer, his arms closed tightly around me and he kissed me. "That should hold you till Friday," he whispered, and turned and left the house.

I stood on the steps with my mouth open to call him back—to tell him I couldn't see him again. But I couldn't make a sound. "I'll tell him Friday," I said to myself, as I went into the house. "One more time can't make any difference."

I saw Angie on my lunch break the next day and asked her about loaning me a pair of overalls. She laughed merrily when I explained why I needed them, and said, "I didn't think you would be able to stay mad at Chance."

I just smiled. I doubted if anyone had ever been able to stay mad at Chance for very long. With the exception of Floyd Perry.

"We may see you there," Angie said. "Chance told Wen a while back to feel free to use the fishing shack whenever he wanted, and Wen said then that we might go down there the Friday night before Old Settlers."

I couldn't imagine why Chance had said we were going fishing Friday night when he knew Wen and Angie were going to be at the cabin. Then I thought he probably figured I would be more comfortable there with another woman along.

"That'll be fine," I said, as I turned toward the dime store. "You and I can fry the fish if the men catch any."

Angie brought the overalls to the store the next morning before she opened the fruit stand. "You may need to take tucks in them so they'll fit," she said.

Halcie laughed when she saw the faded, oversized overalls I intended to wear, but I assured Angie they would do very well. "The fish won't mind how I look," I said.

"But what about Chance? Won't he mind?"

"I'm dressing to catch fish," I replied. "Not Chance Cooper."

We were still laughing and joking about the overalls when the door to the dime store flew open and Maud Arthur came in like a whirlwind.

Halcie Hissem knew Maud Arthur from a long time back, both as a business woman and one-time friend. And I knew her. But Angie Abram had never laid eyes on Mrs. Arthur before, and she wasn't prepared for her outburst.

Mrs. Arthur pointed a finger at me. "I've talked to the sheriff," she announced in a loud voice. "And if you want to stay out of trouble, you'll tell me where I can find Nancy."

Halcie said quietly, "Maud, she isn't here, and no one has seen your girl lately."

Mrs. Arthur paid no attention to Halcie. She continued to shout and wave her finger in my face. "You know where she went," she screamed. "You put her up to running away with that huckster."

"Now, Maud, get a-hold of yourself." Halcie stepped between Mrs. Arthur and me. "You can't blame Julie for what Nancy did."

"I can and I will," Maud Arthur said. "She's been nothing but trouble to me, and now she's turned Nancy against me."

Halcie turned to me and said quietly, "I thought I told you to go to the post office for my mail." And motioned toward the door.

This was the first I'd heard of the mail. I looked at Angie. She shrugged her shoulders, took me by the arm, and said, "Come along," and we started to walk on by Mrs. Arthur.

Mrs. Arthur put out her hand, as if she would stop us by force. She said to Halcie, "Do you know how old that girl is?"

"Age has got nothing to do with anything, Maud," Halcie replied. "If it did, you wouldn't be making a fool of yourself in my shop.'

"I hope you are eighteen," Angie said, when we were outside the store. "That old woman could get you sent to the girl's reform school if you're not."

"She can't cause me trouble on that count," I replied. "I was eighteen when I came to work for Halcie."

"But Maud Arthur doesn't know that, does she?"

I shook my head. "I'm a couple of months older than Nancy."

Then the thought struck me. "Nancy won't be of age for another month yet," I said, thinking out loud. "She has more than one reason for not wanting her mother to find her. Maud would surely send her to a house of correction if she could get her hands on Nancy now."

"And you'd go right along with her," Angie said. "Maud Arthur could charge you with contributing to the delinquency of a minor just for helping Nancy. And since you're of legal age, there's not a thing you could do about it."

Even though the only help I had ever given Nancy had been a little moral support, since she wouldn't take money from me, Mrs. Arthur would twist it to suit her own purpose. She knew nearly everybody in Greene County, and there were those who would swear to anything she asked just to avoid her enmity.

"Angie, that scares me, and I'm not afraid of much. I wouldn't have a prayer against those kinds of charges," I said. "I never realized it before, but single girls like us are fair game for women like her."

"They don't just pick on the single ones," Angie said. "Some married women are just as vulnerable as we are."

"But they have husbands to stand up for them."

"A man can't do much to protect them if they don't know what's happening," Angie said. "That's why talk is so effective. When the gossip is about her, the wife won't tell her husband for fear he won't believe her. And when she hears stories about him, she's afraid to mention it. Afraid it might be so. And eventually, gossip claims another victim."

A period of silence followed her words. I could understand how what she said could be so. But it didn't say much for the trust between a man and his wife.

After a while, Angie said, "Julie, what have you heard about the way Wen Hazel lost his wife?"

"Only what Chance told me," I replied. "That she drank arsenic in her tea—and it killed her."

"She killed herself," Angie said with feeling. "And her friend Verna Clayton drove her to it with her stories."

We had walked by the post office and we had to turn around and go back to get Halcie's mail. There was nothing important in the box. Just circulars from the merchants in town advertising sale days for the Old Settlers Reunion. The reunion had started when the first families who settled this part of Greene County gathered together to celebrate the harvest. But now everyone took part in the Old Settlers Reunion and the merchants used this time to hold their late summer sales.

When we were on our way back to the store, Angie brought up the subject of Wen Hazel and his wife again.

"Wen said they'd had a terrible fight," Angie said quietly. "He had slammed out of the house and didn't come home for two days. By that time, Gayle was dead. They called it an accident," she murmured. "But it was suicide, and Verna's loose talk drove her to it."

"What kind of talk?" I asked, when Angie paused and showed no sign of going on. "It must have been pretty bad to cause her to take her life."

"To some, it wouldn't have meant that much," Angie said. "But Gayle was spoiled and weak—and so jealous she couldn't see straight. When she heard that Wen was seeing another woman and spending his money on her, Gayle went to pieces. And it was all a pack of lies," Angie added. "Not a grain of truth in any of it."

171

Angie shook her head when I asked if Wen knew this about Verna Clayton. "Then why haven't you told him? He would have run her out of town for it."

Angie looked at me and smiled as if she were humoring the town idiot. "You don't antagonize a rattlesnake, Julie," she said. "You give it a wide berth and hope it doesn't strike you."

She left me at the corner to open her fruit stand, and I went on to the dime store. If it had been her intention to get my mind off Maud Arthur by telling me about Gayle Hazel, she had succeeded. I hadn't thought once of my own problems since we'd left the post office.

Mrs. Arthur had gone, and Halcie Hissem was waiting for me at the front door. "Julie, what did you ever do to Maud?" she asked, reaching for the junk mail that I carried in my hand. "She hasn't a kind word to say about you."

I gave her the mail. "I don't know," I replied. "She seemed to like me when I first went there to live. But after Mom and Dad moved away, she turned mean-tongued and wouldn't have a thing to do with me."

Customers came in then, and we both got busy. Halcie went to the storeroom to mark down prices for the Old Settlers Day sale, and I waited on the customers. Quite a few people came in during the morning; some were buying but mostly, they were looking, and they didn't need any help. I had a lot of time on my hands and I spent it thinking about Nancy Arthur and myself.

I prayed that Nancy could stay out of her mother's reach. Being eighteen wouldn't help her a bit if Mrs. Arthur brought up the money Nancy had taken with her when she left home. And you could bet your buttons that

172

she would. Mrs. Arthur couldn't touch me in regards to the missing money, but she would drag me into it, claiming I had helped Nancy.

I trembled to think what would happen if Maud Arthur and Verna Clayton should ever get together. With two women like that on a girl's trail, there would be no place where she could hide or be safe from them.

Chapter Eighteen

The air was hot and muggy when I awoke on Friday morning, and as the day got older, my room got hotter. I ate an orange for breakfast so I wouldn't have to get dressed and go down to the kitchen. Then while I was still in my nightgown, I cleaned my room and the bathroom that I shared with Verna Clayton. I didn't want the word to get around that I wasn't doing my share. Shortly after noon, I put on an old cotton dress and shoes without stockings and left the house.

On account of my working at the dime store, my face was familiar to most of the women I met on the street, and they smiled and spoke to me.

"My, but it's hot," said the undertaker's wife. "What we need is a good soaking rain to cool things off a bit."

I smiled and agreed with her. Then when I met Opal Empson who worked at the bank, she said," Let's pray that this sunshine lasts through the Old Settlers days, so the folks can all get to town."

I nodded and agreed with whatever they wished for. Rain or shine, it didn't matter to me, but it did to them. There was so little to do in Linton that the people looked to the Old Settlers Reunion with the same excitement and expectation that they greeted the Fourth of July

174

parade each year. Those were the only two days of
summer when they all got together and made new friends
and renewed old acquaintances at a carry-in dinner at
the park.

It was cool in the library, and I spent as much time as
possible choosing the books I wanted. When Martha
started getting ready to close the library at two, I took
my books and went back out into the hot sunshine.

Angie's brother was watching the fruit stand for her,
so I stopped to thank him for the loan of his overalls.
"Don't thank me," he laughed. "Thank the good Lord
that I had an extra pair to loan."

I bought a bagful of wild purple plums and a couple
of apples from him, then went on toward home.

Esta Allen was leaning on the desk talking to Mrs.
Brown when I got to the boardinghouse. "If you're not
busy, I'd like to talk to you," she said.

I hadn't seen Esta since I'd left her house and I was
glad to see her. "Sure," I replied warmly. "I'll put these
things away and be right back."

Mrs. Brown smiled and waved my answer away. "Julie,
Esta is like one of the family. Take her to your room
where you can have your talk in private."

I smiled at Mrs. Brown and thanked her. Esta smiled
and thanked her, and we went upstairs together.

Esta sat in the easy chair and looked around the room
as if checking on the welfare of an old friend. I tucked my
legs under me and sat on the edge of the bed, wondering
what she wanted to talk to me about. She didn't keep me
waiting, but came right to the point.

"Maud Arthur paid me a visit the other day," Esta
said simply.

175

I'd hoped that I had heard the last of Mrs. Arthur, but it seemed as though I was never to be rid of her.

"She was under the impression that you were still with me," Esta said. "But I told her you were working for Halcie Hissem, clerking in the dime store."

She paused then, and with a note of apology, went on, "I wanted you to know, should Maud Arthur come down on you with both feet, that I meant you no harm. I spoke before I thought," Esta said. "And I regretted the words as soon as they were out of my mouth."

"Don't worry about it," I said. "She has been here and gone. Halcie Hissem got her off my back and made short shift of her wild tirade at the store."

"She may be back," Esta said. "She asked me what day you came to work for me, and when I told her on a Sunday, she smacked her lips and chewed on the words as if I had handed her a feast."

"I don't know why she should care when I got to your house. I was out of her sight, and that's all she seemed to want while I was living with her."

"Who can tell what goes through her mind," Esta replied.

We sat quietly for a while. There seemed to be nothing more to say. Then Esta said, "I'm afraid I told her more than I aimed to. But if she makes something out of it, you know I didn't do it on purpose."

Esta left soon afterwards, but not before she had asked me if I was still going steady with those two men."

"I don't see Floyd as often as I'd like to," I answered. "And I still go out with Chance occasionally. But I wouldn't call it going steady with either one of them."

"I'd heard that you were." She leaned forward in the

chair and eyed me sternly. "If I were you," she said, "I'd quit leading them on and marry one or the other of those two boys."

I smiled to take the sting out of my words. "But you're not me, Esta. I'll get married when I'm ready. Not when someone else thinks I should."

Later that evening down on White River, Angie and I were talking in the cabin, while Chance and Wen tried their luck at fishing. They hadn't caught one fish before supper. Angie had roasted the weiners she'd brought along, and after we had eaten the men went out again.

"Esta Allen came to the boardinghouse to see me today," I said into the quiet that followed the men's going. "She wanted me to know Maud Arthur had been to see her and to warn me that Maud might look me up. I told her not to worry another minute. She'd already been here and gone. Then Esta asked if I was still stringing Chance and Floyd along," I said indignantly. "As if I was wasting their time."

Angie laughed. "The shoe could very easily be on the other foot," she said.

"Meaning they could be handing me a line?"

"Well, yes." Angie hesitated. "Boys do that to get next to a girl." Then she asked, "Julie, has either of them ever asked you to go to bed with him?"

I thought of what Chance had said to me that Sunday evening on the river bank, but I held my tongue. As for Floyd, he wouldn't even think of such a thing.

"Floyd has asked me to marry him," I said. "But he knows how I feel about it, and he's willing to wait."

It was getting dusk in the cabin, but neither one of us

made a move to light the lamp. "How do you feel about marriage, Julie? Are you afraid to go to bed with a man?" Angie leaned toward me, peering into my face, as if to better judge my answer.

I didn't think a woman should say a thing like that to another, but I tried not to let Angie know how I felt. I could only hope that the shock and surprise didn't show on my face. She thought I was a naive greenhorn the way it was.

"Of course not," I answered casually, as if I was used to conversations like this. "But there ought to be more to marriage than going to bed with a man and having a baby every year, like Esta Allen. What about the part of it that consists of living day in and day out with the same man? And knowing that's the way it's going to be for the rest of your life? That's the part that scares me," I added.

Angie laughed softly. "I know I can get along with Wen in bed," she said. "But it's the thought of waking up every morning and finding him still there that makes me hesitate to marry him."

The setting sun laid a band of red against the window and lit up the room for a moment with its glow. I could see the smile that tipped the corners of her mouth and warmed her green eyes, while Angie watched me and waited to see how I would react to her words.

Chance and I should be starting back to town. But if I said so now, Angie would think that I didn't want to be here with her. Not after learning about her and Wen Hazel. We had been friends all summer and I hadn't suspected a thing. Even when Chance told me they were sleeping together, I hadn't believed it. I had thought it was just a tale that somebody had started. Now I wondered why Angie felt that she had to tell me this, and I wished she hadn't.

Growing up with a strict, straitlaced mother who believed there was good and bad, but no in-between, I had been led to think that only a wild, easily persuaded woman of low character would lie with a man before marriage. Now I didn't know what to think. Angie was not that kind of woman. But now I understood why she feared Verna Clayton's tongue, and why Wen Hazel had Verna working in his store. That was one way of putting a muzzle on her and controlling her range of gossip.

I got up, found the matches, and lit the hurricane lamp that was fastened to the wall near the table. "Now the fellows can find their way home," I said. And hoped my voice sounded natural to Angie.

As I turned from lighting the lamp, Angie motioned for me to sit by her.

"Do I shock you, Julie?"

I shook my head and sat down beside her on the daybed.

"I waited for twenty-eight years," Angie said. "And for more than ten of those years I have loved Wen Hazel. But I'd thought of him as a married man, and out of my reach, for so long that Wen had been a widower for more than two years before I could bring myself to go out with him." She paused, then smiled and added, "Even then, we never showed our faces in town together until the first time we met you and Floyd for supper at Peggy's."

When I didn't say anything, Angie's entire being seemed to grow quiet. "Would you have been my friend if you had known that Wen and me hadn't waited to get

179

married? That we seek out-of-the-way places like this so we can be together?"

The room was so still that I could hear the moths and other nighttime insects beating their wings against the hurricane lamp, killing themselves while trying to reach the unattainable light. Like people, I thought. Always wanting what they can't get.

I turned from the light to Angie's quietly waiting face. We had favored each other right from the start. I liked her, and she had been a friend when I had none. Now, without one qualm or misgiving, I nodded my head, silently telling her that whatever she and Wen Hazel chose to do was their concern. Not mine, or anyone else's.

Angie and I were making plans to go to the Old Settlers Reunion when Chance and Wen came in from fishing. If my face showed any of my feelings about what I had learned tonight, they made no sign of it. Wen said he thought as we did, Sunday would be the best day to go to the Reunion. It lasted for three days, but the last day was always the biggest. "That's when they pull the plug on everything," Wen said.

Chance leaned against the door frame, ready to leave as soon as he heard the final plans. He was going home to Bicknell when he got off work the next day, and we wouldn't see him until Sunday. Finally, Wen said, "Angie and I will meet you at the gate to the park around eating time," and Chance and I left the cabin to drive back to town.

Where the dirt road from the cabin met the black-topped highway to Linton, Chance pulled the car to the side of the road and stopped. He switched off the lights, and it was pitch black in the car. Leafy branches from the nearby trees reached through the open window beside me and brushed my arm as I moved close to the door. I took a deep breath, held it, then let the air out slowly.

Chance hadn't said a word since we had left Wen and Angie at the cabin. I had put that down to his concentration on his driving. The deep-rutted lane winding up from the river was the very devil even in broad daylight. But now as I waited, I wasn't sure that was it at all.

Chance moved from under the wheel and turned to face me.

"You know what they're doing . . ."

"No, I don't," I said quickly. "And neither do you."

"Julie, have you ever . . ."

"No!"

". . . thought about getting married?" He finished.

I said no again. But more quietly this time.

"Neither have I," Chance said. "I like to be footloose and fancy free. But that's what Wen and Angie are doing back there."

My relief was so great that I went limp as a rag doll. This was a far cry from what I'd thought he had in mind when he parked here.

"They are talking about it," Chance said. "Wen told me he ought to be married by Labor Day and have this courting business all wound up."

The thought came unbidden to my mind that he ought to have married Angie a long time ago and then courted her. But I didn't say so.

We were quiet for a while, listening to the night sounds and thinking our own thoughts. Then Chance broke the silence.

"Julie, do you think a person can love someone, yet not want to marry them?"

I thought of Floyd, and how dear he was to me. And of Chance here in the dark beside me. In completely different ways, I was sure I loved them both. But not the way I figured a woman should love the man she was going to spend her life with.

"I think so," I answered. "Why?" Then I wished I hadn't asked.

"I love you, Julie," Chance said softly. "But the very thought of being married scares me to death. Do you understand how that could be?"

I said I could. "I'm not in any hurry to get married either," I said. "But for some people, like Wen and Angie, it's the only thing to do."

"But this is different, Julie. I don't think I'll ever marry. Do you remember how scared you were when we went to the class reunion dance," he asked. "Well, I was scared too. I was afraid you'd be like the other girls I'd known and expect to park and neck on the way home. And I couldn't handle that," he added.

His voice coming out of the darkness was so low I could hardly hear him. He hesitated and seemed to choose his words like he had never before put his feelings into words for another person to hear.

"I didn't know that boys ever felt that way," I said, my voice as low as his. "I thought only girls . . ." I let my voice die away. Something was tugging at my memory. Something that didn't ring true with what he had just said. Then I had it.

"If you feel that way about girls, why did you ask me to stay all night with you at the cabin?"

Chance moved closer to me, but he didn't touch me. "I'd heard things," he said. "And I had to know for sure. I didn't want a girl who would spend the night with a man. And that was the only way I knew to find out."

I was exasperated with him. "Why didn't you just ask me? I would have told you!"

"I was afraid you'd get mad at me."

"It didn't bother you when you fought Floyd. And you knew I would be mad about that."

"I fought Floyd for the right to go on being your friend," Chance replied simply. "Until I met you, I'd never been at ease with girls. I didn't date in high school like the other fellows, and I got the name of being an odd-ball. A woman hater," he added. "But you weren't like the other girls I knew, and I didn't want to lose you."

It was hard to believe that Chance—so easy and carefree always—could have felt like this. But it sounded true as he was saying it. I reached for his hand and held it. "That's all I ever wanted, Chance. Just a friend. And we can be friends as long as you want to," I said. "You've earned that right."

We sat there and talked for a long time, then Chance started the car and took me home.

Chapter Nineteen

There were people waiting for the store to open the next morning when I got to work. Halcie Hissem opened the door, and they came in like droves of sheep, one following after the other. I stood behind the cash register taking their money and wrapping the purchases, while Halcie mingled with the crowd to help them find whatever they wanted and to see that they paid for it. She said in a mob such as this, she couldn't be too careful. They were apt to rob her blind.

Around noon the shoppers left the stores and flocked toward the eating places in town. Halcie came to the front desk and said, "Julie, you'd better grab a bite while they're eating. We won't find a better time."

I had learned to bring a snack with me on Saturday. Even when we didn't have a sale going on, Saturday was the busiest day of the week, and we never had time to go out for lunch.

I started back to the office where I kept my lunch bag, and Halcie called after me, "Julie, we've been so busy I haven't had time to ask how the fishing was last night. Did you catch anything?"

I laughed, and answered, "No. And neither did Chance."

I had brought cheese and crackers and some of the wild plums that I'd got from Angie's brother to snack on today. And while I nibbled at my lunch, I thought of Chance Cooper and the things he had told me about himself last night.

The more I thought about it, the surer I was that his carefree, dare-devil manner was nothing but a cover-up, like a boy whistling past the graveyard to keep anyone from knowing how frightened and unsure he was of himself. I was glad Chance had told me how he felt about girls and marriage and all that went with it. Now we could be friends without worrying about it.

Wen Hazel or any other man would probably think less of Chance if they knew how he felt, but no matter what they might think of him I thought Chance was a brave man. It took a lot of courage for him to tell me these things. He didn't have to.

I washed the plum juice off my hands and brushed away the cracker crumbs and went back to work. Floyd Perry was leaning on the counter talking to Halcie when I got to the front of the store. There were a few customers wandering in the aisles. Just lookers, Halcie said. She could tell a looker from a buyer as far as across the room. And a shoplifter from even farther away.

Floyd grinned as I stopped beside him. "Halcie tells me that you've had a busy day."

I lowered my voice, and said, "We've had people coming out of the woodwork since the minute we opened the door."

"I stopped at the hardware store," Floyd said. "I

wanted to talk to Wen. I didn't see him anywhere, but Verna Clayton is sure earning her pay today."

Halcie sniffed. "It's about time," she said.

We laughed. Then Floyd turned from Halcie and said to me, "I came to see you last night, but Mrs. Brown said you'd gone already. With Chance Cooper."

"If I'd known you were coming, I would've waited for you," I said. "We went fishing down on White River with Wen and Angie. You could've gone with us," I added.

"Not likely," Floyd said. Then he turned back to Halcie. "I'm of a mind to buy a car, if I can find one that I can depend on."

"What made you decide that?"

He leaned over the counter toward her and lowered his voice as if it was a secret between them. "Two men courting two girls, with one car to drive, doesn't work out too well," Floyd said.

Halcie smiled, and said, "I can see why it wouldn't."

One of the lookers had found something she wanted to buy and brought it to the front desk. While Halcie took care of the sale, I walked to the door with Floyd.

"I rode to town with Ben," Floyd said. "But if I find a car I like, I'll be staying to see you later."

He hadn't asked me if I'd broken with Chance Cooper, and I never mentioned it. It would've taken more time than I had now to explain why I hadn't. And why I didn't want to ever.

"I'm surprised at you, Julie," Halcie said, when we found a free minute. "Floyd Perry loves you. Yet you think nothing of going out with Chance Cooper, and then telling him about it. How do you think that makes him feel?" she added.

"Floyd knows that Chance is just a friend," I said. Then, so there would be no mistake about where I stood or how I felt about Floyd, I said, "I've loved Floyd Perry all my life. And he knows it."

"Yes, I believe you do," Halcie said thoughtfully. "But I wonder if either one of you realize *how* you love him."

I didn't have a chance to ask her what she meant. The half of Greene County that hadn't been in the store during the morning came in at that time. We were busy right up to closing time at nine o'clock.

Halcie locked the door, and I waited out front while she went to get her car from the alley behind the store. There was no sign of Floyd. The few automobiles that were on the street were leaving town, now that all the stores had closed for the day.

"I guess Floyd couldn't find a car to suit him," I said on our way home, "and he had to go back to Newark with Ben Collier. Now I don't know when I will see him again."

"Cheer up, Julie. Floyd will surely be at the Old Settlers tomorrow," Halcie said. "You'll see him then."

I hadn't noticed being tired while I was working and looking forward to seeing Floyd. But suddenly, I was exhausted. I felt more tired tonight than I had the first day I ever worked at the dime store. Not only my stamina but my spirit as well had hit rock bottom.

"Even if he's there," I said, "I won't be able to talk to him. I've already promised Chance that I'd go with him."

Halcie pulled up and stopped at the boarding house.

I opened the door to get out. "Halcie, what am I going to do?"

She smiled at me. "That's something you'll have to work out for yourself," she said kindly, and drove away.

Every one who had been hoping for a sunny Old Settlers Day had gotten their wish. On Sunday morning my room was hotter than blue blazes before Chance got to the boardinghouse to pick me up, and there was no sign of it getting any cooler. I had never been to an Old Settlers reunion, and I teetered between going now or staying at home. The thought of the cool park decided me. I was ready to go when Chance got there.

Wen and Angie were waiting for us under the shade trees near the park gate. Standing close by were Floyd and Mr. Thompson, smiling and looking for all the world as if they had been asked to meet us there.

"Blast my hide," Chance said under his breath. "Now I'll have to fight Floyd Perry again." But he was grinning as he said it.

Chance pulled off the rutted dirt lane and parked the car on the other side of Wen Hazel's automobile, on a grassy slope where the ground fell away toward the small creek that ran through the park. "Come on," he said, smiling and taking my hand. "Let's greet our welcoming committee."

"It's about time you got here," Wen said with a big grin. "Angie and I have something to tell you all." He put his arm around Angie and drew her close to his side. "We got married yesterday at the county seat."

That wasn't what I had expected. I thought it would

188

be the promise to marry. Not the fact that they had already.

Chance and Floyd seemed to forget their differences as they slapped Wen on the back and congratulated him. Mr. Thompson shook Wen's hand formally and kissed Angie on the cheek.

"This is call for a celebration," Mr. Thompson said. Then he and Floyd brought a wash tub full of ice, soft drinks, and beer from the trunk of the teacher's car and set it in the shade. "Everybody help yourself," he said.

Wen and Mr. Thompson drank the beer. The rest of us had root beer and orange pop. Mr. Thompson raised his bottle and toasted the newlyweds. "Now if she can cook," he told Wen, "you've got yourself quite a woman."

Angie laughed and turned to me. "We'd better spread the cloth and put dinner on, or the men will start eating out of the basket."

We left the men and went to get the picnic baskets from the car. Chance had brought a hamper of food from home for our dinner. I got it out of the car and put the fried chicken, potato salad, and chocolate cake on the table with the sandwiches, pickles, and sliced cantalope that Angie had brought.

At first, I was fearful and uneasy having Floyd and Chance Cooper at the same table. But it didn't seem to bother them any this time. They ate everything at hand, then wheedled the teacher into giving them the wishbone to break, and the last piece of chicken. I stopped worrying about it.

Chance motioned toward the people who had finished eating and were now clearing the tables. "They are anxious to start the horseshoe games," he said, "and get the tobacco-spitting contest under way."

We had just started on the chocolate cake. I said, "Yuk!" And put my plate down.

Angie made a face. "Chance! That's disgusting!"

Chance laughed. "At the Old Settlers Reunion you're apt to see anything."

"You'll excuse me if I don't look," I said.

He laughed again and got to his feet. Floyd and Wen were standing nearby, just waiting for Chance and the schoolteacher to finish their cake. Chance looked at Mr. Thompson still sitting beside Angie with a plate in his hand. "Come on, Teach," he said. "Let's you and me show this storekeeper and big log-roller how to pitch horseshoes."

Floyd and Wen guffawed at the idea. "Teach an old dog to suck eggs," Wen said.

Mr. Thompson put his plate aside and rose to his feet. "I'm with you." He nodded at Chance. "We'll see who gets the horse laugh."

The men left then to find the horseshoe games. Angie and I cleared the remnants of our dinner and put the baskets back in the car.

"When I saw Floyd here," I said, "I was afraid he would make trouble. But so far, he's behaving himself."

"Wen talked to him earlier," Angie said. "He told Floyd that you'd be here with Chance, and he didn't want any fuss about it."

"And Floyd agreed to behave? Just like that?"

Angie smiled. "Not right away," she replied. "But when the teacher spoke up and said he would help beat some sense into him if he started anything, Floyd agreed."

It should have been me getting a talking to on how to behave myself, not Floyd. He had every right to be upset when he found out I hadn't kept my promise to him. And that's what I told Angie.

"I meant it when I told him that I would break off with Chance and not see him any more," I said. "But I like Chance. I don't want to stop seeing him right now."

"You're going to have to make a choice between them sooner or later," Angie said. "It might as well be now."

"But why do I have to choose one? Why can't I be friends with both of them? Liking Chance Cooper doesn't change the way I feel about Floyd. That's something altogether different."

"Have you told Floyd how you feel?"

"I told him last spring that Chance was just a friend, and he said he understood. But he doesn't. I don't think he tries to understand how I feel."

Angie took my arm and we walked to where the crafts table was piled high with homemade quilts for sale. "You could use a little understanding on your part too, Julie," she said in a low voice. She fingered the raised pattern on a cross-patch quilt and didn't look at me. "Without considering Floyd's feelings at all, you showed up here today with Chance and made Floyd look small in front of his friends."

I started to say that I would never do that to Floyd, but I stopped myself. Angie was right. I had done it already. I had put Floyd down in front of his friends, whether I meant to or not.

We moved away from the homemade quilts and on past

tables and chairs loaded with fancy pillows, bedspreads, and hand-hooked rag rugs. We stopped and looked at these things, but neither one of us was of a mind to buy anything, and we moved on again.

Finally, Angie said, "Julie, are you mad at me for saying what I did? We've crossed the park and you've not spoken to me since then."

I shook my head no. I wasn't mad at Angie. I was thinking.

I said, "Angie, my very first memory is of Floyd Perry. He was my hero all through school, and he still is. Until you brought it home to me just now, I wouldn't have believed that I could ever slight him."

"Maybe Floyd didn't see it that way at all," Angie said, trying to make me feel better. "I shouldn't have said anything, but I wanted you to realize that understanding was a two way street. You both have to participate to make it work."

"A lot of good that does me now," I said petulantly. "It can't change what has already happened."

Angie smiled and slipped her arm through mine. "Julie, don't let what I said ruin your day," she said. "We're supposed to be having fun. So smile now, and forget I said anything."

I smiled for her, but I couldn't forget it.

Floyd and Wen Hazel found us at the far end of the park, where they were holding the team-pulling contest. Two matched pairs of farm horses were hitched to a tree stump, and they were straining in opposite directions trying to pull the stump out of the ground.

Wen said, "This is what I've been waiting to see. Look at that team of grays pull!"

192

"It's too much like work to suit me," Angie replied. "I've held the reins of plow horses and seen enough of them to last me a lifetime."

But she stayed beside Wen to watch the pulling contest.

Floyd took my arm and we moved away from the others. "I want to tell you something," he said. "I would've told you sooner, but I didn't want to take anything away from Wen and Angie's announcement.

"I got myself an automobile yesterday," he said proudly. "But before I can drive it, I find I have to put a license on it and get a driver's license for myself."

"Floyd, that's wonderful! When you didn't come by last night, I thought you couldn't find one you liked."

"I wanted to tell you as soon as I got it," Floyd said. "But Ben said if we hurried we could get to the license bureau in Bloomfield before it closed. So we drove over there."

Floyd paused and shook his head. "We hurried," he said. "But it didn't do a darn bit of good. The place don't even open on Saturday."

"What will you do now?" I asked. "A car isn't much good if you can't drive it."

"I've got that figured out already," Floyd said. "I'll leave the sawmill at noon on Friday and ride to Bloomfield on the logging truck and get it all taken care of. If I get done in time, I'll come by the boardinghouse and take you for a ride," he added.

"I'd like that," I told him. "I'll be looking for you."

"Have you two noticed the looks of that sky?" Wen Hazel said from close behind us. "There's a storm brewing, just as sure as shooting."

We hadn't, but now we did. It seemed like even while we watched, the dark clouds got blacker, the light changed to a yellowish green, and the sky took on the color of an old bruise. We didn't see the lightning, but thunder rolled and rumbled in the distance and we knew it had to be somewhere.

Everyone else seemed to be watching the sky also. They moved restlessly as they waited for one or the other of the struggling teams to uproot the tree stump and bring the contest to an end.

"Wen, we'd better start home," Angie said nervously. "We don't want to get caught in this storm."

"We're going," Wen answered. "Just as soon as this team pull is over."

Just then the huge team of matched grays that Wen was betting on gave a powerful lunge, and the tree stump came out of the ground. The grizzled old farmer who held the horses, stroked their heads and gentled them for the walk to the edge of the woods.

Suddenly there was a loud clap of thunder, and the horses reared and broke away. But no one seemed to be watching them any longer. There were startled cries from the women and children as they hurried for shelter, and more uneasy glances at the lowering sky from the men. Wen and Angie headed for their automobile on the run. Floyd and I held hands and raced after them.

A gust of wind blew dust into my eyes, blinding me for a moment. Lightning flashed and thunder cracked around us, as raindrops the size of silver dollars pelted us, soaking us to the skin before we could reach the shelter of Wen's car.

"We might as well wait out the storm here," Wen said. "Nobody could see to drive through this downpour."

While he was speaking, the wind blew a hard curtain of rain against the car window, and a broken branch went sailing by, riding the wind till it lodged in another tree.

"I wonder where Chance and the teacher have got to?" I said, speaking my thoughts out loud.

"With any luck at all, that Chance has got himself lost," Floyd muttered in my ear.

"The last I saw of them," Wen said. "They were yonder across the creek, getting into burlap bags for the sack race."

I shivered in my wet dress and wished I was back at the boardinghouse. In my opinion, this hadn't been much of a day. Wen and Angie had got married. Floyd had got an automobile. But all I had gotten out of it was a bit of advice from Angie and a soaking.

In the midst of the downpour, we saw Chance and Mr. Thompson come slogging through the mud and water and pile into Chance's car.

"It's a good thing the teacher left his car at the end of the dirt lane," Floyd said. "After this hard rain, you all may have trouble getting home."

Wen shook his head. "I've got tire chains," he said. "I won't have any trouble getting to the main road. But I would bet my bottom dollar that Chance never saw a tire chain. That boy doesn't even carry a jack in his car in case of a flat tire," he added, with a laugh at Chance's carelessness.

The ruts in the mud road were hub-deep with water when the rain finally stopped. Wen and Floyd put chains on the rear wheels of Wen's car. Then they went to help the teacher and Chance try to push his car over the rise to level ground.

When the men had gone, Angie turned to face me over the back of the seat. "Julie, as soon as Wen is finished there, we will take you home. Chance may be half the night getting his car out of here," she added.

I said I would appreciate it. "A hot bath and dry clothes will feel good to me," I said. "And the sooner, the better."

Angie smiled and turned to face the front again.

We had lost the easy friendliness that we had started this day with, and now we had nothing more to say to each other. I turned to the window and watched the men as they tried to push the car and keep their footing on the rain-slick hillside.

Chance had spun the wheels to get up the hill, and now the car was stuck in deep muddy ruts that the wheels had cut into the soft earth. The more he gunned the motor, the deeper he dug the ruts. Finally, Wen threw up his hands and motioned for Chance to shut off the motor.

When Chance joined the other three men behind the car, Wen said, "Those tires are as bald as a baby's butt. No traction." He touched a smooth-worn tire with the toe of his shoe. "You will have to ride to the hard road with me," he told Chance, "then bring my tire chains back and put them on. With chains and a little pushing, you shouldn't have any trouble getting the car out."

He gave the worn tire another nudge with his toe, then turned toward his own car. Floyd stood for a moment as if undecided, then he followed Wen.

Floyd leaned in the car window, and said, "Julie, wait

supper for the teacher and me. We won't be long here."
I nodded my head and said I would. Without another
word, he turned and went back to where Mr. Thompson
stood beside the mired-down automobile.

Wen Hazel made it to the highway without any trouble
at all. Chance thanked him for taking me home, and the
loan of the tire chains all in one breath and, five minutes
later, Chance was headed back down the mud lane swinging a tire chain in each hand.

"That's the most irresponsible boy I ever saw," Wen
said, with a shake of his head. "But you can't help but
like him."

I smiled to myself. At the beginning of the summer,
Wen Hazel couldn't find a good word to say about Chance
Cooper. He still didn't. But what he said now was spoken
in an affectionate way. He wasn't finding fault with
Chance, but excusing the faults he found in him. And I
liked Wen for that.

Wen and Angie were quiet on the way home, and I
had nothing to say either.

When Wen stopped the car at the boardinghouse,
Angie turned to me and said, "Julie, you've been so quiet
on the way home. Are you worried that Chance will come
while Floyd is here, and there will be a big fuss between
them?"

I opened the car door and got out. "I don't think
there'll be any trouble tonight," I said. "They're both
going to be too tired to raise their voices, let alone their
fists."

Angie smiled. "You could be right," she said, and they
drove away.

I heard voices in the parlor when I went by on my way

to my room, but I didn't see anyone. I hadn't seen anyone at the boardinghouse to speak to since Saturday morning. Not even Mrs. Brown, who was almost always at her desk in the front hall.

I didn't know how long it would be before Floyd and Mr. Thompson would get there, but I figured they could wait for me if I wasn't ready yet. I took a leisurely bath and washed my hair. Then when I saw the state my shoes were in, I cleaned and polished them. It was after eight o'clock when I went downstairs to meet Floyd and the teacher.

They weren't there yet. I went to the parlor where there was a window facing onto the street and sat down to wait for them. Every time a car went down the street, I jumped up and looked out the window. But none of them stopped. When Mr. Thompson's car finally pulled up in front of the house, I was out the front door and waiting on the porch by the time he got out of the car.

I felt a shiver of misgiving when Floyd and Chance Cooper both got out of the back seat. But they seemed peaceable enough, so I didn't say anything. I was surprised to see all three of them looking so neat and clean. They had been a muddy mess when we left them at the park.

Mr. Thompson smiled and came up the steps to meet me. "We had to leave Chance's car at Andy's garage," he said. "And while we were there, Andy offered us the use of his bathroom to clean off the mud." His smile grew wider as he took my arm and helped me into the front seat to sit next to him. "That big truck stop at the Junction is the only place we can get supper," he said. "And we couldn't go in there looking like we had just come out of the pigpen."

I felt funny sitting up front beside the teacher, with Floyd and Chance in the back seat. And I wondered what they thought about it. They hadn't objected when Mr. Thompson seated me here, so it must have been arranged between them before they ever got to the house.

After a while, I heard Chance say, "I think the clutch has gone out on my car."

Then Floyd mumbled that he wasn't surprised. "The way you rode the clutch out there," he said, "it's a wonder it lasted an hour."

They argued back and forth. Mr. Thompson smiled at me and jerked a thumb toward the back seat. I smiled in reply. I had found out one thing. Floyd and Chance weren't brooding about where I was sitting. And I was glad of that. It was good to know that they had found something else to argue about besides me.

The parking lot at the restaurant was taken up by the big freight-hauling outfits and stock trucks. There was no place left where the teacher could park. Chance said he could leave his car at the cabin he shared with Bill Bundy and directed Mr. Thompson to one of the small cabins at the rear of the building.

As we walked around to the front of the restaurant, Chance pointed out the cabins that housed the men who worked for the light company. "Those other cabins are rented to the long-distance drivers who just want to get off the road for an hour or so," he said.

Neither Chance nor Floyd mentioned that I had stayed

in one of the cabins earlier in the summer, and I saw no reason to bring it up.

It seemed like everyone in the restaurant knew Chance and Mr. Thompson and stopped to speak to them. Floyd held my hand under cover of the table and said very little. But I knew by the way he looked at me that he wished Chance and the teacher a million miles away so we could be alone.

When we were at the car, ready to leave, Chance said, "I'll trust you fellows to get Julie home without my help. I'm bushed." He waved a hand and went on to his cabin.

"Don't know how we'll manage without him," Floyd said under his breath, and got into the front seat with me and Mr. Thompson.

It was after midnight when they left me at the door to the boardinghouse and drove away.

Chapter Twenty

It was good to be alive on a day such as this. Even the leaves on the old trees along the street seemed perkier, as if they too were happy to be starting the new week with a fresh, clean day. I wanted to skip and sing, like the kids who were prancing and playing hopscotch on the walk ahead of me, but I thought eighteen was too old for that.

Halcie Hissem smiled as she unlocked the door to the dime store. "I'm glad to see that you're in better spirits now than you were when I saw you last," she said.

For a moment I was mystified as to what she meant. Then I remembered Saturday night and how low I felt then. "Oh, that!" I said. Saturday seemed a long time ago.

Halcie flipped on the front lights so the public would know we were open for business, then she turned to me and said, "Need I ask? How was your day at the Old Settlers?"

I laughed. "Fine," I said. "Just fine."

While we waited on customers and restocked the shelves after Saturday's sale, I told Halcie everything that had happened at the reunion, from the beginning to the end of the day. But I didn't mention that Floyd had bought a car. I'd let him do that when he drove it to town on Friday. I didn't mention either that Wen and Angie had been married. That was *their* news to tell.

"Floyd and Chance got along like brothers," I said. "They argued about everything! I would've had to have four wheels and a faulty motor to get any attention from either one of them."

Halcie laughed, then turned away to stack bolts of yard goods onto a shelf that I couldn't reach.

"Did Angie say whether or not she would keep on working her fruit stand, now that she's married to Wen Hazel?"

My mouth dropped open with amazement. I couldn't believe it. I had been so careful not to mention Wen or Angie's news while I was telling about the Old Settlers, yet Halcie knew they had gotten married. It was beyond me how she could have found it out so soon, unless Angie had told her. And I thought that was unlikely.

I answered Halcie's question with one of my own. "When did Angie tell you they were married?"

"She didn't," Halcie replied. "A neighbor of mine who works in the clerk's office at the court house told me that Wen Hazel and Angie Abram had taken out a marriage license Saturday morning." She turned from the shelf to face me. "I just figured that Angie wouldn't waste any time using that license," she added. "It was long overdue."

I ignored that last remark, and said, "Angie will be hurt not to have been the one who told you."

"Far as Angie will ever know," she said, "she'll be the first to tell it." She lowered her voice, winked at me, and whispered, "I know when to keep my mouth shut."

I believed that she did, at that.

When Angie came in later in the day to tell Halcie that she was married, Halcie exclaimed as though happily surprised.

"I've hoped for this day," she told Angie. "And I couldn't be happier for you."

Angie blushed and suddenly seemed embarrassed by the attention she was getting. She turned to me and said, "Tell me, Julie, did the boys behave themselves at supper last night?"

"They had to," I replied. "Mr. Thompson took us to that truck-stop at the Junction, and he made them sit together in the back seat of the car. Chance lives out there in one of those cabins," I added, "so Floyd got to sit up front on the way home."

Halcie and Angie exchanged glances. Two women were sampling perfume at the cosmetics counter, too far away to overhear, but Halcie lowered her voice anyway.

"Julie, you should be more careful about where you go. People will start talking, and there's no telling where it will end."

I smiled at Halcie and assured her that my conduct had been above reproach. "My reputation won't suffer from having supper with Floyd Perry, Chance, and the school-teacher from Newark, surely," I said.

I turned to Angie. "I told you that Halcie reminded me of my mother. Well, now she's talking like her."

"Someone has got to talk to you like a mother," Halcie said. "And it might as well be me."

The perfume testers had gone. Halcie locked the front door, pulled down the blind, and hung the closed sign in the window. "Now, we won't be disturbed," she said.

Halcie sure had to be upset to close her store in the middle of a working afternoon and risk losing business, but I couldn't understand what I'd done to bring this on. Then I reminded myself that Halcie Hissem was my boss, and I needed this job. Whether I liked it or not, I would have to listen what she had to say. There was no getting around it.

Halcie sat on the step-stool and motioned for Angie and me to sit on the unopened packing cases. "My business here depends on the reputation of my help," she began. "I have to be careful about who I hire. I can't bring a trollop in here to work for me. The women wouldn't shop here, nor allow their menfolk to step foot in the place."

"I doubt that anyone would mistake me for a prostitute," I spoke up. "I don't dress well enough for that!"

Angie frowned at me.

Halcie said, "Julie, I had no such thing in mind."

"That's how it sounded to me," I said. Then, "What did you have in mind? What do you disapprove of?"

I was impatient to get this over with. If it had anything to do with my work here at the store, a mistake I'd made on the cash register or my attitude toward a customer, I would be more than willing to sit still and hear her out. But as far as I could tell, this had nothing to do with my work. It was my personal business that she was concerned with.

"Well?" I said, when Halcie didn't answer me.

She gave an impatient sigh, as if I should have known without asking, then she said, "Julie, it's what other folks will think of you being at the Junction with three men that worries me. And they'll hear of it," she added. "You can bank on that."

"How could it possibly matter that I was at the Junction?" I was making an effort to control my temper and speak calmly, but my irritation crept into my voice. "I wasn't the only one there," I said. "The place was packed with people eating their supper."

Angie started to speak, but Halcie held up her hand to stop her. "Let me explain this," she said.

I wished someone would explain something. I couldn't sit still through much more of it.

"I'll tell you why it matters to me that you were at the Junction truck-stop," Halcie said. "You're a stranger around here yet, and you wouldn't know about it. But when you let three men take you to a known sporting house . . ."

"They took me to a what.   !" I couldn't take any more. I was on my feet, heading for the door, when Angie caught my arm.

"Julie, hear her out."

"I've heard enough!"

I jerked my arm away, and turned to go to the office for my purse. I was leaving. "She can fire me," I mumbled to myself. "But I won't listen to another word from her."

Angie followed me to the back room and closed the door, putting her back to it so I couldn't get by her.

"Julie, you should listen to Halcie," she said quietly. "She has lived here a long time, and she has seen how loose talk can ruin a girl's reputation. She doesn't want that to happen to you."

"She's the one who said I was at a whorehouse," I said angrily. "And I'd call that a pretty good start toward ruining my good name. And what's more, I think she made it up," I added. "I didn't see anything out of the way at the Junction."

"Julie, use your head for once," Angie said, losing her patience with me. "Those truckers who stop there pay five dollars for one of those cabins and an hour later, they've gone on their way. Now, do you believe they pay that kind of money just to sleep for an hour?"

I thought about what she had said. If that was true, where did the truckers find women to share the cabins with them? Then, suddenly I knew. When we had left there at midnight on Sunday, the second story of the truck-stop had had a light in every window. Just as though someone up there was ready and waiting to be called.

"If it's that kind of place," I said, not yet ready to accept that it was, "the teacher wouldn't have taken us there. And that's where Floyd rented a cabin for me the very first night I was in Linton."

"The teacher's keeping steady company with Belle Bundy, who does the cooking for the restaurant," Angie replied. "No doubt he is used to going there to eat and thought nothing of taking you. Floyd was a stranger to Linton except for buying supplies in town. I'd advise you to keep quiet about being there. For your own good."

I wondered why it was that every time someone gave advice, it was always for your own good. No matter how distasteful it might be.

I gave up with a sigh of resignation and moved toward

the door. If I couldn't fight their standards of behavior, I'd have to go along with them. For a while.

"It's time I got back to work," I said. "If I still have a job."

Angie stepped to one side. We left the office together.

Halcie had opened the store while Angie and I were in the back room, but there wasn't a customer in sight. Her eyes searched my face, then moved on to Angie.

"Did you tell her not to spread it around where she was last night?" Halcie asked Angie. "She should keep it to herself. The fewer who know about it, the better off we'll be."

Angie nodded her head. "We're the only ones who know," she said. "And it can't do any harm unless one of us tells it. Julie won't say anything. And I won't even tell Wen," she added.

I didn't appreciate being discussed as if I was an idiot. Even if they did think I had behaved like one. But I didn't say anything. I kept my mouth shut and just tuned them out. The sound of their voices was in the background, but I didn't hear the words.

I would abide by Halcie's rules, I told myself, and do my job the best I could. But I'd only stay here as long as I had to.

Floyd had his own car now, and he would take me wherever I wanted to go. Even to Terre Haute to find a job up there, if I asked him to. I would get a job close to the college, enroll in school, and . . .

"Julie," Halcie said.

At the sound of my name I jumped, as if I had been awakened from a sound sleep, and gave her my attention.

207

"I said, give me a hand here, Julie," Halcie said. "If we hustle, we can get this all put away before we go home."

I turned to the opened boxes and began to load my arms. I stocked the lower shelves, while Halcie filled the ones that I couldn't reach. Customers came in, and Angie waited on them.

"My brother is watching the stand," she told Halcie. "And I've nothing to do until Wen gets done with his work. As long as I'm here," she added, "I might as well make myself useful."

At closing time Angie walked as far as the hardware store with me. While we went along, she coached me on what I was to say should anyone ask me about Sunday night, and how I should say it. "Keep it simple," she said, "and act natural. Then no one will suspect that it's a put-on."

At the hardware store, Angie went inside to wait for Wen, and I walked on toward home. I didn't hurry. I had a lot on my mind that I had to sort out and decide what to keep and what to throw away and forget.

This had started out to be such a beautiful day, but now it had gone flat for me. Halcie Hissem had taken all the joy and beauty out of it by carrying on so about me being at the Junction.

I would heed their admonition not to tell anyone that I had gone to the Junction. But should I be asked outright, I wouldn't lie about it—I'd tell them. Angie and Halcie would never know the difference. But I would. And if I lied, I could never be at ease with myself.

When I walked into the house, Mrs. Brown was sitting

at her desk fanning herself with an imitation palm leaf. I spoke to her and started on upstairs to my room.

Mrs. Brown nodded to me. "You must have worked overtime," she said. "Verna's been home for sometime now."

"No," I replied. "Usual time. I just poked along home."

"Did you have a good day at the reunion yesterday?"

Her words stopped me midway up the stairs. I took a few steps back down to answer her. "It was great until the storm hit," I said. Then I went on to tell her that Chance had gotten his car stuck in the mud, and he'd had a lot of trouble getting it out. "By the time we'd all had supper and got back home, it must have been nearly midnight," I finished.

"It was a bit after midnight," she said dryly.

Mrs. Brown laid the fan to one side. "I make sure that all my people are safe at home," she said, "before I ever close my eyes at night."

"I'm sorry I kept you up."

My sincerity must have come through to her. She rested her hands on the desk and looked earnestly at me. "Julie," she said softly, "I've lost more sleep since you've been with me than I have with all the others put together. But I can excuse you for it," she added. "You're young."

"I'm sorry," I said again. "From now on, I'll keep a closer watch on the time."

"See that you do."

I gave her a little smile and a wave and ran up the rest of the stairs.

On Wednesday of that week I received a letter from Nancy Arthur. I was surprised. I hadn't expected to hear from her. Now I was eager to know what she had to say.

"I don't like living in the city, Julie," Nancy wrote. "It's not a bit like I thought it would be. There's too many strangers, and I'm frightened here. I guess the only place where I'll ever feel safe is back in the hills of Greene County."

She ended the note with, "I'll be seeing you," and signed her name in full.

I couldn't believe that she meant she was coming home. But it sounded that way. I slipped the letter in my pocket and went on to work.

Halcie greeted me as usual. We discussed the things that had to be done today, then she said she had book work to do and went to her office. Halcie hadn't mentioned the fuss we'd had on Monday or referred to it in any way. And I never brought it up. I just wanted to forget it ever happened.

A few customers came in, but not enough to keep me busy. I had time on my hands and Nancy Arthur on my mind. It seemed foolish to me that Nancy would ever consider coming back. She had made the break and gotten away from her mother once. She might not be so lucky twice.

Maybe time and distance had clouded her memory of what it had really been like at home, I thought. But Nancy should know as well as I that Maud Arthur could make her life a living hell on earth. She would throw it up to her every day that Nancy had stolen money and left town with the bread peddler. And Nancy couldn't deny it. She would have to live with that if she came home.

As much as I would like to see Nancy, I hoped she would think a long time before she really came back. If I ever got out of Greene County, wild horses couldn't drag me back. And I didn't have half the troubles here that Nancy had facing her.

The day dragged by. I thought of the Saturday when I had complained to Halcie about being so busy, and she'd said, "There will be days when you'll wish for this many people, just to have something to do." Well, I thought, this is one of those days.

A few minutes before closing time, Angie came into the store. I was glad to see her. Since her marriage to Wen Hazel, she hadn't worked at the fruit stand, and she had given up wearing the overalls. This afternoon, she had on a pair of navy slacks and a light blue ruffled blouse tucked into the waistband.

Angie bought a ten-cent scouring pad, then waited until we closed for the day and left the store when we did. As she and I walked up the street toward the hardware store where she was to meet Wen, Angie said, "Julie, did you tell anyone at the boardinghouse that you went to the Junction for supper Sunday night?"

"No," I replied shortly. "No one asked me where I went."

"They found it out somehow," Angie said. "Verna Clayton asked Wen today why we hadn't gone to the Junction with you all Sunday night. Wen said that she seemed to think it was odd that we hadn't been asked to go along."

"Why should she think it strange?" I said. "Surely, Wen told her you had gone home long before Mr. Thompson and the boys came to get me."

Angie didn't say anything. She was there, close enough to touch, but I felt like she wasn't with me.

"I hope he didn't say anything to give Verna the impression that we had a reason for not asking you," I said.

"Wen wouldn't do that," Angie said. But the tone of her voice told me that she wasn't as sure of it as she would like me to believe. "You just be careful what you say about it," she added.

Angie went into the hardware store, and I walked on toward home. Angie's brother called to me from the fruit stand, but I just waved and went on. I had too much on my mind to stop and talk foolishness with him today.

I was glad that Verna Clayton knew I had been to the Junction. Now I wouldn't have to try and hide it or worry much longer about what people would say when they heard of it. I would soon know. But I dreaded the day when someone told Halcie Hissem they heard her hired girl had been seen there at midnight in company with three men. Halcie wouldn't like it. Even though she knew it already, she wouldn't like it that others knew about it.

If only there was someone I could talk to, I thought. I couldn't talk to Angie or Halcie. They had their own ideas, and they wouldn't listen to mine. I needed someone my own age to talk to. Someone who could understand how I felt about things.

I didn't know any girls my own age in Linton. Somehow, I had kept my acquaintances down to the few at the boardinghouse, work, and Wen and Angie Hazel. And they were all much older than I was. Even Angie fitted in with the older women. She seemed to think that I should fit myself into their little niche and never do anything or even think anything that they hadn't put their stamp of approval on beforehand.

Maybe that was why Nancy wanted to come home, I thought. Maybe she missed having a friend she could talk to and know that the friend would understand how she felt about things.

Chapter Twenty-One

Until a quarter to four in the afternoon, my day off went the same as every Friday. I hadn't heard any more about Mr. Thompson taking me to the Junction for supper. Or for any other reason. And Halcie had been friendlier to me the last few days than she had been all week. With a light heart, I set about cleaning my room on Friday morning. Then after that was done, I had lunch and left the house to return my library books and do some shopping.

I had to buy myself a pair of silk stockings today, and Wickes was the only store in town that carried them. Halcie sold a kind of silk stocking, but they had so much rayon in them that they stretched out of shape with one wearing. No matter how tight you wore your garters, the hose would slip down your legs and lie in wrinkles around your ankles. It looked awful. At first, I had bought these to work in, but it was a constant struggle to keep them pulled up smooth and work at the same time.

I saw Wen Hazel outside the hardware store as I went by. He said hello first and then he asked, "Are you coming to Peggy's to have supper with Angie and me tonight?"

214

I shook my head. "Floyd said he might be in town this evening," I said. "But he didn't say what time. I wouldn't want to leave the house and miss seeing him."

"Well, if he gets here in time, come on over."

I said we'd see, then Wen went inside, and I went on down the street.

It was getting near time for the library to close, so I decided to go there first and stop at Wickes on the way back.

Martha was putting the returned books on the shelves when I got there, and she didn't have much to say. She brought a couple of books from beneath her desk that she had been saving for me, and murmured, "I hope you like them." Then she stamped my card with the due date and wished me good day.

I thought it was funny that, with her reputation for gossiping, I hardly heard a word out of her. If she had any juicy tidbits to tell, she must have been saving them for others. She had never so much as said boo to me about anyone.

I spent more time, and money, than I had intended to at Wickes. It was after three o'clock when I left the store and started home. While I had been inside shopping, the sky had grown dark, and storm clouds now covered the sun.

As I hurried by the fruit stand, Angie's brother yelled, "Hey, you're going to get your butt wet!"

I laughed and answered, "I wouldn't be surprised!"

There was moisture in the air, and I could smell the rain coming. But it hadn't started to rain yet, when I ran up the steps to the boardinghouse.

Mrs. Brown was in the hall at the foot of the stairs

when I went in the house. She put her finger to her lips and motioned for me to come closer to her.

"Julie, you've got a visitor waiting in the parlor," she said, under her breath, as she nodded toward the closed door to that room.

"Oh, no," I moaned. "Not now. My washing will get soaked."

I had washed a few things early this morning and hung them outside to dry. I'd forgotten to bring them in before I went downtown, and only the threat of rain had brought them to mind now.

"I'll get your clothes off the line," Mrs. Brown said. "You go on in there. She's been waiting close to an hour," she added in a whisper.

I thanked her and laid my packages on the desk. Could it be Nancy? I went to the parlor door and opened it.

"Mrs. Arthur!"

I was so surprised to see her that her name just popped out, sounding loud and harsh in the quiet room. I took a deep breath, then asked, "What brings you here today?"

I could tell by looking at her that Maud Arthur was angry. And evidently the long wait hadn't improved her temper.

"I came here to find out where Nancy went," she said. "And stop shaking your head as if you didn't know."

Until she said so, I hadn't realized that I was shaking my head. I stepped farther into the room and closed the door behind me. I didn't relish the idea of the others in the house hearing every word that passed between Maud Arthur and me.

"I don't know where Nancy went after she left home,"

I said. I spoke calmly, trying not to arouse her temper and make her angrier than she was already.

"Don't bother to lie to me," Mrs. Arthur shouted from two steps away. "I know she came here. And she wouldn't leave without telling you where she was going."

She moistened her thin-drawn lips with the tip of her tongue, and a sly look came over her face. "How much of my five hundred dollars did Nancy give you to keep your mouth shut?" she asked.

I drew in a deep breath and stepped back from her. I had never dreamed that Nancy had taken so much money when she left home. I opened my mouth to tell Mrs. Arthur that Nancy hadn't given me any money at all, then I saw the crafty look in her eyes and I knew she was lying. I should have known at once that Mrs. Arthur wouldn't keep that much money lying around the house where Nancy could find it. She had only said it to shock me and trick me into telling her what I knew about Nancy's whereabouts.

"I don't know anything about your money, either," I said.

The room had grown dark, like early evening, and the rain made a swishing sound as it swept across the window. I couldn't see Maud Arthur too clearly, but her hate and anger were so strong in the room that I felt as if I could put out my hand and touch them.

She took a step toward me. I took two steps back. As I reached for the doorknob, she lunged at me, knocking me up against the door.

"You'll tell me where she's hiding," she said through her clenched teeth, "or I'll wring your neck!"

Mrs. Arthur's face was right above mine, and her eyes were wild and glassy as she stared at me. I knew that I was no match for her. She was a madwoman, long past the stage of reasoning. But I had to try.

I put my hands on her arms to push her away from me. She grabbed me by the shoulders and began to shake me like a weed in a wind storm. Trying with all her might, I thought, to break my neck.

My fingers touched the doorknob, but I was jerked away before they could close around it. I wished I had left the door open. She could kill me in here, and no one would find me until it was too late to do me any good. Self-preservation, or the thought of dying at this woman's hands, gave me the extra strength I needed.

Without thinking of what I was about to do, I kicked Mrs. Arthur as hard as I could with the toe of my shoe. I felt her hands go slack for just a breath of time, then they closed tightly around my throat. I kicked her again. And this time, I heard her gasp of pain, as her fingers left my throat, and she bent over to guard her leg. Before she could recover, I yanked the door open and ran into the hall.

When Mrs. Brown saw me, she gave a startled cry and hurried toward me. Then she stopped, as Maud Arthur burst into the hall ranting and raving and screaming that she would kill me.

Before Mrs. Arthur could reach me, Mrs. Brown was there between us, a shield to protect me.

"What's going on here?" she asked, with a piercing look at Maud Arthur.

Mrs. Arthur seemed to shake herself, much the same as a dog will do after coming in from the rain, and looked

218

around her, as if trying to remember where she was and what she was doing here. She stared blankly at Mrs. Brown and didn't answer her.

"Julie," Mrs. Brown turned to me. "I want to know why you came flying out of that room like the devil was after you?"

I felt foolish making such a statement, but I said, "She was trying to kill me."

Mrs. Arthur suddenly came alive. "You lying slut!" she said, and started toward me. "Let me get my hands on you . . ."

"Hold it right there!" Mrs. Brown raised her arm and pointed to the door. "There's the door," she said. "Now you get out!"

Maud Arthur spluttered and choked, trying to find her voice. Finally, she screeched, "You ungrateful little bitch!" She shook her fist at me. "You won't always have her to hide behind, and I'll fix you yet," she threatened.

I stepped around Mrs. Brown to where I could face Mrs. Arthur straight on. I wasn't afraid now. I was mad.

"You lay a hand on me again," I said, my voice low and shaking so I could hardly speak, "and I'll tell everyone in Greene County what sort of person you are."

She dropped her clenched fist and turned away muttering to herself. At the door she looked back at me, and said, "I should have run you off the first time you ever stepped foot in my house. I'll get even with you yet."

Mrs. Arthur slammed the door as she went out muttering threats and obscenities to herself.

Suddenly, I was shaking all over, and my legs wouldn't hold me. I sat down in the middle of the floor, covered my face with my hands, and cried.

Without a word, Mrs. Brown helped me to my feet and walked with me to the foot of the stairs. Then she handed me the packages I had left at the desk earlier. "You take a nice long bath," she said, patting my hand. "It will relax you. Then when you're ready, come downstairs. I'll have some nice cool tea for you."

I nodded my head and gave her a small smile of thanks as I started up the stairs.

"Julie."

I stopped and waited for her to say what she wanted.

"What did Mrs. Arthur ever do that just your threat of telling everyone about her would scare her away?"

"Nothing special that I know of," I answered. "But she was awful to me when I boarded there—suspicious and cruel. And to her own daughter as well. That's why Nancy couldn't stand living at home any more. And everyone has secrets," I added. "Some have secrets they would rather die than have anyone know about. Maybe Maud Arthur's like that."

"In her state of mind," Mrs. Brown observed quietly, "she can more than likely imagine a raft of things that would disgrace her should they become known."

I went on up to my room.

My wash basket was sitting outside my door, the clothes all dry and neatly folded. I silently thanked Mrs. Brown for another favor as I unlocked the door and took the basket inside.

The rain had stopped, but there was a steady dripping from the eaves. A measured drip, drip, like the ticking of a clock, or a heartbeat.

I looked at the round face of Big Ben sitting on the table beside my bed. I was surprised to see that it was just a few minutes after four o'clock. It seemed like hours had passed since I'd raced the rain home and found Mrs. Arthur waiting for me in the parlor.

I thought of all the things I should have said to Mrs. Arthur as I put the clean laundry away, and what I would say should we ever meet again. By the time the basket was empty, I had talked myself into a bigger turmoil than I'd been in when I came upstairs.

I drew a full tub of water, as hot as I could stand it, threw off my clothes, and got into it. Almost immediately, I could feel the tension leaving my body. I sat in the tub and soaked myself until I was wrinkled as a dried apple and the water was lukewarm. Still, only the thought of Verna Clayton getting home and wanting the bathroom could get me out of the water and into my clothes.

I brushed my hair, put on the green-striped cotton dress, and went downstairs to have the iced tea that Mrs. Brown had promised me. I could use it, I thought. My mouth was as dry as a cotton sock.

"Do you want to tell me what that commotion was all about?" We were sitting at the kitchen table. The iced tea, made with a sprig of fresh mint, was low in the glass. "You don't have to talk about it, though" Mrs. Brown added. "Not, if you don't feel like it."

"I'm all right now," I said. "And I don't mind telling you what ailed Mrs. Arthur."

I went on to tell her how I had happened to be living at the Arthur house and Mrs. Arthur's attitude toward me after the family moved away. "I left there as soon as school was out," I said. "Then about a month later, her daughter Nancy ran away from home. Mrs. Arthur accused me of putting her up to it," I added, "and she thinks that I know where Nancy went."

"Do you?" Mrs. Brown asked softly.

I shook my head. "But she won't believe me. She was trying to choke the information out of me, but I got away from her. And you saved my skin," I added, "by keeping her away."

"Poppycock!" Mrs. Brown said. "I was just there."

We were still sipping tea and talking when Floyd Perry knocked at the door, then opened it and stepped into the hall, just as if he was at home. Both Mrs. Brown and I got up and went to meet him.

Floyd smiled and refused Mrs. Brown's offer of iced tea. "It sure sounds good," he told her. "But the fact is, I can't take the time to drink it."

I had been dying to ask Floyd about his car, but I couldn't get a word in edgewise between him and Mrs. Brown.

He reached for my hand and nodded to Mrs. Brown. "I'll have her home early," he said, and pulled me toward the door.

Mrs. Brown smiled at Floyd and touched his arm. "Take your time," she said, and turned back toward the kitchen.

As soon as we were out the door, I said, "Do you have your own car tonight?"

"I sure have." He pointed to the automobile sitting in front of the house. "What do you think of it?"

It was a plain black Ford, just like every other automobile to be seen on the street. I couldn't have picked it out from all the rest of the cars.

"It looks good," I said, telling him what he wanted to hear.

"Just wait till you hear that motor." He grinned from ear to ear and helped me into the car. "The brakes need adjusting, and the tires ain't much, but there's power to spare when it comes to climbing these hills."

Floyd got himself settled to his liking behind the wheel, started the motor, and headed out of town. "This is more like it," he said. "No more having to hurry home now, just so the teacher can go visit his girl at the Junction."

"He got me in dutch with Halcie Hissem by taking us to the Junction Sunday night," I said. "She seemed to think it would give me a bad name to be seen there. Especially," and here I mimicked Halcie's voice, "when it was that late at night, and alone with three men."

Floyd turned his eyes from the road to look at me. "Julie, you've got to be joking. No one could be that narrow-minded."

"Halcie is afraid that when her customers hear about it, they'll stop coming into the store if I'm there."

"That's the stupidest thing I've ever heard," Floyd said. Then, "I wonder how she found out about it."

"I told her."

"You didn't!"

He jerked the steering wheel and the car ran off the road and into the high weeds along the edge. He shut off the motor, then turned to me. "Now," Floyd said. "Who else have you told about going to the Junction?"

"Nobody. Halcie and Angie told me not to tell anyone," I said. "But Verna Clayton knows about it. She asked Wen Hazel why he hadn't gone with us."

With just a trace of a smile, Floyd moved his head slowly back and forth. "Julie," he said. "I don't know what I'm going to do with you. Anyone can tell you anything, and you believe them." He put his arms around me and held me close. "You need someone to take care of you."

It had grown dark by now, and I couldn't see his face, but I knew by the sound of his voice he was smiling. What he really meant, I thought, was that I needed a keeper. And I smiled to myself.

After a while, Floyd said, "The fellows from the power lines were at the sawmill this week for another load of light poles. And from the way one of them talked, this would be the last load. I gathered from that that their work around here is about finished. He said their next job would be stringing wire in Orange County."

"Then we won't see much more of Chance Cooper," I said, thinking out loud.

Floyd didn't bristle at the name, the way he once would have, but went on talking as if Chance was a mutual friend.

"Not till they knock off work for the winter," Floyd replied. "They couldn't string electric lines through those hills and hollows down there when the snow comes."

He laughed softly, as if at some private joke of his own. "Last I heard," he said, "Chance was riding to work with Bill Bundy and still waiting for Andy to get his car fixed." He chuckled again. "We may not see Chance Cooper again till the snow flies."

I didn't say anything. I was content to leave things the way they were. But I knew Chance wouldn't go away without seeing me and telling me where he was going. He was too good a friend to just leave town without a word.

Chapter Twenty-Two

Floyd was quiet on the way home, and I sat silently on the seat beside him. After my horrifying experience with Mrs. Arthur this afternoon, it felt good just to be there safe and cared for.

I didn't tell Floyd that Mrs. Arthur had been to the boardinghouse causing trouble. There was nothing he could do about it now. And I could see no sense in both of us worrying about what she would do next.

When he stopped at the house, Floyd turned to me and said, "Julie, I've been thinking. Will you go to the Flat Hollow Church with me this Sunday?"

I went cold and still all over. I hadn't been inside the Flat Hollow Church since the day of Jamie's funeral. And I didn't want to go there now and be reminded of that day. I had been prepared to take flowers to the cemetery for Jamie's grave, but I hadn't counted on going into the church for a service.

"Whatever made you think of going there?"

"I've wanted to go to the graveyard for a long time," Floyd said. "We didn't get there on Declaration Day, and I thought you might want to go now."

I felt a rush of shame that I had ever hesitated. What difference did it make if we went to the Sunday service, too? "Of course, I'll go," I said.

But the service was over, and the last automobile was leaving the churchyard, when we got to the Flat Hollow church that Sunday. "I didn't think you wanted to get there for the sermon," Floyd said, and smiled.

He stopped the car off to one side in the shade of the churchhouse, and we walked around back to the graveyard. I hadn't been to Jamie's grave since the day we had buried him here, and now my feet dragged and I held back from going on.

Floyd took my hand, and after a few steps, he said, "Look, Julie," and pointed toward Jamie's place in the cemetery. "What do you think of it?" he asked quietly. "Do you think your mom and dad would be pleased?"

The raw red clay that I had remembered was covered now with a heavy stand of fresh clipped grass. And at the head of the mound of earth stood a small marble stone.

"Oh, Floyd." I dropped his hand and ran ahead to kneel beside Jamie's grave. I touched the headstone, then I traced Jamie's name, birth date, and the day he died gently with my hand. Beneath the line with the two dates, the words UNTIL THE DAYBREAK were inscribed in the stone.

I felt the heartbreak of Jamie's drowning all over again, and warm tears trickled down my face. I couldn't look at Floyd. I hadn't thought of a stone for Jamie, and he was my own little brother. But Floyd, who had only claimed him for a brother, had set a monument here to mark his resting place.

Floyd came and sat on his heels beside me, quiet and ill at ease because I was crying. I wiped my face dry and turned to him with a shaky smile.

"Floyd, it's beautiful," I said. "But I didn't expect this." I touched the cool stone. "Mom went away from here fearful that she wouldn't be able to find Jamie's piece of earth again. She will rest easy knowing that you have marked his place."

He moved uncomfortably and plucked at the grass that had grown all around the stone. "I was looking to get a marker for my dad," Floyd said quietly. "Then Ben talked to this stone cutter in Rosebud, and he struck a deal with him. We got us two stones, and the stonecutter's debt was squared with Ben at the sawmill."

"I should pay for Jamie's. Dad would expect me to take care of it."

Floyd shook his head. "Julie, all that matters is that one of us kids saw to it," he said. "I was here close by, and I wanted to do this for the folks."

We stayed a few more minutes with Jamie, then we went to look at Jase Perry's marker. It was the same size as Jamie's, but there was just his name with the dates 1890 to 1933 carved on it.

"He didn't have to do that," Floyd said, speaking of his dad's suicide. "He could've found something, some way to see us through the hard times."

"He didn't think so," I said. "After all that time, Jase must have thought it would never end."

"But if he had just waited."

"That's what Mom said, time and again," I told him. "But there's no sense fretting about what you can't change. It's better to forget what Jase did at the end, and just think about the good times you had with him."

"I know," Floyd said.

He got down on his hands and knees then and started pulling the weeds and tall grasses that the mowing machine had missed around Jase's headstone. I knelt down and helped him. It was cool and quiet in the cemetery, and we went about our task without talking and disturbing the silence.

Clumps of daisies, black-eyed Susans, and tiger lilies were blooming along the stone wall that bordered the graveyard. When we had cleared the weeds and high grass from both markers, we picked huge bunches of the wild flowers and made bouquets to place on Jase and Jamie's graves.

It was late afternoon when we left the Flat Hollow Churchyard, but Floyd wanted to drive by the old house where we had lived last summer. "Let's get rid of all the ghosts while we're at it," he said.

No one lived in the house now. We had been away from it just shy of six months, but it looked as if it had been vacant for years. The garden spot that Mom had taken such pains to clear had gone back to plantain and ragweed, and we couldn't see the path to the barn for the weeds. There was no sign of the path that ran to Lick Crick and on to the house where Floyd used to live.

"Let's just go back to Linton," I told Floyd, when he asked if I wanted to stop and look around. "I said my good-bye to this place when the folks left here."

Floyd turned the car around in the barnyard and we started home. At the foot of the long hill, just out of Newark, we had a flat tire, and Floyd had to patch the inner tube. "It's a good thing that didn't happen in the middle of the hill," he said, when we were on our way again. "I don't know if these brakes would've held on the hill."

We had another flat before we got to Linton, but Floyd just pumped up the tire and we went on. It was dark when we pulled up in front of the boardinghouse.

"I won't go in with you," Floyd said. "I don't trust these tires to hold up." He kind of laughed. "I may end this day by having to walk home."

I gave him a hug to send him on his way. Then I went into the house.

I stopped in the kitchen and fixed myself a cheese sandwich and took it up to my room with me. I was too wound up and tired to eat now, but I knew I would be hungry as soon as I rested awhile and put the thoughts of this day away from me.

There was one thought that I couldn't put away from me. And that had to do with my feelings for Floyd Perry. I would have to tell him. But I didn't know yet how I could.

Until today, I hadn't thought of the kind of love I felt for Floyd. I just knew that I loved him. But while we were clearing the weeds from Jamie's and Jase's graves and decorating them with field flowers, I realized we were like brother and sister—family, doing for our dead and sharing the sorrow.

It was late in the day on Monday that I learned Nancy Arthur had come back to the hills. Halcie Hissem and I were putting the store in order, getting ready to close for the day, when Angie came hurrying in. We both stopped what we were doing and went to see what she wanted.

"Have you heard about Maud Arthur?" Angie stopped to catch her breath. "Her daughter came home this morning and found her lying in a heap at the foot of the stairs."

"Dead?" Halcie was astounded.

I had heard what I wanted to know. Nancy Arthur was home. But I kept quiet and listened in case Angie had something more to say about Nancy.

"No, Mrs. Arthur's not dead," Angie said. "But she might as well be. She can't speak a word or raise a finger to help herself."

"What on earth happened to her?" Halcie wanted to know.

Angie spread her hands as if to say it was beyond her. Then she said, "A man from Newark told Wen that they figured Mrs. Arthur had had a stroke sometime Sunday and just lay there until Nancy came in and found her."

Halcie turned to me. "Julie, didn't you say Maud Arthur was at the boardinghouse the other day?"

I nodded my head.

"Well," she said. "How did she act then?"

I swallowed, then I moistened my lips. I didn't want to go over all that again. But Halcie was waiting.

"I told you," I said. "She was mad at me and hell-bent on getting even with Nancy for leaving home. She was blaming Nancy and me for all her troubles, but they were all of her own making."

"That's true of most ills," Halcie said quietly. "Folks bring them on themselves. But I wouldn't wish Maud Arthur's trouble onto the devil himself," she added.

"She's lucky that her daughter came home when she did," Angie said. "She will have somebody to take care of her."

I thought that in one sense, both Nancy and Mrs. Arthur were lucky. Mrs. Arthur would get the care she needed, but she couldn't rail at Nancy or get her hands on her while she was there.

Angie talked for a few minutes, then she said she had to get back to the hardware store. "Wen and Verna Clayton are going out of their minds trying to get the customers waited on so they can close the store."

As she was leaving, Angie said, "Julie, have supper with us at Peggy's. We'll pick you up after Wen closes the store."

I said, "Fine. I'll be ready when you get there."

Halcie Hissem locked the door to the dime store as soon as Angie left, then dropped me off at the boarding-house on her way home. Martha was leaning on the desk talking to Mrs. Brown as I went upstairs. When I came back downstairs to wait for Wen and Angie, Verna Clayton had joined them.

I started on by, but Mrs. Brown called and stopped me.

"Verna was just telling me that Maud Arthur's girl has come back."

"Yes," I said. "I heard Nancy was home."

I started toward the front door, aiming to wait for Wen and Angie on the porch.

"You can rest easy now that Maud Arthur has had that stroke," Verna Clayton called after me. "You won't have to worry any more that she will come here for you."

I stopped and faced her. "I have never lost any sleep

yet, worrying about Mrs. Arthur," I replied. I turned away, just half listening to the voices behind me.

"She's a cold-blooded one," Verna said. "She never turned a hair when I mentioned Maud's stroke. And it's more than likely," she added, "she brought it on by fighting with her."

I realized suddenly that Verna was talking about me. I whirled around and marched back to the desk. "Verna, you have no room to talk about me," I said curtly. "Not after what you did to Wen Hazel's first wife!"

I heard a gasp behind me, then Angie whispered, "Oh, Julie."

I wanted to go through the floor. Any place where I wouldn't have to face the Hazels. I hadn't heard them arrive and, in my anger, I had spoken without thinking. I turned to apologize.

Without so much as a glance in my direction, Angie took Wen by the arm and they left the house.

"You little fool," Verna said.

But I had no time for her now. I ran out the door and down the walk after Wen and Angie. I felt like I had to explain the words they had overheard, or they would never speak to me again.

I caught up with them just as Wen started the motor, and the car roared away down the street. It looked to me like they were trying to put as much distance as possible between themselves and this spot where I was standing.

The street was quiet after they had gone. Not a dog barked, and even the locusts had stopped their grating call for a while. I didn't want to go back to my room, but there was no where else to go. I could go to Peggy's

Cafe, but I would have no one to eat with when I got there. I stood alone on the sidewalk just looking at the millions of stars overhead and listening to the quiet around me. It was the lonesomest feeling I had ever known. I turned and walked slowly into the house.

Mrs. Brown was at her desk, but Verna and Martha were no where in sight. I started on up the stairs. I didn't want to talk to anyone.

"It looks like that woman is still causing trouble," Mrs. Brown said softly.

I nodded my head. "She seems to be getting a lot of help from Verna and me tonight." I replied, and went on to my room.

Chapter Twenty-Three

Tuesday was the kind of day that I would have been glad to skip all together. And with no more business than we had at the dime store, I could have. No one would have missed me.

When I got home from work that evening, Mrs. Brown looked up from the papers on her desk, and said, "Did you have a good day, Julie?"

Before I could answer her, she went on to say, "Verna tells me they didn't have enough business at the hardware store today to pay for the lights."

She didn't mention the fuss of the night before, or even act like it had happened.

I returned her smile. "That's the same kind of day that we had," I said, and went on upstairs.

I waited until I heard Verna Clayton moving about in the room next to mine, then I went down to the kitchen to fix my supper. After one look at the leftover macaroni and cheese, I threw it out and made a meal on Jello salad and cottage cheese.

Old Miss Edwards came into the kitchen just as I was leaving. "It's too hot to cook and eat," she complained, as she rummaged through the pantry and refrigerator.

"But Millie will be starved when she gets in from work, and she don't like waiting for her supper."

I smiled and made the proper responses to her remarks, then I left her to do her cooking. I hadn't seen her niece, Millie Edwards, a half dozen times this summer. I had spoken to her once about her job as a schoolteacher, but that was all. She left the boardinghouse before I got up in the morning, and she didn't get home until late in the evening. And if Millie Edwards had any interests in life, other than working and eating, I had never heard anyone mention them.

I sat in the parlor for a while, looking at last year's movie magazines and glancing hopefully toward the street every time I heard a car slow down or stop in front of the house. I didn't expect to see Floyd. Not so soon after Sunday. But it did seem to me that Andy should have had Chance's car repaired by this time. And I felt sure that Chance would be here, just as soon as he got his car out of the garage.

Verna and Martha came downstairs and went on out the front door. I watched as they walked up the street toward the neighborhood grocery. Millie Edwards came home and went straight to the kitchen. I listened to the murmur of their voices, as the two Miss Edwardses put their supper on the table, then sat down to eat.

I was beginning to feel like an eavesdropper, or a peeping Tom. If Chance was coming by tonight, he would have been here already. I tossed the magazines to one side and went upstairs to my room. It was nine o'clock. I turned back the bedspread and started getting ready for bed.

The knock on the door startled me. Then Floyd whispered, "Julie, it's me, Floyd." As if I wouldn't know his voice anywhere in the world.

"Just a minute," I answered.

I slid my shoes on, buttoned my shirt, and went to open the door.

"Mrs. Brown told me you had just come upstairs," Floyd said, the moment the door was opened. "She said I should knock, then wait for you out here."

My first thought was that something had happened to one of the family, and Floyd had been sent to break the bad news to me.

"What's wrong? Has something happened to the folks?"

"Sh . . ." he said. "I'll tell you when we get outside."

I kept quiet and didn't say another word, until we were in his car and headed toward the edge of town. Then I asked him again.

Floyd said, "Julie, have you heard that Mrs. Arthur had a stroke on Sunday?"

I was exasperated! "Did you drive all the way here to ask me that? Of course, I've heard. Who hasn't?" I had to stop and get my breath. Then I said, "I'm just sorry that Nancy had to be the one who found her."

"You may have more than that to be sorry about," Floyd said grimly. "Nancy didn't find her mother. She was fighting with her when it happened."

"How do you know they were fighting? Is that the story being told around Newark now?"

Floyd had startled and upset me with his unexpected visit tonight, and even though I knew now there was no cause for alarm, I was still perturbed.

"I don't know what they are saying anything about

it in town," Floyd replied calmly. "I only know what Nancy told me."

He turned the car onto the dirt road that led to the park and stopped. He switched off the lights, then shifted around in the seat to face me.

"Earlier this evening," Floyd began, "Nancy Arthur walked all the way to the sawmill to beg me to come here tonight and warn you. She said she was afraid it would be too late tomorrow."

I shivered, though the night was warm, and rubbed my arms as if they were chilled. Floyd moved closer to me and took both my hands in his.

"Julie," he said softly, "we've got trouble. And I can't see any way in the world to stop it now."

"Mrs. Arthur has mailed letters to everybody she knows in Linton," Floyd went on. "She's claiming that you stole money from her and turned her home into a . . . a brothel. That's why Nancy was fighting with her," he added. "Nancy wanted her mother to call the letters back."

"And now she can't," I said, stunned by the extent of her evil. "When Mrs. Arthur left the boardinghouse, she said she would get even with me, but, Floyd, this will destroy me."

I was ready to cry.

Floyd moved slightly, just so my head would rest on his shoulder. "Why didn't you tell me that Mrs. Arthur had been bothering you?" Then he said gently, "You don't have to put up with someone like that."

"Floyd, I was sure I could handle Mrs. Arthur. But I can't handle her lies. Only the people who get the letters won't know they are lies," I cried. "They'll believe her! Halcie Hissem won't keep me on at the store," I went on. "And if I'm not working, I'll have to leave the boardinghouse. Then, what will I do?"

"Hush, Julie. Hush, now, and let me think." Floyd's tone was gentle, but firm. "There's got to be a way we can throw a monkey wrench into that woman's scheme," he said.

The moon had risen since we had left the boardinghouse and now it seemed to be lodged directly above us. It lightened the field around us bright as day, but inside the car it was dim and dusky. Floyd was just a shadow beside me.

"No one would dare to slight you, if you were my wife," Floyd said quietly. "We could get married tomorrow, and it wouldn't matter a whit then what Mrs. Arthur does. You'd be safe," he added.

"Oh, Floyd. I wish it was that simple."

Hot, hurting tears gathered and spilled silently down my face. I'd known that this moment was inevitable, but I had hoped it wouldn't come so soon. I moved my head from his shoulder and swallowed the tears in my throat.

"I can't marry you tomorrow, Floyd. I don't think I can ever marry you."

Floyd looked crushed, like the world had fallen on him. I couldn't have looked any better. I had cut my ties to a safe life, and I felt as if I had just stepped off a precipice.

"Julie, don't you love me any more?"

He sat there still as death waiting for my answer. I wished a cloud would come and cover the moon. I needed the privacy of darkness for what I had to say to Floyd.

"I'll always love you," I said softly. "I can't ever

remember a time when I didn't love you. But it's not the
feeling for a sweetheart, Floyd. It's more like the love
I feel for my family. I don't think you realize it yet," I
said, "but I knew Sunday at the Flat Hollow graveyard
that you feel this same way about me."

Floyd gave a painful moan of denial, but I pressed on.
If I had to hurt him, I wanted to do it quickly and get
it over with. I took his hand and held it tight, willing
him to understand what I had to say.

"Floyd, I know you love me," I told him gently.
"You have proved that time after time. But it's the love
of a brother for his favorite sister. If we had felt about
each other the way a man and woman do who intend to
marry, you would never have allowed me to go with
Chance Cooper. You would never have made peace with
him."

Floyd started to draw away. "And I wouldn't have
wanted to go with him," I finished quickly.

"Are you in love with Chance Cooper?" Floyd asked.
"Is he the reason you won't marry me?"

"No, I'm not in love with Chance," I answered quietly.
"But if I had never met him, I would never have known
there was any love other than what I feel for you."

It was late when Floyd started the car, and we headed
back to town. The moon hung low in the sky, almost
directly in front of us. "Mrs. Brown will lose sleep
again tonight," I said, speaking my thoughts aloud.
"And I'll hear about it tomorrow."

Floyd turned from the road to smile at me. "My
offer is still open," he said. "As my wife, you wouldn't
have to worry about a place to live or a job. They both
come with the territory."

"Thanks," I said, and smiled too. "But I'll take my chances where I'm at."

A painful look crossed Floyd's face, then he said, "Damn that man! I hear his name every way I turn."

At the boardinghouse, Floyd got out of the car and walked to the door with me. He stood awkwardly for a moment, then he put his arms around me and hugged me close, just as though nothing had changed between us.

"Don't worry, Julie," he said, his voice low. "I'm not going to give up trying to find those letters that Mrs. Arthur wrote. I'll talk to Nancy again. Maybe she has some notion of who her mother would've sent them to, and she'd go with me to talk to these people," he added.

For the first time in my life, I felt uncomfortable in Floyd's arms. I made a move, as if to pull away, and he opened his arms at once, letting me go.

"Julie, don't shut me out of your life now," he said softly. "Give me time to get used to the way you feel about me. I'll abide by whatever terms you set, but let me go on seeing you."

"Oh, Floyd. I was afraid you wouldn't want to see me any more, after what I said, and I wouldn't have anyone to rely on if you weren't here."

"I'll be here," he said. "You can depend on that."

He turned then and went back to his car. I went into the house and quietly up the stairs to my room.

Chapter Twenty-Four

I slept badly that night. The next morning, my eyes were dull and puffy from too many tears and not enough sleep. I wished aloud that I didn't have to go to work today, but I went right ahead and got dressed.

I couldn't afford not to go. There were still too many people without work, and they were just waiting to step into any job that opened up. And, I thought, mine might be up for grabs sooner than I would like to think.

"Lord, you look like warmed-over death," Halcie Hissem said, when she let me into the store. "Don't you feel well this morning?"

I shook my head and didn't answer.

Halcie switched on the big overhead ceiling fan to start the stale air moving about the room.

"You just take it easy," she said. "There's no hurry about anything here today."

I took the bills of lading from her desk and went to the stockroom. As I opened boxes and checked in the merchandise, I wondered how long it would be before Maud Arthur's letters would be delivered to her friends here, and how soon afterwards Halcie Hissem would get the message. The way news traveled in this town, I knew it wouldn't take long.

I worked in the stockroom until it was time for Halcie to go to lunch. Then I went to the front of the store to relieve her at the cash register.

"How are you feeling now?" Halcie wanted to know.

"I'm all right," I replied. "I just needed to wake up."

"Well, sorting orders will do that for you," she said. "But not much else, I'm afraid."

"I like checking in the new stuff we get here," I said. "But I was surprised to find so many school supplies in this order. I hadn't realized the summer was so far gone," I added.

"It will soon be Labor Day," Halcie said. "Then we'll have the school kids in here, pilfering every thing they can get away with. But," she smiled, "we'll worry about that when the time comes."

She put the order sheets I gave her onto their spindle, picked up her handbag, and went to lunch.

I hoped that Angie would come to the store while Halcie was out. I wanted to explain to her, while no one else was around, about the words she had heard me say to Verna. I didn't want her to think I repeated everything she had told me. But for the next hour, the only person who came in was a heavy-set woman who bought two yards of outing flannel and a packet of straight pins.

I went out for lunch as soon as Halcie got back. Wen Hazel was just leaving the hardware store as I got there.

"Is Angie at home?" I asked him. "I wanted to talk to her."

Wen seemed surprised to see me. For a moment he looked blank, then he said, "Why? Was there something she hasn't told you already?"

He dropped his head, murmured, "Excuse me," and walked away.

"I just wanted to talk to her," I said. But I was talking to myself. He was gone.

I didn't need Maud Arthur, or anyone else, to make trouble for me, I thought to myself. I did quite well in that department without any help. I got a baloney sandwich from Mr. Burns at the grocery store and went back to the five and ten to eat it.

Somehow, I got through the rest of the day. Halcie Hissem offered me a ride home, but I refused it. "I've got some thinking to do," I told her. "And I think better on my feet . . . walking."

She gave me a funny look, but she didn't say anything. She just got into her car and drove off.

I should have accepted Halcie's offer of a ride home. The walk didn't do me a bit of good. I was just as puzzled, confused, and upset when I reached the boardinghouse as I had been when I left the store.

Mrs. Brown got to her feet when she saw me come in, and I knew just as sure as breathing that she had been watching for me. I braced myself for whatever was coming and went to meet her.

"Verna lost her job because of what you said here the other night," Mrs. Brown said.

"And I lost two good friends," I replied. And walked on by her.

"Wait a minute, Julie."

I stopped in the middle of the stairs and looked back.

Mrs. Brown was standing at the foot of the stairs with a look on her face that said she had a duty to perform and she was going to do it, come hell or high water.

"Usually, no good ever comes of dredging up the past," she said. "But it might, this once. There's something you ought to know about the first Mrs. Hazel, and I aim to tell you. If you'll let me."

I figured that nothing could stop her from telling me, so I waited to hear what was on her mind.

"Gayle Hazel was a beautiful girl," Mrs. Brown began. "But looks was all there was to her. She was a shallow, selfish girl, who had no more trust in herself or her husband than I'd have in a pig. Verna Clayton never told her a thing about her husband." Mrs. Brown's eyes met mine squarely. "Verna only agreed with whatever Gayle had to say about him."

Mrs. Brown rubbed her hand across her mouth, as if to wipe away a bad taste, and said, "There. It's done, and we'll hear no more about it."

"It was none of my business," I said. "And I'm sorry I ever brought it up. But Verna had no right to talk about me the way she did, either."

"Verna knows that now," she said. "Just don't think any more about it."

"I didn't start it, Mrs. Brown. Verna did. Why don't you tell her to forget it?"

"I've already spoken to her," Mrs. Brown said, as if reasoning with a contrary child. "She won't cause you any more trouble here."

"Then neither will I." I turned and went to my room.

Mrs. Brown hadn't mentioned how late I had come in last night. And I'd figured that was what she had in mind when I saw her waiting for me. I suppose, with all this fuss about Verna and me and Gayle Hazel on her mind, she had forgotten to bring up my late hours.

When I went by the hardware store the next morning, the blind was pulled on the door, and a big CLOSED sign hung in the window. It looked to me like Wen and Angie Hazel had both left town.

Halcie Hissem would know where they had gone. I'd ask her. But when I told her the hardware store was closed up tighter than a drum, she put a surprised look on her face, and said, "Well, what do you know about that? They must have just packed up and lit out somewhere during the night." And then she went on about her business.

It puzzled me. But I didn't worry about it. As the day dragged by, I found myself thinking more and more that packing up and lighting out of here wasn't such a bad idea. I told myself that I was looking for a job when I came here, and I could always find a better one some place else. By the end of the day I had convinced myself that anything would be better than what I was doing. I felt like I was just passing the time, waiting for Mrs. Arthur's bag of lies to land on me.

I was still in this frame of mind when I left the dime store and saw Chance Cooper pacing back and forth, waiting for me.

Chance looked just the way he had the first time I'd ever seen him. An old baseball cap sat on the back of his head, and he was wearing a dirty, sweaty tan uniform and dusty boots.

"Bill Bundy brought me from work to pick up my

car at Andy's," he said. "The garage closes at six, so we didn't have time to go by home first."

He took my arm, and we crossed the street to his car. "I've got to talk to you, Julie," Chance said. "But not here and now." He put the car in gear and we moved off down the street.

"I'll change my shirt, and after we grab a bite to eat, we'll drive out to the covered bridge. It will be cool and quiet there by the river."

I rested my head on the back of the seat and closed my eyes. "Whatever you say." I sighed, wanting no more than to sit here and rest. "I've had one calamity after another ever since the day we went to the reunion," I told him. "I could stand a quiet evening for a change."

Chance made a sound between a snort and a chuckle. "I heard something of your troubles," he said. "There's not much Bill's sister, the one who's the cook at the Junction, doesn't hear and repeat to us later."

I sat up and opened my eyes. We were in the country, heading straight into the glare of the setting sun.

"Where are we going?" I wasn't alarmed. I was just curious as to why we were away out here.

"I told you," Chance replied. "I'm going home to change my shirt."

He smiled at me, then glanced quckly back at the road. "You can wait in the restaurant," he said. "When I'm fit, I'll meet you there for supper."

I moved uneasily in the seat. I knew I shouldn't. Halcie Hissem would have a fit.

But that's what I did.

I saw no one that I knew while we were eating supper, but a couple of the men spoke to Chance as they were leaving. We didn't linger over the meal and left soon afterwards.

Chance drove to the covered bridge over White River and parked the car among the trees. The sun was down, and it was dusk where he left the car, but light left over from the day lingered in the fields and meadow and lighted our way to the river.

"Let's walk down by the water." Chance took my hand and we walked down one of the well-worn paths to the river bank. "It will be quiet here," he said, as he sat down near the water and pulled me down beside him. "We can talk and not be disturbed."

Crickets were sawing away in the cornfield, katydids and locust hummed among the trees, and from the river bank frogs croaked and leaped into the water with a loud splash. Chance laughed softly. "It might be more quiet in Mrs. Brown's parlor," he said.

"But I like it here," I said. "Crickets and all."

We were quiet then, even if the insects weren't. Chance threw small stones and gravel into the water, then watched as the circles spread and disappeared into the drift of the river. Finally, Chance turned from watching the river and looked intently at me.

"Julie, my work is finished around here," he said. "Next week we'll be stringing wire in Orange County. I'll have to leave here tomorrow or the next day, whenever the other fellows decide to go."

I had known that Chance would be going away soon. Floyd had told me so. But I wasn't ready to hear it from Chance. That made it too definite.

"I'll miss you," I said, my voice low. "I've grown so used to seeing you, and now you won't be around."

"You could go with me, Julie." He leaned closer, as if his nearness could convince me to go. "That's what I wanted to talk to you about. We make a great pair. You don't want to get married, and neither do I. Go with me, Julie. We'll be a safety for each other. I won't hear any more about why I don't meet a nice girl, I'll have a girl. You'll be there for all to see."

I shook my head. "I can't go with you, Chance. It's foolish even to think I would. We've had fun here this summer," I said. "But the summer is about over."

"It doesn't have to be," Chance argued. "We could be together there, the same as we have been here this summer. You could get a job in Bicknell and find a place to live. Then when we lay off work for the winter, I'll come home to Bicknell, and we can see each other whenever we want. I've told my mother about you, and she'd like to meet you."

It was full dark now, and I could no longer see his face, but the eagerness in his voice told me that it would be alight with his hopes for us. I hated to be the one to smash them, but it was pointless to let him go on dreaming that it could be as he wished.

"Chance, I like you. You're everything I could want in a friend. But I don't want to go to Bicknell with you." I reached, and touched his face with my hand. "We don't have to be together to be friends. That will go on being so, no matter where we are."

He moved to get to his feet, then put out his hand to help me up. "It won't be the same as having you to go places with and to talk to," he said. "You're the only girl I ever met that I could really talk to, and now that I've found you, I don't want to lose you."

"You're not going to lose me," I said, trying to make him feel better. "Orange County is not so far away that you can't come back some times."

"No," he said, turning, and starting up the path to the car. "No, once I leave here, I'll never see you again."

Chance hardly spoke a word on the way back to town. He pulled up in front of the boardinghouse and stopped, but he didn't shut off the motor.

"I'll say good-bye to you here, Julie," he said, "I don't want to drag it out and make a big fool of myself." He leaned over and kissed me. "I'll never forget you," he whispered.

I don't know how I got out of that car and into the house. If there was anyone in the downstairs hall, I didn't see them and they didn't speak to me. I sat on the edge of my bed and cried like a baby for the loss of a friend, the lost summer days, and every other unhappy thing that had happened to me lately. It seemed to me that since I had come here to Linton, I had known nothing but disappointment. I did what I thought was right, but it turned out wrong every time. There was no way I could win.

Sometime during the night, I woke up knowing exactly what I was going to do. I would go to Terre Haute, where the state college was, and take the first job I could find. When classes started this fall, I would be there ready to enroll. I didn't wonder where I'd get tuition money, or even if I could get it. The main thing was to get to Terre Haute. With that settled in my mind, I went back to sleep.

I could think of nothing else while I got ready for work that morning. I'd have to tell Halcie Hissem that I was quitting my job. But I couldn't do that today. It was too close to the time when Chance Cooper was leaving town. And I didn't want to give anyone the impression that I was going with him. Yet it would have to be soon.

I wanted to go home and tell the folks what I had in mind to do. Mom would say it was impossible, but, "Have it your own way, Julie." Dad would remind me that it wouldn't be easy working and going to school at the same time. And they couldn't help me. I knew there were others who were working their way through college, and I'd tell Dad, "If they can do it, then so can I." He wouldn't stand in my way, once he knew that I had my heart set on it.

I would have to get word to Floyd Perry, somehow. I couldn't have him worrying about me and wondering where I had gone to. Besides that, Floyd might want to go home with me to see the folks. Dad was partial to Floyd, I thought. He would look more favorably on my going to college, if he thought Floyd had a hand in it.

"Lord, I'm glad you gave up your day off to work today."

I had day-dreamed all the way to the dime store. If Halcie hadn't mentioned it, I would have forgotten all about this being my usual day off. I'd had my mind on other things when she asked me last night at quitting time to come in today, and I couldn't have said whether it was Friday or Monday.

Lucky for me, we were unusually busy at the store, and I had no time to think of myself. Halcie and I took turns on the cash register, and we both kept an eye on the customers, helping them to find what they wanted, and exchanging the things they brought back. At the first lull of the traffic in the store, Halcie sent me out to lunch.

When I came back, Angie Hazel was ringing up a sale on the cash register, while Halcie flew up and down the aisles like a chicken in a wind storm. I stopped dead still in my tracks with surprise. I didn't even know Angie was back in town.

I started on back to the office to put my purse away, but Angie saw me, and lifted her arm to call me over to the desk.

"Every store in town is doing a landslide business to-day," she said, just as though nothing had ever happened. "Wen even broke down and called Verna back to work this morning."

Never a word about where they had been or why they had left in the first place. "I'm glad Verna got her job back," I said. "If I'd kept my big mouth shut, she wouldn't have lost it."

"We won't talk about that now," Angie said. "That's all been forgotten. And as far as anyone has to know, Wen closed the store so we could all get a rest from it. Lord knows," she added, "Wen and Verna needed a rest from each other's company."

"They are not the only ones who need a vacation from one another," Halcie Hissem had come up just in time to catch the tail end of what Angie had been saying. "And I'm about ready to make it a permanent one," she added.

She motioned toward me. "I've been wondering all week what ailed Julie," she said. "And now I find out that she's aiming to quit me. Running off with Chance Cooper, with never a word to me about leaving," she added, turning an accusing look on me.

I couldn't deny that I was planning to quit my job, but not for the reason she thought. I wondered where Halcie had ever gotten the notion that I was leaving with Chance.

"I have been thinking of quitting here," I said quietly. She hadn't raised her voice, so I kept mine low. "But it's not so I can go to Orange County with Chance Cooper."

Angie Hazel had moved away from us to speak with a customer who came in just then. Halcie Hissem and I were alone near the front of the store.

Halcie's eyes met mine, hard and black as coal. "After last night," she said, "You may have to go with him. I heard just now that you were at the Junction with him last night. We warned you about going there, but you went in spite of it."

"I went there because it was handy for us," I replied. "Not to spite you or anyone else."

I looked for Angie, hoping she would come and break this up, but she was keeping busy and staying as far as possible from where Halcie and I were talking.

"For whatever reason you went there," Halcie said, "I can't excuse it."

"I'm sorry," I said. "I wanted to tell you that I was leaving. Give you time to get help. But I can see now it's not necessary." I turned and started toward the door.

"Julie, you leave here now and you're through."

"Then I'm through," I said over my shoulder. And I left the store.

I fussed and fumed at myself all the way home, then slammed the door behind me when I got there.

"You're home early today," Mrs. Brown said, by way of a greeting.

I just mumbled a reply and hurried on up to my room.

"My feet aren't nailed to this floor," I said aloud to myself. "I could leave here tomorrow and be home before dark." I went to the closet and pulled out my old suitcase.

I emptied the dresser drawers, cleaned out the closet, and started packing. I found my rolled up diploma and placed it carefully at one end of the suitcase, so it wouldn't get damaged. Should things work out right for me in Terre Haute, that piece of paper was going to be my ticket to a teaching degree.

I closed the battered old suitcase and set it near the door. Then I sat down and took a long look around the room. Other than the clothes I would wear when I left here, the room was bare of my belongings.

Chapter Twenty-Five

I had no more than sat down when there was a rap at the door and Halcie Hissem walked in.

"Mrs. Brown told me that you were here," Halcie said. "So I came up."

"That's all right," I said. I gave her the chair, and I sat on the edge of the bed.

Halcie fidgeted uneasily in the chair, and I waited for her to say why she was here. I had nothing I wanted to say to her.

"I must have lost my reason a while ago, to speak to you so," she said, by way of apology. "After you had gone, I asked my cousin just when it was that he had seen you leaving one of them cabins. And when he said it was way last spring, I could've cut my tongue out. I knew then it was when you first came to town and had no place else to stay."

My mouth dropped open, and I just stared at her.

"Oh, Julie," she said, "I've known about that all along and understood the need for it."

Halcie glanced around the room, then nodded toward the bulging suitcase. "Looks to me like you're all ready to go," she said, with no inflection to her voice at all.

"I'm going home to see my family."

"When do you figure to be back?"

"I'm not coming back," I replied shortly.

I wished that she would go. But she sat there, solid as an oak tree, and never took her eyes off me.

Finally, she said, "I'm sorry to hear that, Julie. You and me, we worked well together."

Halcie got to her feet and moved over to lay a brown envelope on the dresser. "I've given you two weeks pay," she said, "in place of a notice. I'd hoped that it wouldn't be necessary."

She opened the door and left the room before I could thank her or even wish her well.

I slept late the next morning and awoke with a start. It took me a minute to remember that there was no need to hurry today. I didn't have a job to rush to.

But there were things I had to do today. A bus ticket to buy, and books to be returned to the library. The bus station was just around the corner from the library, and I could do both these things in one trip.

I put on the same clothes I'd worn the day before and went downstairs to fix my breakfast. I hoped that I wouldn't see Mrs. Brown until after I had my bus ticket and was ready to leave town. But she came in while I was eating and let me know that she already knew I was leaving.

"So you're going away," she said.

I didn't stop to wonder how she had found it out. "Yes," I answered. "I'm going home."

She smiled and nodded her head, as if to say she understood how that was. "Will you be gone long?"

"Yes," I answered again. Then, "I won't be back."

Mrs. Brown sat down at the table with me. "I'm right sorry to see you go, Julie. You have brought some life into this old house since you've been here." She clucked and shook her head.

I got up from the table and carried my plate and glass to the sink. "I've liked living here," I said. "But it's time now that I went home."

I turned to face her. "I really don't have any choice, Mrs. Brown. Halcie Hissem has fired me, and I don't have a job."

Mrs. Brown made a brushing motion with her hand, as if dismissing the matter. "Fiddlesticks, girl. Halcie told me that herself as she was leaving here yesterday," she said. "And that she wanted you back but you wouldn't come. Then Verna told me last night that Angie Abram was helping at the dime store until Halcie can find someone. I said right then," Mrs. Brown added, "Halcie Hissem won't soon find another girl like you."

I had to smile. Her last remark could be taken more ways than one. Halcie Hissem probably wouldn't be looking for another girl like me, I thought.

"It's all right," I said. "I was thinking of quitting there anyway. Besides," I added, "Halcie likes to have an older woman working in the store with her."

Mrs. Brown got up then and started out of the kitchen. "I'll hold your room for you," she said. "Once a girl has been on her own, she's not content to live at home with her folks."

"Please don't," I said. "You'll need the money. And when I leave here, I won't be back."

She stopped at the archway to the hall and turned

back to me. "Does Floyd Perry know yet that you're going home?"

I shook my head. "I've mailed him a note," I said. "But if he should come looking for me, will you tell him where I've gone?"

She smiled and nodded and left the room. I turned to the sink to finish my dishes.

Shortly after noon, I left the house to return my books to the library and go on to the bus station.

When I got to the corner where Angie had her fruit stand, there was nothing left of it except a stack of boards and two-by-fours, which Angie and her brother were loading into an old pickup truck.

"I thought you'd be working," I said to Angie.

Her brother laughed, and said, "What do you call this?" And rubbed his back.

Angie was wearing her overalls again today. She brushed her hands on her hips, and said. "The store's not open. Halcie's doing inventory today."

She told her brother to keep loading the truck. She'd be right back. "I'm going to walk a piece with Julie," she said.

"Halcie told me you were going home," Angie said. "And I was real sorry to hear it. I'll miss you, Julie."

"I'm going to miss you too," I said. "You and Halcie, and Chance Cooper. I'm going to miss everyone I've known here this summer."

Angie smiled at me and caught my hand, swinging it as we walked down the street. "I've grown so fond of you," she said. "Having you to buddy with this summer has been the nicest thing that ever happened to me."

She stopped before we got to the hardware store and

turned back to help her brother. I didn't understand Angie, but I liked her. I waited for her to look back, then I waved at her and went on my way.

At the library, Martha said she had heard that I was going home and wished me a safe journey. "I've never traveled more than forty miles from here," she said, and patted the books under her hand. "Except through these pages," she added.

I smiled. "That's a good way to travel." And I went out the door.

I found out at the bus station that the bus didn't go to Jubilee. The nearest I could get to Jubilee was to take a bus to Oolitic. I had no idea where Oolitic was, but the station attendant told me that if I could find a ride out of there to Jubilee, I could be home before dark.

I paid him for a ticket to Oolitic and left. I didn't know how far it was from there to where Mom and Dad lived, but I would get there. Even if I had to walk every step of the way.

I'd had my supper, and I was cleaning up afterwards when Floyd and Nancy Arthur walked into the kitchen. Nancy's eyes were shining with excitement, and Floyd wore a smile as wide as my hand.

"Oh, Julie," Nancy said, first thing. "Look what we have here." She waved a bundle of envelopes. "These are Mother's letters. She forgot to put stamps on them, and the mail carrier brought them back. Isn't that rich?"

I dried my hands on the dish towel and hugged Nancy. Floyd put his arms around both of us.

"I can't believe it," I said, laughing and crying at the same time. "I was scared to death that Halcie Hissem would get wind of what was in these letters, and now that you've found them, it doesn't matter."

"We knew you'd be worried," Floyd said. "That's why Nancy brought them along."

"I wanted you to see the letter destroyed, right before your eyes," Nancy said. "That way, you'd know they could never turn up or cause you trouble later on."

Floyd was looking at me as if he had just realized what I'd said. "What do you mean by saying that it doesn't matter anymore?" he asked. "Of course, it matters."

"Not where Halcie is concerned," I said. "I don't work for her anymore. But I'm glad you found the letters," I added. "I'm leaving here tomorrow, and I wouldn't like to think of that kind of stuff following me around."

"But why leave now?" Nancy was puzzled. "There's no sense in going away."

I smiled at Nancy, then turned to include Floyd. "It makes sense to me," I told them. "More sense than anything else has for a while. I thought I would go home for a few days," I explained. "Then go to Terre Haute and get a job there, close to the college. I want to go back to school," I added.

"Julie, wait till next week to go home," Floyd said. "And I'll take you. That's the Labor Day weekend, and I'd have three days there with the folks."

I shook my head. "I've got my bus ticket already, Floyd. The bus leaves at ten in the morning, and I'm going to be on it."

He glanced uneasily at Nancy, then leaned close to me.

"You know what we were talking about the other night," he said in a low voice. "Does that have anything to do with you going away?"

I took his arm and held it close to my side. "That has nothing to do with it," I said softly. "You know I would never run away from you. Not for any reason in the world."

"Then it's settled," he said. "I'll be here in the morning to take you to Jubilee. And don't you leave without me," he added, with mocking sternness.

We took the dreaded letters outside and burned them, one by one. And Floyd ground the charred paper to ashes under his shoe.

"She'll not write another one for a long time," Nancy said grimly, when the last letter was nothing but ashes.

Floyd and Nancy left for Newark soon after that. I hugged them both. Then I told Nancy, teasingly, "With those old tires on Floyd's car, you may end up walking home tonight."

"It would have to be the tires," Nancy replied, laughing. "Otherwise, I don't walk."

Floyd ducked his head, embarrassed at our teasing, and said he wasn't worried about getting her home. "I got a couple of good used tires from Mr. Thompson," he said. "And Ben and me worked on the brakes. They still grab at times, but I think they'll hold on the hills."

We all laughed then, and I waved them on their way.

Chapter Twenty-Six

I went to bed feeling good, yet I slept fitfully. Dreaming, then coming awake, only to sleep and dream the same thing over again. I was glad to see daylight. I could get up now and dress, without disturbing anyone.

When the knock came at the door, I was ready to leave for Jubilee and just waiting for Floyd to get here. I said, "Floyd," and swung the door wide open.

Ben Collier and Mr. Thompson stood there. Ben's hand was raised, ready to knock again.

"I thought you were Floyd," I said.

Then I noticed the drawn, weary look on their faces, and I knew they weren't carrying good news for me.

"What is it?" I whispered, suddenly breathless. If it hurt them so much, how could I bear to know?

They came inside and closed the door behind them. Ben took off his hat and stood wadding it with his hands.

"Julie," Ben said. "There ain't no easy way to say this. Floyd won't be coming for you. He's dead."

I started backing away from him. "No," I said. "No!"

Ben Collier caught me in his arms as I fell.

Later, Ben told me about Floyd, speaking soft and

gentle, the way he had spoken to Seely after Jamie had been drowned.

"Two boys, squirrel hunting in that ravine on the other side of Newark, found him about daylight this morning." Ben had to pause to clear the huskiness from his voice. "His car had missed a curve on that long hill, skidded in the loose gravel," he said. "The car went over the hill and smashed up on the rocks at the bottom of the gulch. We figured that Floyd must have died almost at once," Ben finished.

His voice was so low that I could barely hear him. And I didn't believe what I did hear.

There was a long silence after Ben Collier stopped speaking. I couldn't think about what he had said. And no one else seemed to want to talk about it.

"We should hold the service for Floyd as soon as possible," Mr. Thompson said. It was the first time he had spoken since they had gotten here.

"Ben thought Sunday, at the Flat Hollow Church. Is that all right with you, Julie?"

I nodded my head. Let Floyd lie next to Jamie in the Flat Hollow Churchyard. I thought. He had been like a brother to Jamie. It was right that they should be near each other. Then it struck me. Like Jamie, Floyd was gone from me forever.

"I never thought there would be a day when Floyd wouldn't be here with me." Then I began to cry.

For a while, Ben Collier held me and patted me awkwardly. Then he put his big hands on my shoulders and held me away from him.

"Dry your tears, Julie," he said gently. "We've got a

lot to do today. And your crying ain't helping you or Floyd."

I moved out of Ben's hands. "I'll just wash my face, then I'll be ready to go." At his deep look of concern, I said, "Don't worry. I'm all right now."

But even while I was saying it, I wondered if I would ever be all right again.

I went to see Floyd Perry for the last time, riding with Mr. Thompson, and sitting beside Ben Collier. He would've said, "Between his truest and best friends."

I thought to myself, if a man has just one good and faithful friend to grieve for him at the end, then he can be considered a success in this life. And here Floyd had two faithful friends, and me, to grieve his going.

When it was over, and I'd gotten Ben's promise to give Floyd a stone like Jamie's, Mr. Thompson drove me to the bus station to catch the bus to Jubilee.

"Don't sorrow too long for him, Julie," Mr. Thompson said. "You're young. You'll find another who will make you happy."

I smiled at Mr. Thompson to relieve his mind of worry about me. "I'll be fine," I told him.

I couldn't tell him that Floyd Perry had always been more like a big brother to me than a sweetheart. And a brother couldn't be replaced. I would carry his loss with me for as long as I lived.